This story of facing up to challenges is dedicated to my wife, Lidia, my son, Arthur, and to my granddaughter, Brady.

Winner of the
2024 Joshua Tree Novel Prize
and recognized as

Pacific Northwest Writers Association 2023 Finalist
Reader's Favorite 5-Stars
Royal Palm Literary Award 2nd place

also by
Arthur M. Doweyko

Algorithm

As Wings Unfurl

My Shorts

Captain Arnold

WIND IN TREES

a novel

Wind In Trees © 2024 by Arthur M Doweyko
No part of this book may be used or reproduced in any manner whatsoever without permission except in the case of brief quotations embodied in critical essays or reviews.

Attention schools and businesses; for discounted copies on large orders please contact the publisher directly.

Kallisto Gaia Press Inc.
PO Box 220
Davilla TX 76523
info@kallistogaiapress.org
(254) 654-7205

Cover Design: Arthur Doweyko
Author Photo: Laura Alexander
Edited by Tony Burnett

ISBN: 978-1-952224-41*6

WIND IN TREES

a novel

Arthur M. Doweyko

Chapter 1

A very great vision is needed and the man who has it must follow it as the eagle seeks the deepest blue of the sky.

Chief Crazy Horse, Oglala Lakota, 1840-1877

Henry fell backward, cracking his head against the concrete walkway.

Three blurred figures hovered over him. "What happened? Little Injun boy no walk so good?" Another said, "Hey, man, don't you know? It's them damned moccasins. They're a tripping hazard."

He felt his shoes get pulled off.

A blotchy red face appeared inches away. "Maybe it's these books. Way too heavy for you, Cochise. 'Sides you bastards can't read nohow."

His book bag sailed into a nearby ditch.

Henry got up to a knee and rubbed the back of his head. "Three against one—a bit unfair, don't you think?"

"Damn. Did Cochise challenge us?" All three laughed.

Henry focused on the tallest one. "Not all of you—just the biggest asshole with the biggest mouth."

One of the others said, "Whoa. Big Jack, he called you an—"

"Yeah, that'd be me, Cochise. This asshole's gonna send you back to your reservation, where you belong."

Henry staggered to his feet. The loudmouth was nearly a foot taller and a hundred pounds heavier. It was an effort to keep his voice steady. "The name's Henry Wind In Trees—a name you'll never forget."

"Woo, woo, woo. Where's your feather, Cochise? You gonna do a war dance for us?"

Henry looked beyond the titan. The university dorms seemed miles off, as did the few students walking to classes, cell phones in hand, oblivious to their surroundings, unaware of the unfolding showdown. "It's you who's going to dance, Shorty."

The giant's face turned a deep purple and he lunged. Henry sidestepped the brute and landed a sidekick to his butt, using his momentum to send him careening headlong into the sidewalk.

"You're gonna pay for that, chief." Big Jack came at Henry, swinging fists the size of anvils.

Henry ducked beneath the charge and let loose a punch to the side of Big Jack's head. An electric jolt exploded from his knuckles to shoulder. The man's head had to be made of wood.

Big Jack sneered. "Is that all you got, Cochise?" His forced smile sent shivers through Henry.

"Hey! Stop that! I'm calling the police."

A red-headed girl some twenty paces off held a cell phone to her ear and pointed at them. She added, "They're on their way."

Big Jack gave Henry a push. "I ain't done with you yet, Cochise." The other two followed like dogs on a leash.

Henry stared after the three as they rounded a bend. He was still shaking when the girl appeared nearby.

"Are you all right?"

"You didn't have to call the cops."

"You could have been hurt. Besides, I didn't really call anyone."

"A bluff? Nice move." Henry picked up his shoes and scanned the ditch. "And I'm fine."

"Really?"

He retrieved his bag. "That's what I said."

"You might need this." She held out a tissue. "You're bleeding."

"I don't need anyone's help." Henry took a step past her, ignoring the outstretched offering.

"You know, I'm not the one who attacked you. We're not all like those three."

Henry paused, his heart still racing. "I'm sorry. Thank you for what you did." He grabbed the tissue.

"My name's Elizabeth. I'm in your morning math class."

"Yeah, I know. My name's Henry—"

She nodded. "Wind In Trees. Want to grab some coffee?"

Chapter 2

Fifty years later.

"Sir, did you hear?"

Henry lowered his cup of home-grown coffee and watched its vapor leave a swirl across the kitchen window. Ghost-like, it reached outward and retracted, there one second, gone the next. Seth's reflection lingered on the pane—a glossy head leaning in through the kitchen door behind him. The robot's burnished surface gave the impression of a halo hovering over his bronze dome.

"The stuff on the radio?"

"Yes, sir. Systems are on their way."

Henry paused to breathe in the coffee's aroma. The cabin was perched high enough for a clear view of the remaining tower of the Golden Gate suspension bridge jutting up through the morning mist. A defiant thrust against the ravages of time, the rusty red monolith was nonetheless destined to join its moldering twin in the frigid waters of the bay. Henry wondered how long it would be before he joined it.

"Sir, you knew this day would come. Systems claim you are the last model scheduled."

"I'm not a model." Even as Henry spat out the words he wished he could take them back.

"Sorry, sir. My error."

Henry flung the remaining coffee into the sink and washed out his mug. He placed the ceramic antique next to its twin on the counter. The years that had passed could have been days, long days. Still savoring the bittersweet tang fading along the roof of his mouth, he paused at the window facing the forest edge.

A patch of sunlight danced across the solitary headstone nestled beneath the pines at the forest edge. A translucent figure in a blue sun dress sat on it. The sun splashed a quilt of colors across Liz's short-cropped red hair. His wife appeared as she did the day they were married. He shook his head. Her ghost and his robot, Seth, were all he had left.

After the quakes and the epidemic that followed, the radio had announced that the only humans to have survived were prototype cyborgs like him—brains encased in machines. Thanks to the impervious nature of titanium they were immune to the outbreak. How many there were, Henry didn't know, but they were all that was left of humanity in the twenty-second century. Henry tugged his ponytail and wondered what the others looked like. Cyborgs didn't have a need for hair. He liked his. He liked it very much.

"How far away are they?"

Seth opened the kitchen door leading to the porch and pointed. "I can see the aircar. Arrival in about two minutes, sir."

Henry's finger ran along a series of grooves cut into the window frame. Fifty years without Liz. She would have been seventy. After her death, nothing much had captured his interest. He had no use for the civilized world—what was left of it. Years ago he had searched the mainland in hopes of finding others, human or otherwise. Nothing. The image of thousands of rotting corpses became the waking dead of his nightmares. He had chosen a life alone, away from the apocalypse, the chaos. The surrounding forest provided everything he needed. He even had a faithful domestic robot to keep him company. The years came and went, and life had become a fading photo.

He had dismissed the year-old Systems' decree as bureaucratic clap-trap. They had claimed that some cyborgs had fallen ill and died. Apparently, the titanium skull wasn't all it was hyped up to be. The Systems scientists touted a breakthrough in bio-engineering—a fully artificial brain, one hundred percent resistant to biological disease. There would be no need to drink, or eat, or even breathe. Why would there be? The new brain came with its own fuel cell. He tried to imagine a world filled with such cyborgs, and it made his stomach turn.

Fifty years was a very short time for Systems to come up with an artificial brain, considering the devastation. Henry assumed they were military and had some major resources. He still remembered people being overwhelmed with hand-held phones. Robots that walked without falling over had just been invented. How did Systems come up with the cyborg technology? How did Systems survive the virus?

Henry shook his head as he eased into an Adirondack chair on the porch. Seth's four-foot frame stood watch at the head of the wooden steps leading down to the meadow.

"What do you think, Seth?"

The robot's head swiveled as it surveyed a line of tall evergreens.

"Arrival in one minute, sir."

Henry reached out and patted Seth's back. The bronze alloy felt cold and lifeless, but he knew better.

Seth said, "You want to know what I think about the upgrade."

Henry squeezed his eyes shut. "They say it will be identical in all respects—memories, likes, dislikes, the way I talk—even the way I think."

"You are afraid, sir?"

"How can they be sure?" Henry sighed. "I get the part about re-imaging my memories. I get the neural network technology. But self-awareness? Seth, will the upgrade be self-aware? Will my new brain still be me?"

"The Systems scientists claim it, sir."

"I get the feeling that when I wake up—that's it, I don't think it'll be me when I wake up."

"I understand, sir."

An oval object appeared over the tree tops, humming and glistening an aseptic enamel white.

"Whoa … I was expecting maybe a helicopter. What the hell is that?"

"It is an aircar, sir. Much has happened since the destruction."

Henry gave Seth a long look, and before he could utter another word, the aircar landed in his front yard, sending several chickens scurrying into the forest. Two figures in pink uniforms stepped out with logos emblazoned on their chests and shoulders—simple circuit diagrams drawn in black lines within a circle of gold. A circuit—something Henry was about to become. He cringed as the Techs approached. The speckled forest light reflected off their sharp cheekbones. Their morbid sunken orbits housed green pinpoints for eyes. Maybe Systems were all robots. Were all the humans really gone?

The nearest one spoke first. "Good day. You are Mr. Henry Windintrees?" A distinct clicking sound attended each consonant.

"That's 'Wind In Trees.' It's an old family name. And who are you?"

"Systems, sir. You *do* know why we are here?"

Their faces reminded Henry of carved marble, the sort he recalled in pictures of Greek statues, colorless and stone cold. "Yeah, I know." Henry rose from his chair. "But, before we go any further, I'd like to ask you—"

The two walked to the back of their aircar. When they returned, one carried a container about the size of a human head, and the other, a black satchel. "We will need to go inside."

"I wanted to ask you a question—you know—about the procedure—what you feel after the procedure. I mean, you guys went through it, right? Do you still feel like yourselves?"

They glanced at each other and the one with the satchel said, "Please relax, Mr. Windintrees. The procedure will take but a few minutes."

"But that's not what I'm asking about. I don't think you—"

While one held the porch door, the other grabbed Henry by the arm and led him inside to the kitchen. The satchel Tech said, "Please lie down on the counter."

Henry heard the satchel snap open. He sat on the counter and took hold of the Tech's shoulder. "Are you still the person you were?"

"Silly question, Mr. Windintrees. Lie back down." The stone face hovering over him showed no signs of emotion or interest in pursuing the matter any further.

The Tech with the case lifted out a silvery sponge with thin wire tentacles dangling from beneath it. "Here it is—the new you. Beautiful, isn't it?"

A feeling of dread rose within Henry—an anxiety he had almost forgotten he was capable of. "I don't. I don't like it. I want you to stop. I've decided I don't want the upgrade."

The Tech held him down and pulled out a small pointed instrument. "Now, now, Mr. Windintrees. This is a Systems mandate. You do not have a choice." The implement caught a shaft of light outlining a razor-sharp scalpel.

"I said *no*." Henry squirmed, turning away. A line of pressure ran across his temple. Something cut through his artificial flesh. The other Tech said, "Make more room."

He heard something shatter on the floor—the sound of splintering ceramic—coffee mugs—her mug—one of the few things he had that reminded him of his wife. In that moment, Liz loomed behind the Tech who was holding him down. She had never come into the house before. She peered over the Tech's shoulder, her face dispassionate, her eyes wide.

"You're not listening. I said no. What's wrong with you people?"

"Stay still. It will be over before you know it."

Henry tried to push himself up to get out from under the Tech. Where had Liz gone? The Tech rolled onto his chest and turned to the other. "I think I'm going to need some help."

A black case slapped down next to Henry's head and a syringe-like device flashed by.

"Please be still, Mr. Windintrees."

"What, what are you doing?"

Henry felt his shirt sleeve pulled up. He beat the Tech atop him with his free arm, but he might as well have been slapping at stone. He closed his eyes and prepared for the inevitable. He would become them, lost in an electronic matrix, no longer Henry, but something else. *Would he even remember this?*

He heard a sharp metallic sound. The suffocating weight of the Tech lightened, and then slid off. Henry remained lying on the counter, afraid to open his eyes. He ran through the day's events and remembered everything. Maybe the upgrade wasn't so bad after all. He still knew who he was and where he was.

"Are you all right, sir?"

"Seth?"

"It is I, sir. You may consider opening your eyes."

Henry sat up. Two bodies lay on the floor of the kitchen. Seth's diminutive frame stood between them. His short arms waved a baseball bat as if he expected they might wake up any moment.

"My God, Seth. What did you do?"

Henry swiveled off the counter. A closer look at the bodies exposed fist-sized dents on their alabaster pates. Seth said, "It was necessary, sir. You were in distress."

"Are they dead?"

"Offline, sir. The shocks to their brain cases were sufficient to initiate a reboot. They will likely return to working order momentarily."

Henry kneeled alongside one of the Techs. "How do you know they're rebooting?"

"I have a large database, sir."

"They look dead to me."

"They were never alive, sir. They are robots."

"Not humans? I mean, I thought these Techs were upgraded hybrids—like what I was about to become."

"I detected no empathy, sir. Their actions led me to conclude they are robots like me."

"Seth, they're nothing like you."

Henry picked up a shard from what was left of a coffee mug. It sported most of the letter 'L'. Liz appeared at the kitchen table, still wearing her summer dress. She took a step forward and said, "You need to run."

Chapter 3

"**Is** she here, sir?"

It was the first time she spoke. Henry struggled to look away. "Yes, yes."

He dreaded Seth's response. It wouldn't be the first time he'd have to endure a sermon about the fallacy of ghosts and the likelihood of his imminent full-blown schizophrenia. He had lived a very long time alone and he was aware of the edge.

"Did she talk to you, sir?"

Henry nodded and averted his eyes from the robot. "She wants us to leave."

"Should I gather up some food and water, sir?"

Seth's reaction threw him. He didn't know whether to stay or run. Why bother? He had chosen a life of isolation. The world didn't matter. Survival didn't matter—unless it was for a reason, "Good … good idea, Seth." Henry headed to his den and spoke over his shoulder. "No lecture? Are you starting to believe Liz is real?"

Seth paused a few seconds before answering, as if he needed time to think. "There are some things my artificial mind will never comprehend and I have classified Liz as one of them."

"Does that mean you accept her?" *What if she was still alive?*

Seth appeared at the doorway with a distended backpack strapped over his shoulders. "If Liz is real to you, sir, she is real to me."

Henry shook his head. "Sometimes I wonder if you're as artificial as you claim."

Something moved in the kitchen—the sound of scraping —stone on wood.

"Sir, we need to hasten."

Henry lowered a sack loaded with books and personal items to the floor. While donning a deerskin jacket, he gave his den a final sweep. He reached for a framed picture of him and his crew standing in front of an Abrams tank. A remembrance of his exploits in the Middle East and Russia weren't likely to help him. Instead, he grabbed a pair of binoculars and then paused at another wall-mounted display—an 1873 Colt single-action revolver. According to his Lakota Sioux family tradition, the gun was picked up by an ancestor at the Battle of Greasy Grass, known to the white man as the Battle of Little Big Horn. It was passed down through generations over the course of three hundred years—a reminder of what once was and would never be again. He hefted the revolver, lifting it to take in the deep blue of the barrel. The sweet aroma of gun oil filled his nostrils.

"Sir, can you be sure it still functions?"

Henry slid the Colt into his sack along with a box of ammunition and slung it over his shoulder. "There are times when we need to rely on faith, Seth. By the way, be sure to take that bat with you. It has sentimental value."

The sound of crunching from the kitchen turned both heads.

Henry strung a long bow, and slipped it and a quiver of arrows over his shoulder. He caught a reflection of himself in a wall mirror and chuckled.

"What is funny, sir?"

"I look like an Indian. Like the ones in the old movies."

"You forgot your feather, sir."

"Did you pack your oil can?"

As the two stepped out the back, Liz beckoned to them from the mouth of a deer trail. The front screen door slammed. Henry motioned for Seth to follow and the pair loped onto the trail—a mile long switch-back which led down the side of the mountain to the bay.

They had gone no more than a hundred yards when they heard heavy thumping and branches breaking behind them. Seth said, "It appears that at least one of the Techs is pursuing us."

"Let's keep moving. I have an idea."

Henry veered off the path, a course which led the two through thick brambles. Liz turned to look at the two and her face contorted in confusion.

"Sir, I do not think this is a sound idea."

Henry pushed aside a tree branch. "Hide in here."

Seth crouched in a bed of pine needles behind a narrow tree trunk. Henry pushed aside the brambles to get a better look up the trail.

"Sir, the Tech will see you."

The thrashing sounds grew louder.

"Shhh."

The Tech came into view and rushed at Henry like an enraged bull.

Henry yelled, "Stop! Don't do that!"

The Tech sprinted forward with arms outstretched. Henry stepped to the side as it lunged and exploded through the brambles behind him. The ashen head twisted and stared back with one green eye, while its legs continued to pump in mid-air. It dropped off the cliff without a sound and disappeared into the mists below. Henry stared at the swirling haze, half-expecting a pasty-faced specter or some cursed banshee to emerge.

Seth broke the silence. "Do you think it's strange that the Tech was so easily out maneuvered?"

"Come to think of it—yeah. It was almost as if it was really mad at me, like it lost its mind. You'd think it would be more careful."

"Probably a fault of its programming, sir."

"Pretty damn fallible."

"Not every machine is meant to be clever."

"What about you, Seth?"

"I am but a humble servant, sir."

"There's nothing humble about you, but there's definitely something about Systems I don't trust." Henry swung back a pine branch. "If the other one's coming, it's taking it's time."

"Perhaps it is not as angry, sir."

"I don't get it. So what if I die from the Yellowstone? Why the hell do they care?"

"Perhaps they are motivated by some other reason."

"I'm not hanging around to find out what that is. Let's go."

The pair paused every once in a while to listen. There was no pursuit. The fog thickened, forcing them to slow down and feel their way through the trees. They followed the lazy sounds of breaking surf to the peninsula's rocky shoals. When they reached the shore, the gloom lifted a few feet to reveal undulating shallows and an overturned rowboat propped up on a set of logs.

Henry jogged across a narrow strip of sand. "Everything's here. Hop in."

Minutes later they bobbed on the gentle waves of Francisco Bay while Henry rowed. Seth asked, "Sir, how do you know which way to go?" Henry peered over his shoulder. Liz, perched at the prow of the boat could have been a mythical figurehead warding off evil spirits, raised her arm to point the way.

"I just know, Seth. I just know."

After about an hour, Henry eased off. Seth reached into his sack and produced a loaf of bread and bottle of water. The fog had lifted high enough to see a quarter mile out and a mild breeze cajoled ripples into frothy waves. It also brought with it a chill, a portent of yet another short summer. Liz lowered her arm and continued to stare into the glowering horizon.

It seemed like it was yesterday when they had ventured out into the bay for a summer's picnic—Elizabeth and Henry, two newly married grad students sharing precious moments together, little prepared for the hell storm to come. They had beached their kayak on a sand bar, barely an islet. Henry puckered his mouth as he recalled the cheap wine. Elizabeth's laughter echoed in his mind. Then her smile contorted, her eyes widened. The sky darkened. A distant rumble set Henry's neck hairs to attention.

"Sir, we should resume."

Henry blinked. "You're right."

No sooner had his oar entered the water than he heard a pounding come from the boat's wooden frame as if they had run into some rocks. They came to an abrupt stop and boat's aft end dipped. Four blanched fingers emerged from the water and gripped the stern.

Henry spat. "Damn it all." A second set of fingers appeared on the gunnel, and the boat rocked as a zombiesque visage rose from the water—a misshapen head crowned with several cracks in its plastic housing. The one green eye blinked. It was the Tech who had swan-dived off the cliff.

Henry waved an oar. "Leave us alone. Go back to Systems and tell them Henry is not interested."

The Tech's mandible lolled to one side. It wheezed, gushing out garbled words which sounded like the gurgling of a clogged sink drain.

"Get the hell off my boat." Henry unlocked the oar and smashed it onto the Tech's forehead, sending several porcelain-like fragments flying. The robot lolled from side to side and threatened to spill the boat as it raised itself up. When its one good eye winked out, it lunged into the boat and clamped its arms about Henry's torso. Henry flung himself forward and curled his fingers around the Tech's hands, trying to break its grip.

"A little help here!"

Seth stepped over the yoke. Henry gasped. "Well?"

"It should not be long, sir."

Before Henry summoned his wits enough to ask, the Tech's hands loosened and its arms fell away. Henry gulped in some air and stared at the inanimate body sprawled across his seat. "What just happened?"

"You may have produced a fatal blow."

"How did you know? I mean, you said, 'not long'."

"A guess, sir."

A humming sound cut into further conversation. With each passing second it grew louder, coming from high above the thinning fog.

Seth grabbed the Tech's torso and levered it over the side into the water, leaving behind a small gathering of bubbles in its wake.

"Are you sure it won't be bobbing up again?"

"Certainty is a fleeting concept, sir."

Henry stared up at the opaque cloud cover. "How did they—"

"The other Tech may have tracked its partner."

"But it might find us using other means."

"Perhaps, sir."

Throughout the ordeal, Liz had remained sitting on the bow, oblivious to the struggle behind her. Henry settled back into the stern seat. She gave him a quick nod and raised her arm again, pointing the way. They moved off and the fog continued to lift. The overhead thrumming lessened with each heave of the oars. Minutes later, they glided in silence, headed to a destination known only to Liz, and she wasn't talking.

Chapter 4

The last time Henry had ventured across the bay was a few years after the blow up, about a half-century ago. He and Liz had survived the quakes, and figured that one or more of the fault lines had given way. Electronic communication disappeared for a while, but with the help of a resurrected transistor radio, they listened to sporadic broadcasts over the months that followed. The news was horrific, describing a grisly devastation of the mainland and multiple outbreaks of a deadly disease. They hunkered up in their cabin to wait out the chaos, to wait for help to arrive. No one came. They were isolated. Given the pandemonium on the mainland, staying put for a while seemed like the best idea. The clouds never cleared and summers grew shorter. Many trees withered and died. Henry relied on his wits and bow skills to hunt for food, which became scarcer with every season.

They called the asteroid Icarus. It fell to the Earth like its mythical namesake, but instead of plunging into the sea, it chose Billings, Montana. The impact was enormous, strong enough to trigger major tectonic shifts along the volcanic Cascades. Vast stretches of the Pacific coastline moved away from the mainland. The Marin peninsula was spared, but all the bridges spanning the bay collapsed. When the shockwave reached the Yellowstone caldera, the magma, held back for the past 640,000 years vaporized the better part of Wyoming. The enormous volcano ejected a pyroclastic cloud a hundred miles into the air, and the ash spread to the south and east, blanketing most of the Midwest. Some reports described similar meteorite or asteroid strikes in other parts of the world. After a while the radio produced more static than anything else.

A deadly virus showed up at about the same time. The news called it the Yellowstone Fever—airborne and fatal. Liz's cough grew worse and she was burning up. Early on, the looped instructions on the radio identified a location on the mainland Henry knew—the Palace of Fine Arts, where medical help would be available. A boat ride across the bay brought them to the 1915 World's Fair structure. Its enormous rotunda had been laid flat by the devastation, leaving behind only two rose-colored columns complete with their Corinthian capitals. The rest of the once magnificent building lay in ruins, as did most of San Francisco.

A van pulled up at the shore as if Henry and Liz were expected. A medic in a white uniform stepped out and said, "Please get in. We have no time to lose." Henry noted their black and gold logos, but was too bewildered by their appearance to ask any questions. The smell of death hung in the air—the remains of bodies, tattered clothing and bleached bones were scattered in the streets amid the rusting hulks of automobiles and buses. Henry was aware of Yellowstone, and knew it to be quick, but so quick as to kill drivers in their cars?

They pulled up to a single-story structure surrounded by piles of broken concrete, much of which appeared to have been pushed aside. They followed a curved walkway to a set of double doors. The overgrown grass and the distant howl of a coyote underscored the inexorable march of Nature as it reclaimed its land.

The medic lifted Liz out and walked ahead with her draped across his arms.

Henry asked, "Is it true what they said on the radio? This Yellowstone thing, this disease, did it really spread around the world?"

Liz's head turned toward Henry's voice, her eyes remained closed and her breathing had become a series of hoarse eruptions. Henry kissed her on the cheek. "Hang in there, Liz. "

The medic said, "It's true. Yellowstone is one hundred percent fatal."

Sweat tickled Henry's palms. "So why are you people still here? How come you're alive?"

The medic pushed through the entrance while another two carried Elizabeth off to a different hallway.

"Where are you taking her?"

"She's contagious. We have a special unit designed for such cases."

Henry watched her disappear through a swinging door. "I'll see you soon, honey!"

The broad layout of the place reminded him of an emergency room—a military guard stood at the door and a nurse at the counter faced several rows of empty chairs. At least they had the look of a guard and a nurse.

"What's going to happen now?"

Henry felt a stab at his arm. The room wavered. For a moment he thought it might be another quake. Two other men in cherry red uniforms appeared and braced him up. He opened his mouth and his legs gave way. He thought it was lucky that the two in red showed up when they did. The floor rose and Henry shut his eyes.

<>

"Who are you?"

Blurry figures moved across his field of vision.

"Here, take a drink." He focused on a female nurse who produced a cup with a straw. "It's water. My name is Sandra. This fellow is Mike." Henry sucked up the fluid. He was parched. The odd taste made him grimace.

"It's okay. You'll get used to it." Henry recognized Mike; he was one of the male medics in the van.

Henry lifted the cup. The skin of his hand caught his attention. It was smooth, wrinkle-free, and there was something about its color. While the cool liquid descended along his throat, he raised his other hand and took a closer look—no scars, perfect manicures. He remembered cutting his thumb a year ago, and he always had dirt under his fingernails. And his skin hadn't been a light shade of blue.

"I think there's something wrong with my eyesight."

Mike said, "You're fine."

"How long have I been out?"

Sandra said, "Henry, you've been sedated for several weeks. It was necessary for the transfer."

"Transfer? What transfer? And what about Liz, you know—my wife? We came in here together."

Mike placed a hand on Henry's shoulder. "I'm afraid we have some bad news for you, Henry. We tried everything to save her, but she was too far along. She did have Yellowstone. She died a week ago."

Henry dropped the cup and slumped back into the bed. His world shrunk to a singularity. A deep and obscure abyss pull at him, at his heart, at his whole being.

Sandra said, "I told you."

Mike said, "It had to be done. Help me get him to sit up."

Henry felt his arms get pulled, his head and shoulders braced up with a pillow. He inhaled several times, holding the air in and exhaling slowly each time.

Mike said, "Henry, I know this is a bad time, but we need to tell you more. You asked about the transfer."

Henry heard the words but little was getting through. The medic's face moved in and out of focus. All he saw was Liz's face, eyes closed as if asleep, her mouth moving, forming silent words.

"You had the initial symptoms, Henry. You had Yellowstone, too."

Henry wiped his chin with the back of his hand. "Then I should be dead. Why didn't you let me die?" Liz's smiling face appeared before him. Then just as quickly, she disappeared. For a moment no one spoke.

"We couldn't let that happen. You should be thankful that we were able to save you."

"Why did you bother? Without her … Anyhow, I thought the virus was fatal."

"A new technology. Maybe you heard about it? The disease hadn't reached your brain."

"I don't get it. What did you do—give me a new body?" Henry's voice trembled as he forced out a nervous chuckle. Then he looked at his hands.

Sandra said, "That's exactly what we did."

It was a punch in the stomach. Henry flexed his fingers, moved his hands over his chest, his face—the too smooth chin, the hair pulled back. His tongue ran across his teeth, perfect teeth.

"I'm having trouble believing all this. I never heard of such technology."

Mike paused before going on. "Military research—secret stuff. Anyway, there was no time to lose. The transfer was performed the same day you arrived. Over these past few weeks your brain, your biological brain, grew accustomed to your new body's neural network."

Sandra cut in. "The brain is an amazing organ. Everything isn't quite the same as before, but it manages to adjust to the differences and presents those sensations as if they were normal."

"And what's with my skin?"

Sandra said, "It's a light shade of blue—a consequence of the artificial blood—"

"Which is blue?"

"Precisely."

"But I can taste. I was thirsty and there's the cold water going down my throat."

Mike said, "You will need to eat, drink, and breathe to satisfy your brain's biological demands. All the body's basic functions have been replicated—internal and external. Your blood may be artificial, but works much the same as blood carrying nutrients and oxygen."

Henry flexed an arm. "And my muscles—what are they? Springs? Rubber bands?"

"Nothing so crude. Your skeletal system is made of titanium, which includes the brain case. Your muscles are made of biopolymers and behave much like the originals, though I think you'll find they're a bit more powerful and recover faster."

"What do I look like?" Henry swiveled and looked at a reflection in the window. "My face. How did you get it to look like my old one?"

Mike grinned. "That's one of the amazing things about the transfer, or I should say, about the plasticity of the human brain. We needed to be sure we got the major features right—your ponytail, the color of your eyes, and so on. After a few weeks, your brain acclimated to the new you, your sensations, the general feel of your body. At this moment it's convinced that you always looked like this."

"Damn."

"One other thing. You won't be able to procreate, but you can have sex."

"And that's something I'm worried about?"

Mike added, "Don't feel too bad. In theory these bodies can last hundreds of years. Your titanium skull along with the filtered plasma will protect the brain against all disease and radiation, which means it should last as long as you feed it. So don't go all depressed on me. You're alive, and that's more than we can say about most everyone else."

The realization that his body, his life, had become so alien settled in. Henry tensed his muscles, his artificial muscles in an attempt to remain calm.

"What are you saying? What about everyone else?"

Mike lowered his head. "Few humans are left alive. By our estimations the only ones to survive have had your procedure. That's why Systems have sent our teams out—to save what's left."

"Systems?"

"Our military, Henry. It's the civilization we have left."

Henry shook his head and leaned back. "What about you people? Shouldn't you be dead by now?" When no one answered, Henry whispered, "You're cyborgs, aren't you?"

Mike waved his arm back and stepped into the light from the window. "We all are, Henry."

Henry should have noticed the blue tint earlier. He rubbed his arms and legs. "What happens next? We get boxed up and stored in some underground bunker until the world gets its shit together?"

"We've been on a rescue mission for the past three months. By the time we got here, most folks were dead. We hoped that a few might have been lucky enough to be isolated and survived in this part of the world due to the prevailing westerlies. You're free to do whatever you want." Sandra reached around and extended a bundle of clothing.

"What about Liz? Can I see her?"

Sandra said, "I'm afraid that will be impossible. Her remains were incinerated. It's the law."

Henry bolted to his feet. "Law? Whose law?"

Mike said, "Easy, easy. It's a Systems decision. Disposal is more of a policy to help slow down the spread."

"Everybody's dead. Seems your policy wasn't very effective."

Sandra said, "We can do nothing more than try."

"Her ashes." Henry choked on his words. "I want her ashes."

"That won't be a problem." Mike nodded to a medic at the door.

Henry wondered if the tears he felt at the corners of his eyes were actually there. He sucked in a mouthful of air, trying to hold back, to keep from blubbering. The world would never be the same again. Liz was his life. She was everything to him. "And, you're headed where? Back east?" Mike said, "We've got just a few operations left out here. Some major cities along the Atlantic coast have power. We're not aware of any on the west coast. Maybe you'd want to come along? There are survivors living there—like us."

Cities run by cyborgs. The more the thought cycled through his mind, the less appealing it became. Henry finished getting dressed and shook the medic's hand. "What you did was a miracle. For that I thank you." Empty words. *Saving Liz would have been the miracle.*

They walked. Henry was surprised at how fast he gained control over his movements.

Mike appeared at the doorway with a plastic bag. "Sorry, we don't have anything more formal. We leave tomorrow, first thing in the morning. If you decide to join us—"

"Don't wait for me. My home is here—" Henry snatched up the bag. "—with Liz."

<>

The years were a daydream. Henry had withdrawn from what was left of civilization. There was simply nothing about it that attracted him. As far as he was concerned, the world, or what was left of it, could go to hell. He looked at his hand, his arm—not a trace of wear. He thought it odd that science progressed so far after the devastation.

Liz pointed at a rock formation ahead. The fog had lifted.

"We're here."

"Is she still with us, sir?"

Henry guided the boat onto a finger of land, jumped out, and dragged it into the rocks. "She's always with us, Seth." His personal phantasm, some twenty paces beyond the rocks, beckoned them to follow.

"Has she told you where we are going?"

"She doesn't speak much."

Seth nodded. "That's unfortunate, sir."

"It certainly is, Seth."

Henry gathered up his gear and hiked up the embankment. "I know where we are."

Liz reappeared at the base of a pair of rose-colored columns and then walked away toward a street strewn with rubble.

"And I know where we're going."

Chapter 5

The pair weaved through decayed buildings that reminded Henry of overturned toy blocks strewn across a carpet. Crumpled toy cars and desiccated toy bodies positioned along the streets, sprinkled with sand and dust, added to Henry's growing dark mood. He glanced up at the gray sky, wondering if some giant child might at any moment appear.

A one-story cement structure sported a faded Systems logo above its entrance. "This is the place, Seth. This is where Liz and I were brought."

"Are you sure it is where Elizabeth wants you to go, sir?"

The double door entry stood ajar, its cracked glass encrusted with grime. A spiral of cold air followed the two inside and kicked up a short-lived dust devil in the reception area. Henry's gaze darted from the overturned chairs to an inner set of doors—doors through which he once entered as a human being, and through which he left as a machine.

"This way."

The stiff pneumatics squealed as the pair pushed through. Muted bands of light fell across the grimy hallway flooring. Henry dropped his backpack and motioned for Seth to follow.

He stopped at the second room. Except for a fine coating of ash, the bed was as he left it—covers folded at an angle, pillow still propped up against the frame. He even thought he saw the imprint of his head in the pillow. *Ghosts*. A gust of wind whistled across cubicle's lone window. The sound reminded him of an aircar.

"Seth, will you please get back to the foyer and look out?"

"As you wish, sir."

"I've got a bad feeling."

Why would Liz lead him here? The medical outpost abandoned for a half-century would have little to offer. Perhaps he was supposed to find something—a clue discarded like a bread crumb on a forest trail.

He was about to leave when he heard a squeal followed by a thud. The air in the room shifted. Someone must have entered through the emergency back door. His mind raced as the sound of crisp metallic footsteps grew louder. He pictured his Colt ensconced in its leather holster deep inside his bag—the bag that was in the hallway. It might as well have been a thousand miles away. The bow slung about his shoulder promised little in the way of defense. He unstrung it, hoping for inspiration, when a pale white oval of a face leaned into the doorway. Its glittering green eyes hummed as they shrank into pinpoints.

"Hey, Henry. It's me, Mike."

The string hung from Henry's fingers and he leaned back into the wall by the headboard.

Mike said, "You remember? When you and your wife, what was her name … Elizabeth? When you and Elizabeth came here—man, that was a while ago. What … about fifty years?"

"Mike? But you're—you're—"

The mechanical mouth clicked as it opened. "Upgraded. One-hundred percent artificial." Mike took a step into the room and Henry found himself pressing his back against the wall even harder. The ceramic-like head had a small dent over one ear hole, and its mouth locked itself into a perpetual smile. "What do you think? Pretty cool, heh?"

"I'm sorry about that dent in your head. Seth said you were a robot."

Mike raised an arm. "That's quite all right, Henry—a misunderstanding. We aren't really robots." He paused a moment, and then added, "If I were in your position, I would have done the same thing."

It was odd that Mike seemed unperturbed about the assault. Henry said, "I'm also sorry about your partner. That robot, I mean, that Tech wouldn't stop coming at us."

"Sandra? No problem." Mike shrugged and his crooked mandible produced a macabre smile. "The water's not too deep where she sank. We'll swing by later and pick her up."

"You and Sandra look a lot different than the last time we met." The air in the room grew colder, more sinister.

Mike kept up his smile as if he was unaware it was still there and took another step toward Henry. "Yeah … as you know, the upgrade became mandatory last year. The Yellowstone virus was getting past the braincase. On the upside, the upgrade means we don't need respiration or digestion anymore. That's a major plus." Mike tapped his chest. "Battery-powered." A slight grind in his throat erupted producing the hint of a chuckle. "We're happy with the change."

"So, you're still you? I mean, do you remember everything? Do you feel any different?" *There's a stupid question.*

"That's what I'm here to tell you, Henry. Everything's the same. There's no reason for you to be frightened of the upgrade. Hell, we're designed to last a thousand years. Think of what that means."

Henry stretched the string, wrapping the ends about his wrists. "Up in the cabin you didn't come across as a human. Now you seem a lot friendlier. I don't understand."

Mike lifted an arm and tapped the side of his head with one of his stick-like fingers. "I guess I needed some sense knocked into me." He ground out another chuckle.

Henry's reaction time was slightly faster than human, slightly slower than robot. He ducked his head as Mike's arm glanced off it and smashed through the wallboard. Rolling beneath the bed, Henry looped the string around Mike's ankles and slid out the other side.

Mike pulled out his arm from the wall sending a cloud of plaster to the floor. "Fast little shit. You're not going anywhere." He took a step and crashed to the floor like a stack of pipes. While Mike churned out more invectives, Henry was already in the corridor with bag in hand.

"Seth, I need some help here."

He reached the lobby with the clanking ogre close behind. Seth was gone. It would take seconds to fish out the Colt, seconds he didn't have. He hefted the sack over his shoulder, ready to swing it and turned to face the motorized ogre.

Mike burst through the pair of swinging doors into the lobby. His head swiveled in Henry's direction and he charged forward. He was two steps in when Seth, who had been standing to the side of the doorway, slammed his bat into both knees. Mike toppled through a descending arc and crashed to the tiled floor. He lifted himself to all fours, green eyes blinking, mouth agape. Henry swung his sack and connected with Mike's head, sending him sprawling into several chairs.

Seth stepped over to the body and said, "I believe it is stunned, sir."

Henry reached for Seth's bat when he heard a voice. "This way." Liz appeared for a moment at a set of doors on the opposite side of the lobby.

"Let's go, Seth."

Henry kept the bat in hand as the two sprinted through the doors. The corridor was a mirror image of the first with rooms to either side. Henry paused at each, wondering where Liz was leading them. He found out at the last room—empty, except for a floor covered with severed heads. At first Henry thought they were human, but closer inspection revealed they were likely creatures like himself—titanium skulls with plastic covers designed to look human. These were cyborg heads, and the semi-dried oily goo at their bases suggested that what remained of their humanity had become a dark smear. He nudged a few to get a better look.

"Jeez."

"What is it, sir?"

"That was me." Mike appeared at the doorway. "That was me before this." Mike used both hands to point at his face.

Henry jumped back and raised the bat. "What the hell is wrong with you? First you're friendly, and the next second you're trying to kill me."

Mike backed up into the corridor. His body trembled and the words came out in bursts. "I'm not trying to kill you. Get outside. Use the aircar." He slammed a fist into the wall again and again. "Get out."

"You're not well. Come with us. Besides, I don't know how to fly that thing."

Mike stopped the pounding and stuttered. "My orders were to upgrade you—make you like me—do you really want that, Henry?"

Seth said, "I can fly the vehicle, sir."

"You are full of surprises, Seth. Let's get out of here." Henry gave Mike a quick glance. "I'm sorry, Mike."

The two ran through the corridor's emergency exit. No sooner had they piled into the aircar than Mike burst through the emergency exit.

"Get the damn thing up, Seth."

Seth leaped into the pilot's seat and toggled several controls. The aircar jerked up, rose several meters and hovered. Mike appeared directly below, pleading for them come back down, that he would help them, that he wouldn't kill Henry. The psychotic soliloquy lasted all of a minute before Mike fell to his knees and smashed his fists at the concrete, launching a cloud of crushed stone into the air.

"Should we help Mike, sir?"

"Forget about it. I don't think that's the Mike I knew."

"Where to, sir?"

"I don't have a clue."

"But I do." Liz leaned forward from the back seat and whispered into Henry's ear.

Chapter 6

Henry sat back in the copilot's seat and gazed out a window panel as they passed over the south end of the bay. Remnants of bridge towers and the bows of several half-sunken ships pierced its cold waters. A colony of gulls, maybe thirty strong, glided below them, unperturbed by the devastation below.

"Lucky for you there are no foot pedals, Seth. How did you ever learn to fly one of these?"

"Learn, sir?"

Henry shook his head. "I don't know if you're being honest or sarcastic."

Seth was the best thing that happened to him. After Liz died, the weight of living alone threatened to undo what little remained of his sanity. Isolation was a cold demon. Coming across Seth saved his life.

<>

On the day they met, a light rain fell, coating pine needles and branches with a translucent glaze. Henry perched about twenty feet up a scraggly pine and his deerskin did little to keep out the sodden cold. He glanced over his shoulder at a feeble glimmering to the east. The gray light of morning was about to arrive, and with it, a clear line of sight. He focused on a sprig of blackberries that he hung at a turn of the trail below and sucked on an apple to keep his breath natural and undetectable. The forest and its residents had taken their time to come back after the Yellowstone blowup.

The sun slipped through the trees, painting the trail with its golden fingertips. At the sound of antlers rubbing against a tree, Henry drew his bow. A black-tailed deer with a small rack, no taller than four feet, trotted along the forest path. It paused to sniff the air, looked about, and moved farther along. When it stopped at the blackberry treat, Henry loosed his arrow.

Whether its trajectory was affected by a slight movement of the tree or a gust of wind, Henry would never know. The shaft struck the deer too high, entering at its left shoulder. It leaped, and the chase was on.

Henry hit the ground at a jog. The deer would lead him on a long pursuit, so he set himself to using the scant light to pick out its tracks. After a half mile the hoof prints veered off the path. A blood smear on a low pine branch and traces of a disturbed needle thatch confirmed the new direction. The going became slower and more tedious. His prey was slowing down as well.

A dark smear across a thick stand of brambles a few feet ahead caught Henry's attention. At the faint sound of uneven and raspy breathing, an image of his ancestors flashed through his mind. He placed each step on clear ground, careful to avoid the crack of a twig. Hunting was in his blood, even if that blood was a liquid polymer. He tiptoed to a stand of trees. The breathing became louder.

Aware of an abrupt drop beyond the trees, Henry withdrew his long knife. A quarry with nowhere to go would be dangerous. The deer lay trembling on its right side. An arrow protruded from its shoulder and blood streaked its dark hide. Antlers swiveled in Henry's direction, and that was the last he saw of the deer.

The earth heaved and swallowed the animal. The rain-saturated cliff edge turned into a river of mud and fell away from Henry's feet. He swung his hand back but only came away with a tuft of grass. He stared at it in amazement as the black avalanche carried him into the ravine. Debris folded about him and the dull morning light winked out.

The world returned with the sounds of the sea—the swish and gurgle of the ocean passing over sand and between rocks. Henry opened his eyes, but saw nothing. He spat out dirt to clear his mouth and shook his head, tossing off a thin layer of muck. The wan light from above took the shape of a jagged opening. He had fallen through a roof.

He knew the house. Abandoned for half a century, the structure had succumbed to the immutable ravages of decay. Weakened rafters likely accounted for his survival. He knew the family that once lived there and recalled a bright young girl, maybe six years old—full of life, full of potential. Where was she now? Her body buried somewhere within the wreck?

A tangle of roots cloyed at him, the wet dirt became quicksand. He pulled his arms and legs free, and rolled off the oozing rubble onto a carpeted floor. The tilted room sent him sliding on the slick rug to a lower corner where he crashed into a crumbling drywall. Faded images of stuffed animals covered curled up sheets of wallpaper. Henry's stomach clenched as he realized it was her bedroom.

The ride wasn't over yet. The doorway was an arm's length away when the floor lifted, hurling him back into the corner. A deep-throated grinding reverberated through the frame house as it lurched farther into the ravine.

Henry flung off the debris, rolled along a wall, and fell through the open bedroom door. He tumbled onto a landing and bounced down the hallway steps. An ocean wave crashed through the missing front door, pummeling him backwards into a kitchen entry.

While grasping the edges of a slimy countertop, a quick personal survey confirmed that his legs and fingers were still intact with no obvious tears in his skin. A deafening crash shook the kitchen and a wall of mud, rocks, splintered wood and jagged wall boards spilled through the doorway. More of the cliffside rubble appeared to have tumbled atop the house, shifting the structure once again. In seconds, he and it would be buried under the frigid waters of the Pacific Ocean.

Henry kicked out the window above the sink. The house groaned and heaved as it gained speed, throwing him back onto the tiled floor. A cupboard door swung wide, and Henry leaped in as the kitchen turned upside down. A beat later the cabinet door slammed shut and the house exploded. Timbers squealed and shattered with a thunderous bellow. He waited for more movement, more noise. The lumber yard smell of fresh hewn wood joined the scent of dead fish seeping into his dark sanctuary. The house became silent. It had reached the bottom of the ravine.

A push on the cabinet door did nothing. He bore his shoulders against the panel, but it would not budge. He imagined a mountain of debris behind it. After several more attempts, he sat back in the dark and let loose a pissed-off sigh. After some time, an hour or maybe more, his feet and knees were becoming wet—seawater. The tide was rising and it was time to panic.

In the darkness the sound of dripping water took on a deadly character. With his clothing soaked, the water's clammy embrace climbed along his back. He slammed at the door again and again.

When the seawater reached his chest, he chanced a shout—the final, desperate act of a man about to die. "Anyone out there? I'm stuck in the kitchen. Can anyone hear me?" He knew the futility—no one would hear. There was no one left to hear.

The sound of his ticking mechanical heart counted off the last moments of his life. An image of Liz flashed by, smiling and unmoved by his predicament, as if she was waiting, waiting for his arrival in the reality to come.

"Damn it all. Not here, like this."

The water had reached Henry's neck when he heard something slide against the cabinet door—shifting mud, maybe the rising water slopping against the wood.

"Can I be of assistance, sir?"

<>

The scattered clouds offered up brief glimpses of the barren landscape below. Henry's mind drifted back to the present. "You remember when we first met?"

"Of course, sir. Is there something specific you want to know?"

Henry looked back at the setting sun. With the wet, dank weather back home, it was a sight he seldom saw.

"Were you as big of a smartass with your previous owners?"

A faint shudder shook Henry, as if the aircar had undergone a minor steering correction.

"I am sure that I was, sir."

A smell of sulfur turned Henry's head. They passed over what was left of the Yellowstone caldera. What was once a haven for tourists eager to see hot springs and bison had become a hundred-mile-wide crater laced with rivers of glowing lava. The crimson rivers ran in several winding traces through a poisonous miasma. Long gone were the bison and the mule deer and Old Faithful. No one would be visiting Yellowstone again for at least a few centuries. Then again, maybe there was no one left to visit.

After an hour feeling sorry for himself and everyone else, Henry asked, "Have you figured out if we have enough fuel?"

The sparse instrument panel appeared to lack any obvious fuel gauge, or any labels.

"That is not a problem, sir. The aircar utilizes a drive which derives its energy from the Earth's magnetic field."

The car shook again and its humming drone wavered for a second.

"What's going on, Seth?"

"Interference, sir."

"Caused by?"

"Perhaps an electrical storm—" Seth's voice trailed off as the little robot's fingers danced on the main display. "I'm afraid it may be more serious, sir."

"How serious?"

"Systems is gaining control of the car. I believe they may be unhappy with us."

"Can you override them?"

"I am not sure, sir."

The landscape below was barren of landmarks, making it difficult to guess where they were. The Yellowstone upheaval had covered much of the Midwest with volcanic ash. The aircar banked left.

"Where are we?"

"Over South Dakota, approximately forty miles west of Rapid City."

"See that clearing coming up? Can you get us there?"

Seth caught on and had his backpack in hand by the time Henry unlatched the side door. They glided over a downward slope and when the car reached the clearing, the two jumped, kicking up coils of ash as they rolled. The car continued on in a wide curve and disappeared beyond a rise. Henry wiped down the robot's eye slits. "Good job, Seth."

"Where to, sir?"

He chuckled. Seth was never dismayed, never showed any signs of stress. He was always the optimist. Henry looked about and fought back a pang of sadness. Gone were the wildflowers and endless fields of tall grasses he remembered as a boy. A blanket of acrid dust took their place, sulfurous Yellowstone ash blown out from hundreds of miles away. A few tufts of yellowed grass led up to a tree line where a small number of stunted pines and firs stuck out as faded green slashes in the pallid backdrop of toppled and debarked trees.

"We're going for a hike, Seth. This is Lakota country, the country of my ancestors. I'm going to introduce you to Chief Crazy Horse."

Chapter 7

"**Y**our coffee, sir."

"Damn, I'm thirsty—and hungry, for that matter." Henry took a long sip and cinched up his jacket against the brisk morning breeze. He moved closer to the heat while Seth grabbed a few dried branches, broke them down and tossed them onto the fire.

"What's for breakfast?"

"Dried meat, sir."

"Sounds great." He held out his cup. "Refill?"

While Seth reached back for the coffee pot, Henry said, "Last night I had a whopper of a dream. Nightmare might be a better word for it." He sucked in the aroma of the brew. "Care to hear about it?"

Seth poured. "I'm all ears, sir."

Henry ripped into a strand of beef jerky. "I was hiking, kind of like we did yesterday. It was getting dark and I needed to find a place to sleep. Up ahead, along a ridge, there was a cave. The light of a campfire, kind of an amber glow, flickered against the rocks."

Henry took a long swallow. "When I got closer, I heard a growl. A dog, a big black dog sat across the opening. So I crept up nice and slow. I didn't want to spook that animal. An old white-haired woman sat next to the beast, humming while she worked on something—a blanket in her lap."

"Was there a pot hanging over the fire?"

"How do you—"

"And was the pot full of a sweet-smelling red berry soup?"

Henry threw the rest of the jerky into his mouth. "How the *hell* do *you* know about it?"

"I just know, sir."

Henry put his cup down. "Am I awake? I mean, right now, this isn't a dream, right?"

"Who can say for sure?"

Henry had quenched his appetite, but his curiosity peaked. "Back to the dream, if it was a dream. I smelled the berry soup. My mom used to prepare it for dessert. This whole scene was right out of a Lakota legend—something you seem to already know."

"Where the dog is supposed to undo the blanket while the woman checks the soup. Then she resumes knitting. If she ever finishes the blanket, the world ends."

"You never fail to amaze me, Seth."

The robot nodded. "But in your dream, sir, something different happens."

"Damn right. I got closer. The woman was up and at the pot. Then it got really weird. I watched myself walking up to the cave. I was naked and embarrassed. The lady smiled. She seemed to be expecting me—like I was an old friend. All of a sudden the dog jumped up, barking, snapping its jaws. My other self grabbed the dog and smashed it into the cave wall. The old woman ignored all the fuss and stirred the berry soup, like nothing unusual happened. Then this guy, me, handed her the unfinished blanket, and she started knitting again. That asshole stood at the mouth of the cave, looking out, looking back at me. I got the impression he was making sure that I wouldn't interfere. And there was this awfully sad look on the old woman's face."

"The dog that kept the world from ending was dead, thanks to your other self."

What did you do, sir?"

"Nothing. I couldn't move. The old woman finished the blanket and sobbed. Things got darker. The dream was breaking up. My double laughed, and dark lines showed up on his face and body. His skin crawled and twisted, and turned into snakes. They slithered away into the underbrush. All that was left was a skeleton, a shiny skeleton. It was made of metal."

"Titanium?"

"Yeah, could have been."

"Quite a dream, sir."

"It's screwed up." Henry kicked at the campfire. "I don't get it."

"The meaning of your dream is straightforward, sir. You feel you are about to end the world."

Henry tossed his cup down. "I think someone's beaten me to it."

The breeze picked up and a cloud of dust swallowed the two. The end of the world rode on that dust. Was he really the last human being on the planet? Was the virus already in his body, like tiny snakes slithering over his titanium braincase, looking for a way in?

"It was an interpretation, sir. I didn't mean to suggest—"

"That's okay, Seth. Not everything has to be about me. It was a dream."

Seth picked up Henry's cup. "To be sure, sir."

Henry gave the bleak horizon a quick glance while rolling up his blanket. Low hanging clouds and the frigid morning air held a promise of snow. Liz, some ten paces away, took up a position in the direction they had been hiking. Her constant presence brought a smile to Henry's lips. Despite the world going to hell, there she was. His heart ached to reach out, to embrace her.

"Is she here?"

Henry nodded. "I know, I know. I see her all the time. I wish she would speak more. She ignores me when I do."

"Conversing with her may be a troubling sign, sir."

"Yeah. Schizophrenia. But what the hell, Seth. There's only me around, and all that counts is what I think. She could be a figment of my dementia. She could be a ghost. In the end, it doesn't matter."

"It must be a comfort, sir."

"Seth, I'm not crazy. I have a feeling that eventually we'll know if she's real. Only time will tell."

"Indeed, sir."

The sky blanched and a thunder boom crashed overhead.

"Time to hit the road." Henry rolled up his gear and the two quickstepped through a winding path headed east. Liz remained several paces ahead despite an occasional attempt by Henry to catch up. A gust of wind roared through the trees, releasing the few leaves yet remaining. He watched them encircle Liz, making it look like she was floating through a magical portal. For a moment, he wondered how much of the world was real anymore.

A snowflake fluttered by. "I think we're going to get some snow. Have you ever experienced snow, Seth?"

"Snow is foreign to me, sir. My first and last occupation was confined to Marin County—where you found me."

"Where you found me, and saved my life."

"I think it could be said that we saved each others' lives that day, sir."

His companion's expressionless eye slit remained inscrutable. A robot programmed with a combination of sarcasm and soulful truth—maybe he read too much into the words. Maybe the whole conversation was all in his mind. Maybe Liz was in there, too.

It was near nightfall when they heard the singing.

Chapter 8

Henry's stomach churned. The machinery inside was unlike his original organs, however the clever people at Systems managed to replicate hunger pangs. His brain cried out for nourishment, and the message came in loud and clear.

"A woman's voice. What do you think?"

"Which sound, sir?"

"Not my stomach, Seth."

The robot sidled up to Henry at the base of a boulder. They were perched on a ridge overlooking a narrow valley blanketed by shadows. A splash of light caught Henry's interest.

"Hard to say, sir. I see a few teepees and a number of figures gathered around a fire. I do not recognize the chant."

"You don't know that song?"

"I am a slave to my programming and memory, most of which was supplied by my creator."

"Aren't we all, Seth. I know that chant. My mom used to sing it." Henry closed his eyes and inhaled the pungent aroma of burning wood; the promised warmth of the campfire was like the soft touch of his mother's embrace. First, she hummed, lyrical and soothing, and when his eyes became heavy, she sang the song of the Great Spirit, a promise of peace and love between mother and child. He wanted so much for it to be real.

"We need to take a closer look, Seth. There's someone down there that shouldn't be alive, never mind singing that song."

The two wended down the icy slope, pausing once in a while in a futile effort to see if they were spotted by who-knew-what. They stood out, dark figures on a snow-covered bank. Having reached the outskirts of the encampment, they dropped to the ground and scampered behind a pair of fir trees. A single woman's voice stroked the melodic tune. Men gathered

in a circle about a large fire pit and hummed to its rhythm.
cante' waste' hoksila ake istimba
hanhepi kin waste'

A single black braid of hair swayed over the woman's buffalo hide robe which was wrapped about her shoulders and the child she held. The guttering flames illumined her and four men with an electric blue sheen. The men wore deerskin and leggings. Traditional Lakota animal hides gave way to modern clothing more than two centuries ago, but judging by such details as their moccasins and beadwork, this group had stepped out of time.

Her voice soared into the darkening sky, as if she sang to an ethereal audience extending beyond the campsite, perhaps beyond the stars.

Henry listened to the repeated refrain, and wondered if it was being sung to the babe in the woman's arms, or to him.

Good-hearted little boy, go back to sleep.
The night is good.

"Sir, are you all right?"

"I don't think so, Seth." Henry shook his head and raised himself on a knee. "The fire ... notice the lack of smoke?"

"It is odd, sir."

"Blue is not the color of burning wood." Henry picked up a dried-out branch and snapped it. The sound echoed off the surrounding trees, but no one in the group moved.

"I think we're watching some kind of animated display."

Liz materialized on the far side of the small clearing next to one of the teepees. She waved and pointed at it as if to say, "Quick, get in here," and then she disappeared.

They jogged past the fireside animatronics. Henry wondered if Liz's message might not be to watch out for something in the teepee instead. Misgivings aside, he entered. His eyes were quick to adjust to the murky interior. A shredded shirt and jeans were spread out on the ground covering a few moldering bones. Henry had seen many human remains over the years, but these offered up something new. The beasts that feasted must have had a special talent.

"What could do that?"

Seth bent over a skull with its top half sliced off. "The edges are fused, sir."

"By the looks of it, these bones have been here for decades." Henry's head snapped back. "What did you say? Fused?"

"High heat appears to have been applied."

A distant thump interrupted the conversation. It was followed by another and another, each time growing louder. Henry pulled back the deer hide a fraction of an inch. The ground shuddered as a metallic grinding joined in.

Seth whispered, "What is it, sir?"

"Too dark to see anything."

When the clatter ceased, Henry peeled back the flap a bit more. The blue flame of the campfire danced its ghostly shadows across the encampment. The positions of the men and the woman remained as before, encircling the fire, oblivious to them or to the noisy visitor. Henry concentrated on the opaque spaces between teepees, pausing at each to allow his eyes to adjust. When he pushed out the flap to check alongside his tent, he saw four green pinpoints of light revolving in a circle. A faint mechanical hum suggested that the darkness concealed something large and heavy, and likely nonhuman.

"P-please return to your seats. D-do not disturb the exhibit."

The voice reminded Henry of a screech of chalk on a blackboard.

"I think it's talking to **us**, Seth."

They stepped out of the tent and took in the green-eyed monster. It was a car, maybe a pickup truck. A pair of headlights flashed on and bathed the pair in amber. A projection atop the hood continued to rotate, its lasers painting the surrounding trees with sparkling green lines.

"P-please return to your seats."

It was a pickup truck and the rear was open to the air, offering up bench seating.

"It's a tour guide. It must think we strayed off."

"The seats are not all empty, sir."

Henry came round alongside. Two mummified bodies with empty socket holes stared back at him from the back row, still clothed and skin attached, and arms wrapped around each other.

"At least they still have their heads."

While Seth lumbered onto an available bench, Henry spoke to the rotating turret. "What's the next stop?"

Its green eyes flashed. "P-please retake your seats. N-next stop— the Z-ziolkowski House."

Henry no sooner than pulled up his sack, when the automated tour lurched forward. A cloud of ash exploded over him as he landed in the laps of the two desiccated passengers. After a short coughing fit, he brushed off his face with his free hand. "At least we don't have to walk."

Seth remained stoic as always despite being thrown to and fro. He peeked over the open rear. "Looks like an axle problem."

"You're not going to ask about Ziolkowski?"

"History was part of my learning, sir. Korczak Ziolkowski began the project—the carving of the mountain. It was he who designed the Chief Crazy Horse monument."

Henry nodded and smiled. They gripped their seats as the tour mobile continued to rock. He wondered what Seth would think if he knew Liz was sitting next to him.

Chapter 9

The morning light seeped through dingy windows and cajoled one of Henry's eyes to flicker open. He swung up from the couch in one motion and pulled back his shoulder-length locks, refastening them. His breath blew out white against the frigid, gloomy interior of the bedroom. Henry knew where he was. The Ziolkowski House was built right after the Monument was completed. He remembered staying in the massive log structure when he was a child, while his mother taught at the school nearby. It was one of many buildings nestled in the valley beneath the monument—all devoted to sharing the culture and history of the Lakota as well as all the other Nations. He wondered what his parents would think about the changes, the desolation, the end of everything.

He shuffled to the window and rubbed away the grime. A light coat of snow covered the log cabins in the clearing outside. Beyond them, looming over the small valley like a Greek titan, Chief Crazy Horse sat atop his horse and pointed to the lands where his people were buried. Despite the maelstrom set off by the Icarus impact some three-hundred fifty miles to the west, the towering giant carved out of a mountain of solid granite remained intact. It never failed to humble him. After nearly one hundred years of sweat and toil, it remained a towering testament to an indomitable human spirit. Henry's jaw tightened as he realized that he might be the last one on Earth to gaze at the wonder—the last one to appreciate its enduring humanity.

"It is magnificent, sir." Seth had sidled alongside him.

"Damn right." Henry threw on his jacket. "Let's get outside. I'm starving and I remember a native-style restaurant up closer to the monument."

"Do you think it still functions?"

"Who knows, Seth. That lullaby group last night was still going strong. Maybe they've got some robot cooks up there eager to serve us a hot, three course meal." Henry scanned the room. "Moreover, I don't see Liz here. She might be outside."

"Perhaps having breakfast, sir."

"Nice."

Minutes later, the two arrived at the Laughing Water restaurant, a single story structure built of logs with large picture windows, dark against its bleak gray exterior. Glass shards hung from several openings.

"It's not looking too promising, Seth."

"I agree, sir. However, let's keep our chins up."

Once inside, the cheerless gloom persisted in spite of a brightening sky outside. Tables and chairs were scattered about the floor. The charred remains of what might have been a campfire dominated the center of the expansive room. A desiccated body sat upright on a chair in a far corner. Henry half-expected it to rise, overjoyed at their arrival. Instead, it remained fixed in place with moldy orbs continuing their long and lonely vigil.

"Can I place an order, please?" Seth sat at the counter facing the kitchen.

"What are you doing?"

A pair of swinging doors parted.

"May I be of service?" The automaton that emerged wore a mildew-saturated toque canted at an angle, a soiled double-breasted jacket and checkered pants. With hands on hips, it leaned forward as if to take a closer look at its guests.

Henry noted the discolored face and the distended nose. Its plastic skin hung loosely from its chin. "Are we too early for breakfast?"

The nose wobbled as it spoke. "We have a full breakfast menu. Can I start you off with coffee?"

It couldn't hurt to ask. "Yeah. Just for me. Seth, here, isn't hungry."

The mechanical chef disappeared through the swinging doors, followed by the sounds of metal pots clanging on the floor. Seth looked up at Henry who leaned away from the counter.

"I know what you're thinking, Seth. I want to see what he comes up with."

A minute later, the kitchen doors squealed and the chef reappeared with a ceramic cup and saucer in one hand and a tarnished metal pot in the other. The smell of burned rubber wafted across the counter.

Henry said, "You know what? I changed my mind. I think we'll be leaving."

The robot seemed not hear and set down the cup and saucer while angling the coffee pot. Nothing came out. It then reached under the counter and brought up a container of condiments bristling with an unappetizing display of black mold.

Henry said, "Let's check out the back."

"Sir, customers are not permitted to enter the kitchen."

Henry and Seth picked up their bags and ambled around the end of the counter. The robot chef continued to hold the coffee pot askew and cocked its head in apparent dismay.

"Jeez."

The kitchen tiles might have been white fifty years ago. Dark streaks of mold ran across the floor and walls. Several mechanicals lay sprawled across rusty counter tops. None moved. A gas burner near one flickered with an unsteady blue flame.

"It's a wonder this place didn't burn up years ago."

"It could use some maintenance, sir."

"This place is so far gone, I don't even see any rats."

As Henry stepped over a pile of pots and pans, he heard the sound of footfalls.

"Did you hear that, Seth?"

"I did, sir."

"Stay here." Henry dropped to all fours and crawled along the center counter which ran the length of the kitchen. Mid way along, he rose to his knees and hazarded a peek. A dark shape, taller than a man, bolted to the rear entrance. Clippety-clappety footfalls brought to mind hard-heeled boots striking stone tiles.

Henry got to his feet. "Hey, come back. We mean you no harm."

The figure ran out the rear door. By the time Henry and Seth emerged, there was nothing to see but a small clearing and the forest beyond.

"I wonder who that was?"

Seth bent over and pointed at the thin snow cover. "Perhaps, sir, it was more a what than a who."

The markings were unsettling—three-toed footprints.

<>

Anth opened the door to her home pod a tiny crack. Father was still wrapped up in his warming robe, while mother cleaned the foraging table.

"Where have you been? And close that door."

Anth stilled her panting and stepped inside, grateful for the heated air.

"Will you answer my question?"

"I was out for a walk. You know, exploring … nowhere special."

"The morning meal is over. There will be nothing to eat until tonight. When your father wakes, you'd better have a good reason for your wandering. He looked for you all over the house and outdoors. You've got chores."

"Don't worry. I'll do them." She hissed the words out.

"Watch your mouth. If your Father ever heard you speak that way …we've told you over and over again that you should never go exploring alone. There is no telling what dangers you might run into."

An image of a dark figure leaped to Anth's mind—one accompanied by a small metallic creature. The taller one had arms and legs, but lacked a scaled head. Instead, it had a grotesque growth of black hair. She was familiar with hair, as her duties at the archive center had exposed her to many a human specimen. The creature was repulsive, but she nonetheless would learn more about it. It was the first living human she had encountered since their arrival.

"It was just a walk. There was no danger. When will you allow me live my own life?"

Her mother paused wiping the table. "Were you with that boy, Genz? There's plenty of time for that sort of thing."

"No, mother. I told you. *Just a walk.*"

"I'm sorry dear, but because you're of age is no reason for you to continue to disobey us. We have been chosen for this mission. That means you too. We all have been tested and qualified for colonization. Don't forget the people back home depending on us. Our success will rely on discipline and close adherence to the guidelines set forth by the Elders. Exploring on your own jeopardizes this mission. Even though all the humans are long gone, don't assume it's safe out there. There are dangerous animals, artifacts, all kinds of things. Do you understand?"

Anth strode past her mother, entered her room and slammed the door behind her.

Chapter 10

Beyond the shadow cast by the restaurant, the dull warmth of the sun thinned the remaining strips of snow, and with it, any further trace of three-toed footprints.

"Seriously? That's what we followed out of the restaurant?"

"The markings resemble some fossil tracks, sir."

"That was no fossil. It looked like a person, like you or me—well, like *me*." The forest ahead curved up the side of the Monument. Henry shook his head. "No use trying to track it; too many rocks up there."

"We could proceed in the general direction it took. Perhaps we'll get lucky, sir."

Henry sighed and let out a chuckle. He was about to lecture Seth on the art of tracking, when Liz stepped out from within a crag and walked up into the ponderosa stands beyond.

"Maybe you've got something there, Seth." Henry swung his sack over his shoulders. "Let's give it a try."

Halfway up the slope, the pair slowed down. Henry sensed a growing weakness in his limbs. He hadn't eaten since the evening before. Even a mechanical metabolism demanded input as did its biological predecessor. Seth said, "We can take a break here, sir. I have some more dried meat—"

"Why didn't you tell me that before we went to the restaurant?"

Seth canted his body as if shrugging.

"Yeah, yeah—I didn't ask."

A half-hour later they reached the foot of the Monument. The raised foreleg of the giant stallion loomed overhead, and beyond that, Crazy Horse's outstretched arm.

"Whew. I've never been up here this close."

"It is quite impressive, sir."

"Near six hundred feet high."

Henry clambered up a pile of jagged granite rocks and stopped to take in the brisk air. His gaze drifted over the hills in the distance, taking in the wisps of color embedded in the tall fir. A hawk flew over the treetops below and threw Henry a cry that echoed across the narrow valley. He might be the last human on Earth and that thought left a kind of hollow feeling within him, one he wasn't sure would ever go away.

The hawk's cry still reverberated within his mind, when a twinkle of silver, perhaps reflected sunlight, caught his wandering gaze. The short-lived glint came from the valley floor.

"Something's out there."

Henry pulled the binoculars from his sack.

"What do you see, sir?"

"We need to find some cover." He threw the field glasses into his pack and skipped over the rubble. "There's an aircar coming our way."

Seth leaped after Henry, landing on each rock with remarkable precision. "Sir, we can hide in the access tunnel."

Henry stopped short. "Access tunnel?"

"According to my memory, there should be an entrance beneath this statue. It was used by the stone workers for storing supplies."

Henry surveyed the way down. The sharp outcroppings promised a tedious descent. "Is it far?"

"Here, sir." Seth pointed up at a dark cleft beneath the horse's hoof only a few yards away. The two scrambled back up and ducked into the alcove.

Henry heaved at a rust-mottled iron door. "Locked."

The unmistakable drone of the aircar drew nearer.

"Do you think it's the one we used?"

Seth leaned his dome of a head past the edge of the entryway. "Hard to tell, sir. It does appear to have identical markings."

A metallic clang turned both heads back to the iron door in time to see it swing open about a foot. "Get in." The voice carried with it a hint of an echo.

"Did you hear that, Seth?"

The little robot nodded. He glided past Henry and disappeared behind the door. "Come, sir. We've been invited inside."

Henry reached into his pack, wrapped his fingers about the revolver, and followed Seth into the gloom. His nose flared at the stench—a mix of tobacco and rotten cabbage. The door squealed shut behind them, cutting off all light.

"What are you?"

46

Henry spoke in the direction of the voice which seemed quite near. "How about some light?"

"You're with 'em, out there in the valley, ain't that right?" The voice came from everywhere.

"I don't know who 'them' is. We've been travelling for a couple days, hiking you might say. We're from San Francisco."

After a pause, it spoke again. "Frisco? That's no couple-a-days hike."

"It's a long story. We stole an aircar."

Another pause. "Are you human? I mean, 'sides your little robot, are *you* human?"

"Another long story. My body's artificial, but my brain is the original. I think that qualifies me as human."

"Damn. You're one of 'em. Come to finish me off, ain't that right?"

Henry heard a double click—the unmistakable sound of a round entering a chamber. He pulled back the hammer of his Colt and eased the weapon out. "No, no. I don't even know what you mean by 'one of them.' I told you, we were passing through and—"

"Whatever you are, you ain't gonna get me."

Henry heard a yelp from the doorway followed by a sound a sack might produce when hitting the ground.

"It's all right, sir. Our host is still alive."

Henry uncocked his gun and pulled out a small flashlight. The beam caught Seth waving his bat, and at his feet, a body of a man covered in animal skins. A black automatic, which looked a century old, lay just beyond his fingertips. Long, scraggly gray hair with beard to match hid the man's face.

Henry was about to step closer to get a better look, when Liz appeared before him. Her eyes were wide and locked on his. Her mouth fell open as if to say something. Then the world turned black.

Chapter 11

Henry recalled what pain was all about and rubbed a temple in a reluctant tribute to days long gone. His body told him he had undergone a shock, a result of the blow to his head, which his fingers confirmed by running over a slight depression over his right ear.

He opened his eyes.

"Ah, you're back. You fellas sure are made to last."

The man speaking to him was the one who Seth had laid out. His silver hair ran in long glistening tangles over his eyes, catching the guttering light of a candle set on a wall shelf. He rocked back and forth on a stool with its front legs rising with the motion.

Seth appeared to be seated next to the man. The little robot was propped up against the wall like a lifeless doll.

A woman wearing coarse-knitted clothing leaned against the wall. As gray a shadow as the man, her brief smile revealed a startling row of missing teeth.

Henry said, "Who are you two? I thought everyone was dead—done in by the Yellowstone."

The woman shook her head while the man stood. "The name's Mick, but you won't be needin' to know that much longer. Those Systems people are damn good, ain't they, Jaynie?"

Henry tried to rise, but found his torso and arms were tied with a rope to a pole at his back. That was when he got a closer look at Seth. His little companion's head drooped over his chest, revealing an open metal flap.

"What the hell have you done? We're no threat to you."

"Yeah, right. Jaynie, bring over them pliers for me, will you hon?"

"Hold on, hold on. We are not from Systems. *I'm* human, not one of their robots. In fact, they were after *us*. And Seth there—he's my friend, a domestic robot." Henry pulled at his bindings. "You better have not hurt him."

"Did ya hear that, Jaynie. 'Not *hurt* him?'" The old man coughed up a witch's cackle.

Jaynie said, "Maybe this feller is a might loose in his head."

"Loose is right. And about to become more loose."

The two laughed as Mick drew nearer. "This here robot of yours is no human invention, and neither are you. Friggin' blue skin is a dead giveaway." The man rubbed the top of his head. "And this here bump must've been my imagination. We'll soon see how human you really are."

Mick brought the pliers up to Henry's head. "I have to admit, you're a damn fine piece of work. A little tinkering, and who knows what we'll find. I think I see the seam. Jaynie, hold its head steady."

Henry jerked away. "Check my bag. There's stuff in there that'll prove I'm human."

"Already have. Impressive collection and I especially like that Colt. My granddaddy used to have one just like it. You've been busy."

"It's not a collection, damn it."

The pliers winked in the dark like some silvery lizard intent on having dinner. Henry heaved against the rope when someone or something struck the door with a heavy, metal-on-metal clang.

Mick said, "Your friends? Come to rescue you?"

Henry whispered. "If they're coming for me, it isn't a rescue."

Jaynie glided to the door and uncovered a peephole. "Damn System robots." Her voice faltered. "We're done, Mick."

The clanging got louder.

Mick turned back to Henry. "Son of a bitch. You brought 'em here." He leaned over Henry and said, "Lights out, champ."

Henry felt a nip at the elastic skin at the base of his neck.

Jaynie screamed. "They're coming through."

Mick twisted his body around enough for Henry to see a deep red glow appear near the door lock. A moment later, a flash of yellow filled the room. Henry heard a wet gasp as Mick fell against him and slid to the floor. The odor of seared flesh wafted up from his body. The woman's wild screams ebbed, becoming more like the mournful bleats of a doomed animal.

Henry shifted his torso, aiming a turn of rope into the narrow beam of light coming through the door. A second later, everything went dark, except for a smoldering round hole in the door. He strained at the burning rope and snapped it.

The stricken woman was somewhere near the door.

"Jaynie, is there another way out of here?"

He heard her gasp. "What do you care? Mick … Mick." A sharp double-click followed. "This here shotgun'll put them tin cans to bed."

Mick's body had taken out the single candle when it fell. Henry used the shaft of light streaming in through a hole where the door lock had been only moments ago to spot Seth sprawled on the floor. "Take it easy, Jaynie. You've got to believe we're no threat to you."

"Them that's outside is all I care about."

"I think they might only be after me. Don't do anything crazy, and maybe they'll leave you alone."

Henry caught the gleam of the shotgun barrel. Jaynie hefted it to her shoulder and whispered, "There's a reckoning to be had."

A shudder ran through him. Things were about to go from bad to very bad. A rattle at the door jerked him into motion. He fumbled with the flap at Seth's neck, restoring several connecting plugs.

"I'm back, sir. What is the situation?"

"We've got visitors—probably the ones from the aircar."

The door squealed in fits and starts. Something pushed against it, bending the iron cross brace inward. A narrow band of light slipped through a crevice at the door and fell across Jaynie who sat propped up nearby. She steadied the shotgun, aiming it at the door. Blood pulsed through a jagged line across her bodice.

"Jaynie, you're hurt."

She wheezed, "Get out. I'm a goner. But I ain't goin' quiet. If you really are human, get out. There's a back door … a ladder—"

The door slammed against the bracing, almost lifting it off its loosening hinges.

"Let's go, Seth."

Henry found his revolver on the floor and grabbed up his quill and bow. "Leave the bags, Seth." The two raced to the back of the room. Henry swung open a wooden door to a shadowy maw.

"Jeez. The smell."

"My senses detect waste matter, sir."

Henry swung the door closed behind them, and heard the iron entryway collapse, followed by a shotgun blast. "I can't see a thing. Jaynie said something about a ladder."

A suffuse red light moved along the wall in front of them.

"Damn, Seth. I forgot about your built-ins."

Seth turned his head in an arc, allowing the light from his eye slit to paint a clear picture of the space ahead which illuminated a vertical shaft with a rusty ladder bolted to its side.

"So, do we go up or down?"

Seth pointed downward with his bat. "The smell is coming from there, sir."

Henry marveled at the bat, but there was little time to comment. "Then it's up."

He lifted Seth onto the ladder and clambered after him. They climbed for a minute before hearing the sound of breaking wood from below.

"How much farther, Seth?"

"A few more rungs, sir. I see the outline of a round seal above us."

The ladder vibrated.

Seth pushed up on a curved metal lid and in seconds they clambered atop Chief Crazy Horse's flowing mane. Henry lowered the cover and braced himself against a towering lock of granite hair. "They're coming. Where the hell do we go next?"

Seth ambled around the undulating precipice and raised his bat. "I suggest we prepare ourselves, sir."

Henry caressed the Colt at his belt. The ladder shook as the sound of footfalls along its rungs grew louder.

"Sir, we have company."

Henry pivoted while withdrawing the revolver.

The creature stood about eight feet tall with arms and legs proportioned like a human. Yellow-green scales covered the length of its body, a naked body, while a Mohawk-like protrusion of silvery scales erupted from its head giving it an unsettling twentieth century feel. The scaling smoothed out and became darker at its hands which displayed three long and thin fingers. Henry's attention was drawn to its eyes, slitted and dark green, set in yellow orbs.

"Who are you?"

The creature's mouth opened to a set of pointed teeth. It hissed, producing a silky serpentine sound—an effect underscored by the intermittent appearance of a pink, forked-tongue.

The lid swung up. The reptilian leaped past the two and slammed the hatch back down with a leg. The movement caused a set of membranous wings to unfold from beneath its arms. It bounded back to Henry and wrapped its legs about his torso. The hatch's cover flew up and a silvery head emerged from the shaft.

When Henry's feet left the ground, he called out. "Seth."

He and the reptilian glided down into the valley and plunged through the leafed canopy. His last glimpse upward caught the tip of Seth's bat moving as if waving to him.

Chapter 12

Fierz extended his arms. The wrinkled membranous wings stretched from wrists to waist. Now stiff and useless, he recalled at time when they billowed in the balmy updrafts that ran alongside his mountain dwelling back home. Gliding through canyons and valleys, unbound, invincible, with the heady confidence of youth, the world had been his.

He blinked away the memory and lowered his arms, allowing the ephemeral ghosts of times long ago to fade. Reality held him in its vice-grip, trillions of miles away from home. Even the miracle science of stasis had not held back the effects of countless years of travel. He shook off the past with a shrug, for he was the vanguard of his people for which no sacrifice was too great. The colony was everything. So much depended on its success.

He entered the examination room where Anth awaited. "What have we here?"

His daughter leaned over the table. "A curious artifact, father. I found this specimen at the great statue."

"That's far beyond our perimeter. I told you to stay close to our base. There's no telling what dangers await us here. We have Soofysh machines to do the searching for us."

Anth bowed her head. "I am old enough to take care of myself."

"Old enough?" Fierz thought about giving her yet another lecture, but dismissed the comment with a brief snort and instead fixed his attention on the humanoid stretched out before him. Anth's posture suggested that she was about to speak again, no doubt more drivel about her personal freedoms. He raised his hand and said, "I want to take a closer look at this specimen of yours."

After running an oblong device over the chest of the prostrate form and analyzing its output, he said, "It appears this construct has lungs or what passes for such an organ. Curious. A robot that breathes. You say it was conscious?"

"One of the Soofysh trackers forced it to the top of the monument. It may have been struck by a branch when we flew down."

"From the top?" Fierz was certain that his neck coloring gave away his displeasure. "That was reckless. How many times have I—"

"I'm sorry, father, but this creature was most unusual. I had to get closer."

Fierz sighed and patted Anth on the shoulder. "In that, you have a point. How did you come upon it?"

"The trackers breached an entrance at the statue's base. There were two humans hiding there, yet unaffected by the plague."

"Were?"

"Unfortunately, the trackers damaged the humans within. They were dead when I arrived."

Fierz nodded. "Too bad. There is so much we do not know about the biology of these humans. I will direct the trackers to retrieve the bodies."

Anth nodded at a door with a glass panel. "But you have so many specimens."

"There's not much to learn from decomposed tissue. Fresh material will offer valuable insight." Fierz waved the hand-held scanner at the curiosity before him. "Now, this one is a different matter. I think I'll enjoy taking it apart."

"Dinner is ready!"

Mother's voice came from several rooms away, but nonetheless jerked Fierz to attention. "Your mother will not be denied. The hour is late. We can wait until tomorrow for the dissection. In the meantime, why don't you lock it up for safekeeping? Use one of the cages in your menagerie in case it wakes."

Chapter 13

Anth stepped through the sliding doors of the Library.
"A little late, aren't you?" Genz flared his nostrils as he stifled a smile. "Trouble sleeping last night?"

"Don't you have a book or something to file?" Anth averted Genz's eyes and marched past the counter.

"Hey, why the attitude? Last night was special. Did something change?"

"New day. New beginnings." Anth fought off the urge to look back. Genz was pleasant, but there were more important things on her mind today.

The Library was more a warehouse than an organized collection. In addition to books and electronic media, stacks of artifacts covered its walls—the decaying remains of human technology. Anth had been told that no humans had survived the holocaust, that they had succumbed to a fatal disease—one of their own doing. How was it that the two humans in the cave had survived?

Anth felt as if she spent all her life in school—first back home, light-years away, and then in the Library on Earth—an odd name for a planet, which according to her linguistics class, meant soil, and odder still for a planet with so much water. Translating written records was boring, and Anth hated the speech classes—listening to recordings, practicing tongue-twisting phonemes. It was tedious to learn a foreign language, especially since all those that used it were dead. That was what she thought until yesterday.

"Can I help you?"

It was Genz.

"What makes you think I need your help?"

"You've been standing there for a while. Are you lost or in a trance?"

"Don't be funny. I'm just thinking."

"Thinking about me, I bet."

"Get off your pedestal." Anth moved to one of the nearby shelves and pointed. "What are these things?"

"You should get out more often. Translating all those Earth books can't be good for your social development."

"And you're some kind of expert at socializing—here in this dump?"

"You thought so last night."

Anth grabbed a small device off the shelf. "Get serious."

Genz swept it out of her hand. "That's a communications unit. We've found thousands of these—based on electron storage and electromagnetic fields. They used relay towers, some even relied on satellites."

"Given their level of technology, they were clever to come up with that."

"Not clever enough to save themselves."

Anth's neck flushed a pale shade of amber. "Have you ever thought that maybe they didn't all die out?"

"Right." Genz came closer. "If that were true, we would never have come here, and you and I would have never met."

Anth forced her gaze to the hallway. "Is this it? Nothing new?"

"That all depends. The trackers bring in stuff every day."

"What about today?"

"There's all kinds of crap in the back. Follow me." They moved through several rooms, some of which were stacked to the ceiling with piles of relics. "I don't know how we'll ever get through all this junk."

"It may not all be junk."

They arrived at a room that had the largest mound. "This is it. The newest garbage is on top. See anything you want?"

"There's a lot here. You better get back to your desk. I'll call you if I need you."

Genz pivoted and swung his head to Anth, who anticipated the move and pushed him off. "Now is not the time."

"Sorry." Genz's powerful limbs swayed as he walked away with his head lowered.

Anth called out to him. "I'll be back tonight."

Genz continued into the next room without even a nod. Anth whispered to herself. "Sometimes you can be such a lizard." She strolled around to the far side of the pile. It had attracted her attention the moment

56

she'd entered the room—a bronze sheen in the shape of a small humanoid.

<>

Henry ran his hands over the bars of the cage yet again and sat back down to sip up the last of the water in the bowl. Judging by the dim light from a window slit high on a wall, the day was fast ending, or beginning.

The creature behaved kind enough. Saving him from an uncertain fate was a heroic act, and for that, he would be grateful. However, it had offered no explanation. What was it? Where did it come from? At least it seemed to be on his side.

"Patience."

"Liz?"

Henry heard shuffling sounds beyond the closed door. The room had to be a part of a larger complex. Events came back in a blur—the sprint through the woods, the musky scent of the creature, the rush through a darkened hallway, and sleep. His dreams were speckled with visions of aliens probing and taking specimens. The clang of the cage door had stirred him awake. The creature had pushed a bowl into the cage and darted out.

He leaned back against the bars and concentrated on the shadows. The black outlines of his bag, quill and bow were visible on a table across the room. Apparently the creature had explored the storeroom. That there was no sign of Seth worried him. More cages extended to either side, standing several feet high and about six feet wide. In one, a furry animal curled up and raised its head. Sad eyes within dark circles fixed on him. Another cage contained something larger—a ball of fur rising and falling. None of his fellow captives showed any excitement or agitation. Henry rubbed his fingers on the inside of his bowl and wondered what it was he had consumed.

<>

The muted window light was gone. It was evening. Henry wrapped his fingers around the bars and shook them. Survival and escape should have been on top of his list, but he began to obsess about relieving himself. Even an artificial body had its needs.

The lights came on—blinding lights. His neighbors grunted and hissed, knocking their bodies against their cages. Dozens of enclosures lined the walls behind him. He was in a zoo.

Henry scanned the room, trying to gather as much information about his prison and his keeper as possible. Judging by the design of the cages, the scant furniture, even the lights on the ceiling, everything looked human-made.

On the far side, a single door swung open. The zoo keeper entered and said, "Do you understand English?"

Each uttered consonant was bracketed by a hissing sound, the scaly creature could have been in a B-rated Hollywood monster movie. Henry half-expected seeing a zipper running down its back. The illusion was fast put to bed by the pink tunic. Emblazoned on its shoulder was a familiar symbol—a black circuit diagram on gold.

"Yes, I do. Who are you and how is it that you speak English?"

"What is your function?"

What a strange question. "Didn't I see you in the kitchen back at the Crazy Horse Monument? That was you, wasn't it?"

"What are your normal duties?"

"I don't have duties. That coat you're wearing—what does the insignia mean? Who are you working for?"

"The symbol is Soofysh. I do not, as you say, work for them. They work for us."

The last syllable slithered out of the side of its mouth, almost as if it was reluctant to speak.

"Who is 'Soofysh'?"

"A name for our partners."

"Let me guess. Does the English word 'Systems' come close?"

The creature threw Henry a wide-eyed look. "You know of it?"

"Oh, I know of it." Henry swept his arm in a half-circle. "So, Systems and Soofysh are one and the same, and they're keeping a menagerie?"

The creature hesitated before answering. "Menagerie?"

"These animals ... all in cages."

"They do not belong to Soofysh. They belong to me."

"Your pets?"

The reptilian stepped closer, nearly within arm's reach. Its eyes turned a deep green.

Henry said, "Your questions—you think I'm some kind of robot? The color of my skin—I can explain."

It bent over as if to take a closer look. "You look like one, though I have never seen such a one. Are you saying you are not a mechanical construct made to look human?"

"I am human. I was sick, dying. Systems saved my life by putting my brain in this artificial body." Henry paused a moment, realizing how weird he must seem. "I know what that sounds like."

"It sounds impossible."

"There was a robot with me—a small one."

"A robot with a pet robot. How remarkably curious."

"Damn it all. I'm not a robot. His name is Seth. Do you know what happened to him?"

At that moment a second figure entered the room, a bit taller and wider than the first, but wearing the same pink uniform. It launched a string of gurgled hisses at Henry's keeper who stood and pointed back at the door. The keeper responded with a similar volley, but louder. The visitor backed up and eased the door closed as it left.

"Colleague?"

"My father. He does not want his daughter to keep such pets. He feels that these animals are for consumption—for food."

Henry looked about. "Most of these would also serve as food for humans, but I don't think you'll find me edible."

"Oh, my father has a great interest in you, but not for food. He is anxious to begin the dissection. There are few robotics still operating on this planet, your Earth. He loves to take things apart and he thinks you will provide much information about human technology."

"That's rich. I am not so sure that I'm a product of human technology."

"What else can you be?"

Henry thought about the Soofysh, aka Systems. They were the ones that saved his life, but why?

"You must have some kind of scanner, something to see inside my body." Henry pointed at his head. "There is a human brain in here. My titanium skull is the reason I'm still alive."

"Explain."

"Before I do, maybe we can get acquainted—you know, introduce ourselves. It's what humans do. Hell, it's what civilized people do. My name is Henry Wind In Trees. How about you? Do you have a name?"

The reptilian stared at Henry as if deciding what to do with him. Henry added, "I am no threat. You could at least be nice."

The creature lolled its head from side to side, and said, "Anth."

"Only the one word?"

"Family names are held in private."

"You can call me Henry, if it's easier for you."

"You have not explained what you mean by 'still alive'."

"We had an epidemic. A disease was released into the air by the asteroid that crashed in Montana, a part of this continent some few hundred miles west of here. It happened a while ago. The news reports said it was a virus, incurable, that the whole world was affected. It killed off just about all human life. It killed my wife."

"Wife?"

"My life partner. A female human I loved and expected to live with for the rest of my life."

"We have similar relationships. I am sorry she died. But what you said about the disease—that is nonsense. There is no such disease. Humans destroyed each other with poisons."

"Who told you that?"

"The evidence is clear. Everyone on this planet died about the same time. I am surprised that you think a disease was released by some natural disaster that killed only humans."

"Who are you people?"

Anth curled her mouth up into what might have been a smile, if one ignored the row of needle-like teeth jutting from below her upper lip.

"Do you not recognize us?"

"I've never seen the likes of you before."

Anth reached for something on the desk behind her. "Perhaps this will refresh your memory."

A book landed in his cage. Henry gaped at the words emblazoned across its leather cover: 'The Illustrated History of the Cretaceous Period.'

Chapter 14

Henry pushed his waste pot through the narrow opening below the cage door. His physical relief was soon displaced by a dark mood. Yesterday's encounter with Anth served up more questions than answers. After a restless night, he spent most of the morning paging through the book—a treatise on the fossil remains of dinosaurs that lived some 65 to 145 million years ago. The author suggested that most disappeared after an asteroid strike. Henry was aware of the theory—debris tossed high into the air resulted in dense clouds over the entire Earth, cutting off sunlight, and killing critical plant life—a lot like what happened much more recently, but worse. Things were so bad that large animals starved to death. Dinosaurs became extinct.

Anth's three-toed feet brought to mind some of the fossil species described in the book, but her hands had three fingers, and she didn't have a tail, at least not an obvious one. Of course, early humans might have had tails. Besides, she was intelligent—a thinking creature, not a damn dinosaur.

The door opened and Anth approached Henry's cage. "Luck is with you. My father does not wish to disassemble you yet."

"You told him about me? That I'm not a robot?"

"I chose to keep our conversation a secret."

The news was welcome. "He would be killing the last of the human species."

Anth wagged a finger. "You know that to be untrue."

"It's incredible."

"What?"

"That finger wiggle."

"A habit of mine—a leftover from childhood—we learned to erase errors that way."

"Still ... a damn coincidence. So, you knew about the others ... back at the monument?"

"I was surprised as apparently you were to find they were alive." Anth gazed into Henry's pot. "You produced this?"

"If you fed me I could have produced more, but I suppose that would be a waste of time and food. Hell, why feed a specimen that's slated for dissection?"

Anth lifted the bowl and appeared to take in its aroma using a narrow set of openings over her mouth. "An unusual talent for a robot."

"I told you—"

"I'm beginning to think you may be speaking the truth."

"Then you have to release me. Humans are not pets, nor are they for consumption, or for that matter, dissection."

"You are hardly human. A brain in a machine ... I can see why father has such an interest."

Henry pointed to his head. "So he knows what's in here, but still wants to take me apart?"

"He is our leader and chief scientist. His duty demands he understand all the possible dangers to our colony and learn of the technology that may still exist on this planet."

"You must already know, this technology is not human."

"I suspect he knows, and it excites him even more."

"You said colony?"

"I've told you too much." Anth turned away as if intending to leave.

"Are you comfortable keeping me in a cage? Do I amuse you?"

"You do not."

"Even in your culture, you must know what your father intends to do is wrong."

Anth glanced at the door and whispered. "If I let you go ... you will leave, never to return?"

"What if I don't? What if I choose to stay, to talk to your father? Maybe he's more reasonable than you give him credit for."

Anth straightened up. "You do not know him. That would not be brave of you. It would be foolish."

Henry grasped the bars of his cage with both hands. "Then I won't come back. But there's a catch. What have your people done to Seth? He may be a robot, but he's my friend. Don't tell me your father took him apart."

Anth ran to the door without a word.

"Leaving?"

The door slammed shut and the lights dimmed off.

<>

Next morning, the sound of rain pelting against the single window stirred Henry awake. The foul musk of his fellow inmates hung heavy in the humid air. His artificial, but convincing abdominal cramps reminded him of the need for food.

He sat with his back against the bars staring into the semi-darkness, hoping for inspiration; he'd even settle for a dumb idea over none at all. The door swung open and the lights came on. Along with Anth's familiar padding, he heard a distinct clap-clapping on the tiled floor.

"How are you this morning, sir?"

A little bronze head peered out from behind Anth's legs.

"Seth!"

"It is I, sir."

"Are you all right? I thought those Systems robots got to you."

Henry looked up at Anth. "How?"

"Your little robot is quite clever."

Seth said, "When I saw you were rescued, I opted to play dead."

Anth said, "I found him on a pile in the Library. He looked lifeless, that is, until we were alone."

Seth said, "It was then I chanced to reactivate. Anth was kind enough to reunite us."

Henry shook his head. "Does this mean you're letting us go?"

Anth reached for the locking mechanism on the cage. "Tell me … where are you going?"

Henry wasn't about to confide in her that he didn't have a clue, since he was being led by someone long dead. "Not sure." He looked about, half-expecting Liz to turn up." I guess we're trying to locate Systems headquarters." Anth cocked her head as he continued. "To find out why they're trying to kill me."

Her eyes widened. "Tell me more."

It took a few minutes to describe the attempted mandatory upgrade, the escape across the bay and the aircar ride. Anth paced back and forth.

Henry said, "Well?"

"Your Systems … they do sound like our Soofysh."

"I never saw any Systems people that looked like you."

"I work at their Library—a job they provided us, my family. The catastrophe you described, the disease—it all occurred at about the same time we were informed of the availability of this world for colonization."

Henry took a moment. "Quite a coincidence. Maybe they were lucky, being nearby when it all happened."

"I doubt it." Anth's shoulders lowered and her head bowed. "What if they arranged for the extermination of your race? They have that capability."

"Would your people do that? Would they sterilize a planet to make way for colonization?"

"We are not Soofysh. We are not so cruel. The Soofysh are a mechanical, artificial intelligence system of protocols designed to discover new worlds fit for settlement. I think you would call them un-manned probes. They were deployed many years ago, before I was born, to locate solar systems capable of supporting our life."

"But your people built them. You programmed them."

"Even that I'm not sure of. My father once explained that our ancestors … what is the word … contracted their services."

Unsure of what to do, Henry stepped out of the cage and sat on the desk. He scooped up his revolver and quiver. "Why are you doing this

"Did your father agree?"

"He did not."

"You'll be in trouble."

"It wouldn't be the first time."

"How will you explain our disappearance?"

Anth moved from cage to cage, opening each.

"You're letting your pets out? What will you tell your father?"

"There's nothing to tell. I'm coming with you."

Chapter 15

Henry took the lead along a forest path while Anth trudged along with a skip to accommodate his shorter strides. Seth kept up the rear and nodded his inscrutable head in apparent satisfaction. They were leaving tracks. The mid-morning sun made a good show of peeling back a few rain clouds—shafts of light painted the way ahead. Henry thought that would make the going easier for both them and their pursuers.

Anth was at his elbow when he said, "How long before your father comes after us?"

"I doubt my father will. He is old and devoted to the management of the colony. The Soofysh may come. It depends on what my father will tell them. His interest in you may not decrease because we ran off."

"That's not the kind of interest that eases my mind. And wouldn't he come after you?"

"It would be his duty."

What an odd way to put it.

"Did you say your father will talk to the Soofysh? I thought they were some kind of algorithm."

"That they are, but they can take on physical forms. And I think they are still here."

Liz disappeared from the path ahead and reappeared next to Henry. The transition caused him to freeze. He was about to speak to her, when she flitted back to the path steps ahead.

Anth said, "What happened? Did you see something?"

Henry shook his head. "Just a thought … just a passing thought." He wondered if Liz was no more than a Soofysh construct, an implanted vision for reasons known only to some mysterious entity. His stomach recoiled at the idea.

"The Soofysh rarely appear in any form. I myself have never seen them."

"How can you be sure they exist? For all you know, your people invented the concept to justify the carnage and colonization."

"I have seen my father speak to them in his office—using a monitor device."

"What the hell do they talk about?""

"Progress of our efforts at establishing a permanent base."

The reply made Henry wince. "So here you are, making yourselves at home on my planet. There's no one left to stop you. Why the hell are these Soofysh still here?" Henry craved to meet one, to find out exactly what happened to Liz.

"I suppose their work here is unfinished."

Henry waved his arm in a circle. "Look around. I think they're done."

"There must be something else."

"I still don't get why you decided to run away. You're not concerned about your parents? I'm sure they'll worry."

"They are not my actual parents. I call them mother and father out of convenience. They are what you would call guardians. We were all chosen to carry out specific duties … in preparation for—"

"Colonization?"

"We were to gather up details of the Earth's chemistry, technology, resources—"

"And clean up any leftover humans you might come across?"

Anth's eyes appeared to glow.

Henry thought back to the encounter at his cabin and the chase across the bay. "These Soofysh—might they come across as robots?"

"All I know is that they have supplied us with robots—one supervises the Library, and the Tracker you encountered at the Monument. Those mechanicals have specialized functions. I think the Soofysh are different."

"Back at my cabin when Systems came to replace my brain with an artificial one—those technicians might have been human once. Is it possible the Soofysh possessed a human brain?"

"I have no knowledge of such things."

<>

Henry paused at an opening in the brush that led to a glen. The trail ran upward on the far side and disappeared under a line of trees. Liz waved at him from the other side.

"Couldn't you fly us out of here?"

Anth spread her arms. "These are for gliding. I do not fly." The translucent leathery membranes stretched thin and looked more like the webbing a flying squirrel might use.

"You figure that your people back at the colony know what we're up to by now?"

"It is a certainty we will be of concern to them."

Seth leaned out from behind Anth. "If I may, sir?"

"Ideas, Seth?"

"Perhaps we could locate a means of transportation?"

Henry thought of automobiles, but after fifty years, they would be useless—their engines seized with rust and fuel turned into jelly. Even tires made of rubber would crumble. Seth pointed away from the trail and to a break in the ridge surrounding the meadow. Henry squinted, a habit leftover from his human days and caught a glint coming from the valley floor.

"What am I seeing out there?"

"Tracks, sir. They are railroad tracks."

Henry said, "Anth, do you know anything about them?"

"I never had the chance to explore this far away from our base."

Henry wondered at the answer. By his reckoning, they had only traveled several miles—a distance easily managed by a giant reptile, especially one as rebellious as Anth appeared to be.

"I can't believe there are any working trains. They depended on electric power or diesel fuel. Anth, where did you get the juice to run your lights?"

"Juice? Ah, electricity—we have our own generators."

Seth said, "Those are smaller gauge tracks, sir. They were part of a scenic tour built some seventy years ago that used a replica engine from centuries before. They circled the Crazy Horse Monument, with a spur which led to the nearest town."

"Yeah … I recall that, but how the hell did *you* know that?"

"I just know, sir."

"And the engine?"

"A steam engine, sir."

"Which ran on wood or coal."

"What does this mean?" asked Anth.

Henry gave Liz a glance and said, "Seth, I'll tell you what. Why don't you go check out that track? See if it's in working order. Maybe you can find something we can take a ride on. In the meantime, I think it'll be better for us to stay out of sight. We'll wait right here for you."

Seth disappeared in the tall grass. Henry thought about Anth. He was sure she was hiding something. Motivation—why would she up and leave her colony? After all, would he trust two strange mechanical men that happened to waltz out of the woods?

"So, Anth, what's the real reason you decided to play hooky? You know, choose to come with us and leave everything behind?"

Anth turned away, hiding her face. "I had enough of my parents, my guardians. I am tired of all their rules. And there is the question of the Soofysh. I am sure my father knew what they did to your world. And he lied to me, to all of us."

"Knew about what?"

"What I suspect happened here. Something is wrong. My studies of your civilization provided no suggestion of an impending war or release of poisons, not even a viral outbreak, contrary to what we were told by the Soofysh."

"Yeah. But something *did* hit Yellowstone up in Montana. After the earthquakes, just about everyone died, except for folks like me." Henry pointed at his head.

"The truth must rest with the Soofysh. They were the first to arrive. If they lied about the strike—"

"How could they lie? You said they were mechanical, similar to robotic probes."

"If they are, then they *were* programmed to lie."

"By whom?"

"This, I do not know."

"You think someone released the virus?"

"Or a poison."

Henry's plastic insides knotted up—at once impressed by the detail in its construction and enraged by the thought. "Damn it all. Were we attacked by aliens and no one even knew? The news announced a meteorite strike, and I accepted it. The virus or poison … my Liz died from it. Everybody died from it." Henry looked up at Anth. "Your Soofysh aren't explorers. They're goddamn murderers. And you people were dumb enough to go along with their story." Henry took a moment. "Sorry. Maybe you were no more ignorant than we were, thinking the cataclysm was a natural event. The Soofysh may have arranged for the meteorite to strike too. Do you know if there were other strikes?"

"This I can confirm. A total of eleven appear to have occurred about fifty years ago. Each major continent was affected."

Henry sagged against a tree. "And the poison—did it kill everyone on Earth?"

"As you found out recently, most, but not all. For example, the two living under the Crazy Horse Monument must have escaped its immediate effects long enough to survive."

"That means that some others might have survived."

A branch snapped behind the pair.

"I have returned, sir."

"Hey, Seth. Did you find a train?"

The little android stepped out of the foliage and pointed back to the ridge. "In a manner of speaking, sir. Please follow me."

Henry peered up at the trees, looking for his ephemeral wife. Keeping up with Seth was a challenge as the diminutive automaton wound through forest shrubs and trees with a surprising litheness. In contrast, the cracking of low-hanging branches to his rear confirmed Anth's steady progress.

A few minutes later the trio reached the floor of the valley on the far side of the ridge. A line of train tracks curved away in the distance.

"Do you see it, sir?"

"Just tell me what I'm supposed to see, Seth."

No sooner had the words tumbled from his mouth that Henry realized what had gotten Seth so excited. The mid-morning sunlight gleamed up from the railbed. "They're shiny."

"I thought you would be pleased, sir."

Chapter 16

Henry and the reptilian sat at the base of a fir tree, scanning the sky for aircars or anything else that might crop up. An awkward silence had developed between the two. Henry, angry at the reptilians and their Soofysh colleagues, began to feel sorry for Anth. He couldn't imagine the grief she must have had in making a decision to run away from her colony and her family, even if that family was in name only. They were her people, her culture. He gave her a sidelong glance, but she continued to stare out over the valley, lost in her thoughts. With nothing clever to say, the minutes slogged by.

Seth's shouted from the tracks. "I hear something, sir." The robot lifted his head from one of the steel rails, toddled down the rail bed embankment toward Henry. The thought that a train kept running for half a century brought up an image of the chaos in the park's kitchen.

A line of black smoke curled up over the lower tree tops.

Henry said, "It's coming up that bend. I hope it's slow enough. Stay behind these trees until it passes."

"Sir, how do we know if it's going our way?"

"Anything that puts us farther away from here works for me."

The train lumbered into view with a labored chug-chug of its steam engine synced with eruptions of sparks billowing from a smoke stack. The black locomotive hauled two faded green cars and a red caboose. From a distance, the scene reminded Henry of his first toy train streaking along a circular track beneath a Christmas tree. Silver icicles threatened to ensnare it while his Russian Gray cat watched in fascination, stalking the train behind wrapped presents.

"Now!"

The three skittered down the embankment. Anth, first to reach the rear of the caboose, sprung onto its railing and reached back to scoop up both Seth and Henry in one motion. The half-sized train, designed for tourists and children, made it impossible for the reptilian to follow the other two through the windowless rear door.

The caboose was nothing more than an empty shell—streaks of dull brown rust adorned the flaking red paint on the outside, while sand and soot coated the vacant innards. Shattered windows and a half century on the tracks would do that. Henry staggered to the forward door, and with a heave of his shoulder, swung it out. He leaped over the coupling to the rear platform of the second passenger car.

A silhouetted figure appeared at the dusty door window. "Liz!" Henry tugged at the handhold and the door cracked open enough to squeeze through.

The car was empty. A coating of fine grit covered the aisle—no footprints. Five rows of double seats with faded upholstery offered up nothing more than more dust. Henry swayed along the aisle, relieved at the lack of human remains. Cold air swirled in through a broken side window, kicking up the dirt as he shuffled through, sending it out the open door to his rear.

A voice reached him through the clickety-clack. "What do you see, sir?"

"Not much. Stay where you are, Seth. I'll be back in a minute."

Henry flung open the forward door and straddled the coupling to the first passenger car. Its rear door was ajar, jammed open by the boney remains of a human foot. Tattered clothing stretched its way up the aisle before disappearing beneath a pile of ash. The car had passengers, though none appeared animated. Henry loped forward from one seat to the next. He counted five dried-out and dismembered human remains. By the looks of things, they must have been brought down by the virus, or the Soofysh poison, about the same time. The thought of the Soofsyh and their aircars spraying death over the countryside gave Henry a shiver and increased his resolve to find Liz.

A movement at the front of the car interrupted Henry's brooding. A blue capped head rose from the first seat. The shredded remnants of a conductor's jacket hung from its silver shoulders as it straightened up with a distinct series of clicks.

"Ticketsss, pleazz."

It took one step and tumbled to the floor, kicking up a plume of grime. Henry kept his eyes fixed on the automaton's outline. When the air cleared, it was splayed out like a discarded marionette freed from its strings. Henry gave himself a few moments to recover and then stepped over the heap. The spectral image of the locomotive's coal car appeared through the soiled glass of the forward door. He shoved it open and jumped.

With the help of a short ladder at the rear of the car, he climbed up, over, and in. Instead of the expected pile of coal, he landed on a solid surface with a rough texture—black paint blistered over its metallic facade. The locomotive was no steam train. He recalled the crooning Lakota woman surrounded by her braves, metal manikins programmed to entertain, huddled around a gas-powered campfire. Everything in the park was artificial. The irony was obvious. Anth was the only life form present in its natural state.

He crawled on the uneven surface and peered over the front lip of the car. The engineer's head tilted to the right side window, as if to get a better look. Its left arm held onto a chain, which looked ready to blow a whistle. It had no body, only a naked metal torso affixed to a brace. The train ran on automatic and the engineer's arm moved.

The whistle ground out a raspy screech. It had gone the way of everything in time. Henry lurched forward as the locomotive slowed down. The rails straightened out and rooftops came into view. A faded sign meandered by with the name—Custer—a small tourist town some five miles south of Crazy Horse. Henry recalled the place as a child—gunslinger shows along Main Street, stagecoach and wagon rides, lost silver mine tours. His fondest memory was of Everett's General Store, a wondrous storehouse filled with the history of the old west. The air carried the lilac perfume of old, blue-haired Mrs. Everett as she doled out homemade ice cream. His tongue glided over his palate, tasting that ice cream.

The locomotive chugged to a stop at a raised wooden platform attached to a one-story clapboard building—the train station. A white curtain fluttered in the breeze, its end flapping out a window like a languid laced tongue. Human bones and shredded clothing pock-marked the gray wooden deck.

Henry was about to leap over the coal car's wall when something tugged at this leg.

"Sir, did you see it?"

"Damn it, Seth. I thought I told you to wait back there."

"I apologize, sir."

"See what?"

"The window, sir. The one with the curtain."

Henry took in the scene again. He saw nothing out of the ordinary, considering the town was abandoned a half century ago—bones and debris, the rust-streaked dome of a black SUV lurking at the end of the station, some rusting hulks beyond, and the window—the open window of the train station.

"The curtain. You're talking about the curtain."

"Correct, sir."

"A fine, lace curtain blowing in the breeze."

"Which suggests—"

"That window's been opened recently—maybe today?"

"Maybe just now, sir."

The window exploded outward, sending a cloud of splinters and glass across the platform. Two bodies, silver and green, rolled out atop the debris.

"It's Anth and—"

"One of the Systems robots, I believe, sir."

The pair tumbled off the platform and down the embankment leading up to the raised track bed. Henry straightened up to get a better look. Anth wrapped one arm around the robot's neck and with the other tore off its head. She held the sparking silvery orb aloft, as if it was a trophy.

"What happened?"

Anth coughed and said, "This Soofysh device was about to kill you."

"How do you know that?"

She tossed the head and picked up a small oblong object. "A cutting tool like the one that was used back at the monument—the one that killed the humans who were hiding there."

"So they know where we are."

"Sir, they may know our location, but why kill us?"

"That's the sixty-four thousand dollar question, Seth."

Seth gave Henry a mini-shrug.

"Sorry, that's a reference to—"

"An ancient TV quiz show. One that was found to be fixed, sir."

"Yeah, fixed."

Henry swung over the side of the car and dropped to the track bed. "Go ahead, Seth, I've got you."

Seth leaped off the car's rim into Henry's waiting arms. The two shuffled over to the Soofysh robot's remains.

"Was it necessary to destroy it?"

"It is a Tracker, but when I saw it aiming the cutter at you, there

74

was little time to do much else." Anth bent down and reached into the robot's torso. She pulled out a black cube. "It has a device which sends out a signal to the Soofysh." She clenched her fist and the cube crumbled. "Which no longer functions."

"I guess we owe you our lives, and not for the first time."

"There is no debt. You would do the same for me."

Henry nodded, but remained perplexed. The railway had to be operating on automatic for decades. Anth and her people must have known about it, so why didn't she mention it earlier? And he doubted the Soofysh were trying to kill him. They wanted something else.

Chapter 17

"What do you mean, she hasn't called in?"

Genz lowered his head.

Fierz raised his voice, inserting an extra hiss to drive home his anger. "The Soofysh are expecting a report. You and I and Anth all agreed to the plan. Do you know how foolish I will look?"

"I am aware of the potential consequences, sir." Genz wished he could disappear. The accord had been clear and Anth swore she would keep it. She might have even been a bit over enthusiastic.

Fierz stomped across the floor—a vivid sign of distress, and even more significantly, of his frayed temperament. "Tell me that you at least know which way they went."

"I have a good idea."

"I'm beginning to think this was a horrible mistake. I should never have trusted her. We should have processed the cyborg when we had him. How am I going to explain this to the Soofysh?"

"Don't worry, sir. Before the Tracker's signal died, we had them located in a town called Custer—not far from here."

"We can't wait for Anth. She may have used the situation to get away from here—from me."

"Oh, sir, don't think that." Genz wondered if it might be true, but would she leave him? They were a team. "Maybe she's waiting for the right moment."

"The right moment was this morning. Each passing second takes them farther away. We cannot lose them."

"I'll get on it right away, sir. We have a Librarian that I can—"

"No! You will go yourself. Our robots are too unreliable; hand-me-downs from the Soofysh. They were never designed for such work. When you find Anth, you will report to me. If the Soofysh hear of this—you know how they work, and their automatons are very reliable."

Genz swallowed hard and nodded. "Sir, when I find them—"

Fierz turned away and spoke to the wall. "I've worried about her ever since she started collecting local animal life. Pets! She has an unhealthy fascination about the life on this planet, in particular, for the few humans that remain. If she has decided to turn her back on our mission, then she is of no further use to us. More than that, she may represent a danger."

"But she's your daughter." Genz liked her. He hoped she liked him too. When no reply came, he added, "I understand, sir."

Fierz spat. "Do you?"

Genz nodded and hastened out of the office.

<>

Henry squatted over the remains of the robot. "We can't stay."

"How did it manage to find us, sir? And how did it get here?"

"Good point, Seth. Maybe it came on foot or used one of those aircars. Maybe there's one parked nearby." How the robot located them was a question that irked Henry.

Anth said, "Nothing in the back of this building." She pointed down Main Street to a white steeple. "I'll search that way."

A white-washed wooden church building took up the far end of Main about a quarter-mile away. Henry said, "Why don't you go a block in to the right, parallel to Main. We'll take the left side, and meet you at that church."

Anth disappeared behind the railway station.

"I guess we better move, Seth. She's fast."

Half-century old dust-coated cars abandoned on every street gave Henry the impression of toys scattered on a playroom floor. Out of habit, Henry eyed them in the vague hope of spotting one that might yet be operable. Along the way, he and Seth wended between human remains. Judging by the open car doors, many appeared to belong to folks leaving their cars. They assumed the look of wind-blown garbage. Thankfully, the scent of death was long gone. Henry thought about the rest of the world. Were such broken, bleached shards all that was left of humanity? The Soofysh might be a mysterious entity with obscure motivations, but their handiwork screamed of a blatant disregard for human life. To Henry, they were pure evil. He imagined them in the process of cleaning up the Earth, seeing to loose ends—loose ends like himself. And how did Anth figure in all this?

A small can rolled along a raised wooden walkway and clattered onto the street. Its label missing, its silver skin gleamed in the sun. Henry crouched behind a car. Seth said, "Sir, there is something moving inside that store."

The entrance to the building was missing a door. The faded signage suspended beneath a slatted canopy suggested it might have been a grocery store. Seth pointed at the can. "Take care, sir." Several jagged puncture holes prompted Henry to reach back into his jacket for his revolver. A moment later, they heard a low growl. He whispered. "Sounds like a damn mountain lion."

"Too low for such an animal."

"Okay, maybe something bigger, a bear?"

"Based on the modulation and frequency, my guess would be more in line with the *Canis* genus."

"A dog? Isn't a dog smaller than a bear?"

"It's something related." A triangular black head with a pointed nose jutted from the doorway. Seth added, *"Canis lupus,* to be exact."

"A wolf." Henry thought he knew the sounds mountain lions and bears made. He was sure the deep-throated snarl came from such an animal. But there it was—a damn wolf, sniffing the air and craning its head to scan the length of Main.

"Don't move, Seth."

The two took up a position behind an empty horse trough at the end of the walkway. A light wind coming from the wolf's end of the street was in their favor. Even the slight odor of Henry's artificial metabolism would have screamed out their presence. Henry tightened his fingers about the revolver.

The beast took a step onto the walkway and turned its head to the church some hundred yards off. Its coat shone black, and instead of the thin, almost gaunt torso typical of wolves, this one sported an enormous barrel chest, as wide as a man's, with the skin tight against its ribs. Muscles rippled under its short black fur and the tail curled up beneath its body. Henry shuddered as he realized it reminded him of the dog in his dream—the dog that kept the world going.

With his hand over his mouth, he said, "Look at his size. That's why he sounded like a bear."

"Indeed, sir."

It arched its back as it threw a momentary look in Henry's direction. Nostrils flared and gushed torrents of steam into the cold dry air, and then it turned away, jogging toward the church at the end of the street..

"He's caught a whiff of something. I'm betting it's Anth."

Several abbreviated barks erupted from within the store. In that moment, the wolf leaped out into the street. Its size could be described as monstrous—the length and girth of a small horse. Some half dozen others emerged from the storefront and padded alongside their leader. They looked like pups. The pack spread out along the street, several individuals to either side, while their number one trotted ahead. They moved as one and were stalking prey.

"We've got to do something." Henry's words no sooner left his mouth than the flanking wolves disappeared into side streets. The big one slowed its jog as it neared the front doors of the church.

"Damn clever. Anth is big, but a dozen wolves—"

"May be too much for her, sir."

Seth scooted out from hiding, and with bat in hand ran along the middle of the street at the beast which had stopped a mere hundred yards ahead. Henry leaped over the trough and chased after Seth, all the while convinced he had just made one dumb decision.

They got within about fifty yards of the massive animal when it turned. Its lips curled up, white and thin, and quivered as a short snarl escaped. With head lowered and tail tucked, it padded toward them, slowly, methodically, with its eyes locked on Henry.

"Now what, Seth?"

"You should find refuge, sir." Seth tapped his head. "That wolf cannot harm me."

"No way, little guy." Henry raised his gun hand and aimed. Seth took a couple of steps toward the wolf and swung his bat in a circle. They made a fine pair, Henry thought, David and his sidekick facing Goliath.

Several shadows emerged from the side streets. The other wolves glided into flanking positions and the rear. Escape was no longer an option.
.

Chapter 18

Anth stopped when she saw a rear door ajar. She sidled along the clapboard wall and chanced a look through the opening.

"It's me."

"Genz! What are you doing here?"

"Take it easy. It wasn't my idea."

"Father."

Genz stared at the floor. "He wants to know why you didn't report."

Anth stepped into the dark and pulled Genz in with her. "How did you know where we were? You'll ruin everything."

"Oh?"

"I've got the cyborg to trust me. If there are others, this one should lead me to them."

"So, why didn't you report?"

"Because this piece of shit doesn't work." Anth threw a small device to Genz's feet.

"Your father is pissed. He wanted me to—"

"He wanted you to kill me?"

Genz turned away. "I'd never do that. You know that I love you."

Anth draped her arm around his shoulder. Genz was many things, but a murderer he was not. "I know. By the way, did you bring a Tracker with you?"

Genz ignored the question and raised his arms as if to embrace Anth. She pushed him away. "You did, didn't you?"

"It wasn't my idea."

"I'm sure. You need to get out of here. The cyborg will arrive any moment." She opened the door wide. "Get going. Tell my father to be patient. I'll return with his precious prize, and with some luck, much more."

Genz glided his hand to Anth's neck, but this time she did not throw it aside. He rubbed the smooth scales beneath her chin and said, "Be sure you do that and do it soon. You know your father—the longer this takes—"

"The more of a jerk he becomes." Genz avoided her stare. "By the way, you needn't worry about picking up the Tracker."

He blushed a dark blue. "Why is that?"

"It's in the same shape you're going to be in if you don't get out of here right now."

Genz laughed. He patted her on the rump and sprinted out the door. She watched him being swallowed by the shadowy tree line. That's when she heard the growling.

<>

"Hold on, Seth. Don't move."

The four-legged behemoth halted about ten paces away. Thrusting its nose upward as if sniffing out danger, and with a paw dangling in the air, it seemed to weigh its options. Henry hoped the beast would be confused by their appearance—two mechanical men may not be desired menu items, even for a hungry wolf.

The late afternoon sun glinted off its yellow eyes. Its size and the piercing stare reminded Henry of the Lakota legends of skinwalkers— wolves as large as men. He shook off the creepy feel of that thought, but kept his eyes glued to the wolf's ivory canines and the silvery saliva oozing over its lower lip. Henry's grip on the revolver tightened as the creature took another tentative step closer to him, apparently choosing to ignore Seth.

Henry tried a calming voice. "Take it easy fella. Nobody here wants to hurt you." The image of an old woman weaving a blanket flashed through his mind, and in a moment of inspiration, he lowered his gun and pointed it at the ground

"Sir, are you sure that you want to do that?"

"Nothing to lose, Seth. Let's see what happens."

The wolf lolled its head from side to side, as if trying to get a clearer look at Henry's gun hand. A dull throbbing sound filled the air. An aircar rose up from behind the church's single steeple, paused a moment, and then whooshed away over the woods to the south.

The front doors of the church parted and Anth stepped through. The wolf howled at the receding flying machine. The rest of the pack gathered about their leader, and joined in the baying. When the aircar disappeared from view, they were off, chasing after the giant wolf as it galloped past Anth and beyond the church.

Main Street was empty and the quiet that settled in threatened to unnerve Henry. A moment ago he had shared an existential moment. He rubbed a finger over his revolver to confirm it was still there.
Anth asked, "What happened?"
"The biggest damn wolf I ever saw was waiting for you. He must have caught your scent."
"My scent?"
"What about that aircar?"
Anth shook her head. "It took off before I could reach it."

A blurry figure appeared behind Anth and glided through the closed doors of the church.

"Liz." Henry whispered her name. He winced as she passed through the reptilian and continued on past him to the train station.

Seth appeared at his side and whispered. "Elizabeth again, sir?"
Anth asked, "What is it you are seeing?"
Henry shook his head. "Nothing. Just a memory." He shoved the revolver into his jacket. "We need to get back to the station."

On the way, Henry stopped when they came by Everett's Grocery Store. The sign was hard to read, but he knew what it said.

Seth asked, "Sir? Is there something wrong?"
"Hold on a moment. Seth, stay here with Anth. I'll be back in a jiffy."

Henry pushed on the front door and its hinges broke free, setting it to collapse inward and land flat on the wooden floor. He stepped through a cloud of dust and turned toward a white enamel and glass counter. The paint was infected with curling lines of black rust, and the glass was gone. Faded hand-drawn lettering covered the wall above. Henry stopped for a moment, letting his mind feast on memories. Suddenly, old Mrs. Everett loomed up from behind the counter. "What'll it be, son? How about our s-s-special, pis-s-stachio nut?" Henry blinked a few times, but the image of Mrs. Everett remained—her gentle smile—now a clown smile, her blue hair—now filthy gray. Her eyes wandered in different directions, as if looking for little Henry Wind In Trees with his hand waving in the air.

"Sir. Is everything all right?"
Henry reached out to the sputtering mechanical Mrs. Everett, and patted her on her shoulder. "That's okay, Mrs. Everett. Just stopped by to say hello."

She continued to rotate her button eyes. Henry stepped back out of the store and wiped at a corner of his eye. Phantasms had a way of surviving—always nearby, always ready for a conversation.

"Sir?"

"We're getting out of here."

It took but a minute for the three to jog the distance. On the way, Henry checked the side streets. He wasn't convinced all the wolves had left, and the image of the big one sent chills through him. In fact, the whole episode gnawed at him—the robot waiting for them at the station, the just-in-time intervention by Anth—and the aircar. Something was beginning to stink.

They clambered up onto the raised station platform in time to see the train move out. It was on an automated schedule, running the same route for the past several decades on its own, toting phantasms in an endless circle. Why had Liz led him back here?

"Sir." Seth pointed his bat at the receding train.

"What do you see?"

Liz sat on a crate near the rail bed and waved.

"You see that, Seth?"

"Don't you, sir?"

That's when Henry realized what Seth was pointing at—a second set of rails that ran behind Liz, curving perpendicular to the main line and heading south. Sitting atop those tracks was a relic perhaps two hundred years old—a handcar, complete with seesaw handles.

"Whoa. I haven't seen one of those—ever."

Anth said, "A crude vehicle. I know it from your history books."

"Yeah, and it takes more than two to get it going." Henry looked over Anth's build. "But I think we might be able to handle it ourselves."

"Sir, that means we'll be headed south. Is that where we need to go?"

Henry glanced at Liz, who rose up from the crate and walked along the south spur.

"That's what it means, Seth."

Anth gave the crate a long look. "Is there something over there?"

Henry said, "Nothing that any sane person can see." He tossed his backpack onto the car. "With some luck we might be able to get this bugger to roll."

The car was a replica, which meant it wasn't an Old West leftover, giving Henry some hope for resurrection. It took Anth's powerful limbs to unlock the handcar's rust-cratered wheels. When it moved, it gave off a syncopated groan and screech, but with each tug at the handle the pumping became a bit easier and the noise a bit less. There was no telling how long the car would last before it fell to pieces, but until then, they were flying along the southern spur, headed away from Custer and toward a future most uncertain.

Chapter 19

Anth spat out a tuft of fur and wiped her mouth with her other hand. Her rabbit was history. Henry dangled his over the campfire using a tapered branch as a spit.

"You never told us where you're from. I mean, that book back at your personal zoo—don't tell me you're a descendent of the dinosaurs, and your people left Earth millions of years ago, only to return to reclaim what was yours?"

Seeing Anth's eyes widen made Henry laugh. Even aliens gawked. "Only kidding. That's something I made up—right?"

She swallowed and moved closer to the fire. "Where we came from—our planet's name—what we are called—what does it matter? We have explored and settled on a number of other planets. When your planet became available, we took the opportunity. It has a similar day-night cycle to ours, and the atmosphere is compatible. When we learned of the water here, we jumped at the chance."

"We?"

"I mean, our people, our governing body."

"So what did the Soofysh do for you? Did they sell you this planet?"

"I'm not sure 'sell' is the correct term, but they provided the information and the offer to settle here."

Anth looked away, as if expecting Henry to chide her and her people's relationship with the Soofysh. When he said nothing, she continued. "I can tell you it took us a long time to get here. I do not know the exact distance. We were asleep through most of it."

"So you sleep? Like we do?"

"On the ship—maybe sleep is the wrong word. Unconscious—

that's what we were. Under normal circumstances we rest during the day when it is warmest."

"Are you cold-blooded?"

"You mean like your reptiles—your fish?"

Seth said, "I think the question goes to your metabolism. A warm-blooded animal, for example, my master, needs to eat to sustain its inner temperature. Cold-blooded animals have a slower metabolism and require an external source of heat."

Anth edged closer to the fire and took up a lotus position. "Your master is hardly a warm-blooded animal." She extended her arms and formed a kind of umbrella with her membranous wings facing the heat. Her eyes closed.

Henry said, "Isn't she a fountain of information, Seth?"

"Sometimes what is not said is just as informative, sir."

"Damn right." Henry lowered his spit, searing the skinned rabbit meat.

Night had arrived and the air held the crisp promise of snow. It was bad enough that he was conversing with a reptile. He began to question his sanity. Liz had become his reason for carrying on, and as tenuous or crazy as that sounded, he would follow her. *To what end? To discover what happened to the world? Or was there some other purpose that only Liz knew?* He shrugged off the uncertainty. The thought that she might yet be alive was good enough for him. The answers to all his questions were ahead. He was sure of it.

"Sir, your rabbit."

Henry shook off the flames erupting from the shapeless mass of meat and brought it up to his nose. He and Anth had gone the day without food. He marveled at the reptilian's stamina. They had stopped only for water and a brief rest. If the hand car hadn't seized, they might still be rolling.

"This smells so damn good."

Henry devoured the meat. Minutes later he was covered in a blanket of pine needles and lost to the world.

<>

Anth asked, "What do you hear?"

Henry lifted his head from the train track. "I had to try it. I guess I've seen too many movies."

"And?"

"I don't think we need to worry about getting run over."

The rails snaked through an inch or two of the night's snowfall and appeared to continue south. A slight declination made the walking easier.

"These tracks must lead somewhere—" Henry stopped himself from bringing up Liz. She walked, or floated, along those tracks, staying a few paces ahead of the group, always out of reach.

"Sir, a vibration." Seth pointed south along the rails.

The land ahead took on the contours of a shallow basin, rimmed by trees along slopes dotted with emaciated evergreens. Several pines erupted near the track bed ahead. His eye caught movement off to the side. Small dark specs appeared in the distance, growing in number.

Anth said, "What are they?"

Henry straightened up. "I assume you can climb a tree." Against the white of the snow, indistinct dark blobs formed and reformed into murky patches spreading out across the plain. "I think we need to move, and fast."

Henry considered the woods, a good mile to either side of the tracks. A stand of tall Larchmont pines lay straight ahead about a hundred yards off, in the direction of the oncoming horde. Those were closest.

"This way." Henry ran. Halfway to the trees he turned around to see Seth weaving through the prairie scrub, while Anth remained on the tracks staring after them.

"Anth! You need to get out of there. Those are bison and that's what we call a stampede. You'll get crushed if you stay there."

Henry's concern that she may not have heard him through the rising thunder of hooves was allayed when she leaped off the rails and sprinted.

They all reached the pines at the same time.

"What now?" she asked.

"Up. The higher, the better."

Henry broke away some low-lying branches on a nearby tree. On the way up he reached back and pulled Seth up. Anth climbed an adjacent pine in two bounds. Its thin trunk bowed to her weight in an alarming way.

She said, "Is this high enough?"

Henry gazed up at her in wonder. His tree vibrated as the thrumming mass of horned black bison thundered ever closer.

"I hope so. Brace yourself. Here they come." He took hold of Seth's bat as the robot locked its stubby arms about the trunk.

The first beasts to arrive veered around their refuge and galloped headlong toward the rails where the trio had been only moments earlier. More and more bison skirted through the trees. Numbers grew and bodies pressed against each other, some crashing into the trunks. The pounding cranked up and visibility dropped. Henry shook off the volcanic dust and snow kicked up from below. A vague oblong shadow emerged from the cloud debris where Anth had been perched.

He spat out the dirt in his mouth. A crack, louder than the hammering below, turned his head. Anth's shadow moved lower, as did her tree.

"Sir, she needs help."

Henry stepped out onto a limb while holding the trunk. He extended his bat toward the blur. "Anth! Grab this."

Anth's tree leaned farther away, but her distinct shape erupted through the swirling murk as she took hold of the outstretched bat. "Hold on, I'm pulling you in."

A second crack and her tree fell away, swallowed by the rampage beneath. Henry lost his grip on the trunk as Anth's weight yanked him to her. Visions of a quick end dashed through his head—crushed beneath hundreds of hooves. A vice grip caught his loose arm. Seth's hands locked on him while the little robot's legs curved about the trunk.

Anth swung onto a lower branch.

"Are you okay down there?"

Her head bobbed up out of the dust. "I am okay. Thank you, Henry."

Henry pivoted back to his trunk. "Thank you, Seth."

Once Seth regained his upright position, he nodded, "Pleasure to have been of service, sir."

A minute later, the stampede ended. The only evidence that anything dangerous had passed their way was the beaten earth below and the crumpled remains of a fallen tree. Weighed down by the snow, the dust settled quickly.

When the three were on the ground, Henry said, "I think that was the first time you called me by my first name."

Anth shook out her membranous wings. "I owe you my life."

"Aw, hell, there's a lot of owing going on. We should be thanking Seth. He saved us both. And anyway, didn't you save my life back on the Crazy Horse Monument? I think that makes us even."

Anth looked up at the sky. "We need to hide."

"Why? Those bison are gone."

Seth pointed over Henry's shoulders. "Sir, it's not the bison she fears."

"What the hell is that?"

The object on the far side of the valley was disk-shaped and black.

It made no noise as it cleared the trees.

"It's a damn flying saucer."

Anth said, "No. That is Soofysh."

Chapter 20

Images of green-eyed androids, clicking and whirring, manning the controls reared up in Henry's mind. He pictured them scanning the landscape, wheels grinding in their metal heads, twitching digits eager to blast away those few humans still alive.

"You've seen one of those before?"

Anth pulled Henry back behind a tree. "No, but I have read about them."

"I thought you said the Soofysh worked for you."

"It is what I was told. I am just—"

"an invader—happy to move in after your damn Soofysh killed all the inhabitants." The words tumbled out of Henry's mouth before he could shut it. "Sorry. It's not your fault." He sagged against the trunk, not sure what to say next.

"Sir, the object is following the bison trail."

"That explains the stampede. They got spooked by that thing, who wouldn't be? And it's headed straight for us." Henry turned to Anth. "What did your *readings* tell you about that thing? What's its function? How many robots, or whatever, are in it?"

"Robots? There are no robots. That object is a—what do you call it—a drone. It is a remote-controlled device used by the Soofysh to scout and send back information."

"Then it can't harm us?"

"I am not sure."

"Sir, they may be using infrared detection."

"That means you'll be fine, Seth. Maybe if I cover my head with some snow—"

Anth said, "They will detect me, and once they find me, they will find you."

"Sir, I think the question of detection may no longer be an issue." Henry pulled down a sprig for a better look. The saucer sat on the ground about a quarter mile off. Its flat body rose a few feet off the ground while a number of spindly legs sprouted beneath. It skittered like a spider with its black multi-hinged limbs stretching out and retracting, and it headed towards them.

"Did you know it would do that?" Henry withdrew his revolver from the backpack, spun the cylinder and pulled back on the hammer.

"That weapon will do little to stop it."

"Right, but it's all we got."

Seth held up the bat. "I feel I should tell you, sir, that it has been an honor to work with you all these years."

"You've been watching too many movies."

"But, sir—"

Seth didn't watch movies, but he did have access to a formidable historical archive of the arts and sciences. He seemed to enjoy quoting a line to ease the tension—something a human might do. *Wonders never ceased.*

"I feel the same about you, Seth."

The over-sized arachnid came to a stop about a hundred yards away. It's black turret top rotated left and right.

Henry called to Anth. "What do you think it's up to?"

There was no answer. Anth was gone.

Seth said, "She is at the tree line."

"Great."

"Perhaps she is frightened, sir."

"I can't blame her."

He winced at a sizzling sound—bacon on a skillet. A tree limb brushed his head as it tumbled to the ground. Another crackle sent bark erupting from a point closer to his head.

"Sir, it's some kind of energy weapon, maybe a laser."

"Doesn't matter much what kind of weapon it is."

"This may be the end for us, sir."

"Not if I can help it."

Henry lunged out of the stand of trees and zig-zagged toward the Soofysh drone in a wide arc to his left. Judging by the puffs of smoke appearing at his heels, the drone had acquired a singular interest in him and not much else.

Dodging death rays didn't seem a winning strategy, but then, he had little choice. He aimed and fired away, hoping that one of the 45-caliber rounds might find a soft spot. Several more tufts of grass and snow flew into the air as he closed in on the drone. He was close enough to see the turret head's cycloptic eye and at the same time he wondered why such an advanced piece of equipment had trouble nailing him with one of its blasts. His introspection was cut short when he saw Seth's bat weaving through matted stalks of prairie grass.

The drone was no more than ten feet across, maybe three feet high. The turret atop its curved dome appeared to be the business end of those high energy blasts. Henry discovered he was out of bullets just as an orange light flashed from the turret's eye and the edge of his jacket sleeve fell away.

He was out of options and sure that a direct hit was only a matter of time. Seth smashed his bat at one of its spidery legs. In the same moment, Anth loomed up from behind the drone and leaped atop. The distraction gave Henry a chance to drop to a knee, reach back for his bow, and in one motion pull an arrow from the quiver. He let loose the pointed shaft as the turret unleashed another orange flash.

Blinking to clear his vision, he stumbled into a dark void filled with the smell of burning plastic.

<>

"Sir, are you all right?"

A blurry Anth appeared behind Seth.

Henry said, "I thought you ran out on us."

Anth said, "The drone was not interested in me."

"I can't see you. Everything's so gray."

"That's understandable, sir. It's evening."

"What? How?"

"That was a remarkable shot, sir. I mean, with your arrow."

"Seth, what's wrong? That smell—there's something you're not telling me."

"I'm afraid you will need some repairs, sir."

Henry sat with his back propped up against the rough bark of a pine tree. A yellow smear of light danced over Seth's bronze body. He celebrated the warmth of a campfire. Anth moved to the opposite side of the flickering light with her arms and translucent wings splayed open. He flexed his own arms, wriggled fingers and brought his knees up.

"What needs fixing?"

"It's nothing, sir."

Henry ran his hands across his shoulders and neck.

"Higher up, sir."

When his fingers reached his ear, they slid over cold metal and something gooey. "Damn." He brought both hands to his head.

"The damage was limited to your skin covering, sir, over the right ear."

"I must look an awful mess."

Seth held up something in his hand. "I applied some tree resin. I think it should do until your artificial skin repairs itself, sir."

Henry placed the sticky ear to the side of his head, using his fingers to feel for the edges. "How's that?"

Seth nodded. "A perfect fit, sir."

"What about that drone thing?"

Seth brought up a large black disk—the turret. An arrow's feathers protruded from a broken lens on one side. "I believe this is yours, sir."

"How?"

"Anth. When she pulled it off, the rest of the mechanism collapsed." Seth nodded at a pile of spider legs and cables at the base of a tree. "A second earlier, and you might still have your ear, sir."

"Anth appears to have fondness for tearing heads off."

"We all have our proclivities, sir."

"And what might be your proclivity, Seth?"

"Care for a portion of rabbit, sir?"

Typical Seth. "Where did that come from?"

"Compliments of the reptilian."

"I can't figure her out, Seth. I'm sure she knew about the ambush back in Custer. If she wanted us caught, why did she come along? And then she goes and saves my life."

"Puzzling, sir."

"You're no help."

"Perhaps the morning will bring some enlightenment, sir."

Henry looked about. Every time Liz disappeared, the emptiness returned, expanded, and swallowed him. He hated the feeling. He hated the world that took her away.

Seth waved the rabbit leg.

Chapter 21

Fierz slammed a fist against the wall. "She did what?"

The silvery screen blinked for a second and resolved into an image of a dark outline of a figure—an eyeless manikin. Fierz stared at the projection, working hard to conceal his wonder and his fear. It spoke without perceptible movement. He was sure it was designed to relate to his own symmetrical form, but darkened no doubt to impart some level of dread. No one had ever seen a Soofysh in person. For all he knew, he was talking to an algorithm.

"Our drone located the humanoid male and his party. Their capture was a certainty until your daughter disabled the control module."

"Is that all?"

"Prior to that, the humanoid male damaged the energy beam mechanism."

"And how did he do that?"

"A feathered wooden shaft tipped with a steel point appears to have entered the firing port."

"An arrow? You're describing an ancient human weapon used by a people who no longer exist."

Silence followed as if the Soofysh representation considered its next statement. "Nonetheless, the humanoid we seek used such a weapon—an unfortunate and improbable outcome."

"What about him? Was he destroyed?"

"The drone was at least somewhat successful. Its final energy burst appears to have caused some damage, but insufficient to disable the cyborg creature."

"Is that all you have? You don't *know* much do you?" Fierz shook his head. The human or cyborg or whatever, was quick and clever, and still in one piece. "Other drones. You *do* have other drones?"

"They have been dispatched."

"What does that mean?"

"They will reach the humanoid's last location soon."

"Soon? I want that creature brought back to me, and I want him or it alive."

"What you wish is not of our concern. The hunt for the cyborg is an accommodation, a favor. What of your daughter?"

"She's no longer my daughter." Fierz turned away from the screen and muttered to himself. "Alive or dead—it doesn't matter."

"As you wish."

"I trust you will utilize sufficient resources to ensure success this time."

Once again the image paused before responding. "The Soofysh will not chance the further loss of our assets. Our own plans for the cyborg will supercede yours."

The screen blinked off.

Fierz tapped his desk and thought. The Soofysh were useful to a point. That they have plans for the cyborg meant little to him. The technology embedded in that thing would be his. He wondered if they lost the cyborg on purpose.

The door announced a visitor.

"So it's you. What have you to report?"

Genz shuffled into the room, his eyes averting Fierz's unnerving stare. "I caught up with them at the Custer town."

"And?"

"I relayed your message. Anth promised to return with the cyborg. She said she wanted to locate more of them."

Fierz grimaced. "More of them? And you believed her? Did she say when she would return?"

Genz lowered his head even farther. "No, sir. When she found more—"

"Idiot. Your girlfriend is a deceptive creature. She lied to you—and to me."

"She might be on her way, sir."

"Doubtful. The Soofysh found her group."

"Genz's cheeks blushed a deep crimson. "Has she been captured?"

"She destroyed their drone." Fierz canted his head to see what effect the news had on Genz. "Are you pleased?"

"No, no, sir."

"Your relief will be short-lived. The Soofysh are annoyed. Dereliction of duty is a trait they are quick to discourage. To them, my daughter is an extension of our group. Next, they will find me at fault." Fierz took a step closer. "And I will blame you."

Genz opened his mouth.

"Get out." Fierz hunched over his desk, certain his bluster was convincing. He was also sure the Soofysh had a stake in this chase.

<>

Henry asked, "How far did we travel last night?"

Seth turned his eyeless head to Anth, who faced the rising sun and unfolded her wings to take in its heat. "The likelihood of pursuit suggested we get away from the location of the drone attack as fast as possible, sir."

Henry pointed at the drone's remains. "Who carried that?"

"Anth was more than capable, sir."

"So how far did we go?"

"Thirty-one miles to the south, sir."

Henry rubbed the side of his head and wondered if that was the direction Liz would have preferred. He hadn't seen her lately. "That's quite a distance on foot. I don't remember much."

"You were somewhat unaware. Are you feeling better, sir?""

"So she carried me too?"

Anth broke away from her sun-gazing. "You and the drone artifacts posed no unusual physical challenge."

"So, Anth, why?"

"Why what?"

"Why are you helping us? What's in it for you?" Henry hoped the sudden change in topic and tone would coax the truth out of the reptilian.

She stared back with eyes wide like a toddler caught with her hands in the cookie jar.

Henry said, "I only see reasons *against* your involvement. The grand plan to settle my world, the Soofysh and your father … and you can't know where we're going or why we're going there for the simple reason that I myself have no idea."

Henry grabbed his bow and quill. "Don't get me wrong. You saved our skins more than once, and we owe you for that, but I think you should get back to your people, and the quicker the better. For all I know, your father is more interested in you than us."

"I doubt that. Perhaps the time has come to speak plainly, Henry."

A chill spiraled down Henry's titanium spine. Anth retracted her wings and folded her arms in a posture all too human. When she spoke, the words came in a soft whisper. "I knew. I knew what the Soofysh had done. My father, or rather, the leader of the colony—his name is Fierz—explained it to me on our way here. When we arrived about a year ago, my job was to identify the animal life most suited to our metabolism—the best food sources."

It took a moment before Henry replied. "And your English?"

"I was forced to learn your tongue, both in writing and speech."

"I don't get it. If you knew what the Soofysh had done, who the hell were you planning to have a conversation with?"

"We were commanded. The Soofysh informed us that humans were animals of slight intelligence, that they were clever enough to develop tools, some of which were worthy of investigation—possibly of use to our colonization."

"But that's not all, is it?"

"No. I was to locate any surviving members of your race." The creases surrounding Anth's mouth appeared to deepen. "The few humans I found feared me at first, but I convinced them we were here on a peaceful mission. I brought them to our base camp."

"I take it that your guests didn't leave."

"No, they did not."

"What about me? I must have been a quite a find."

"Fierz wanted very much to study you. You are the first, what do you call it? … cyborg, part-human machine … we had ever encountered."

Henry thought back to the encounter at his cabin. "I may not be that unique. So, what about you? Why the change of heart? Or, is this another trick?"

"I am not deceiving you."

"Back there, in the town—you had to know about the ambush at the train station."

"I knew. I was told, and it wasn't my idea."

"Why didn't you allow that automaton kill us? You'd be back in your—in Fierz's good graces. Now it looks as if he wants *all* of us dead."

"I was confused. You—you're the first human that I had a honest conversation with. You're not like the others."

"You mean scared, frightened out of their minds of giant reptiles taking over their planet—eating them?"

Anth sat on the ground and held her head in her hands. "It was all a lie. In the beginning, our people were convinced by the Soofysh the

Earth was vacant—the backward inhabitants had destroyed themselves using weapons beyond their control. The few remaining humans were no more than unintelligent violent animals, better off dead than alive."

"The only good injun is a dead injun."

"What?"

"Nothing. I still don't see why you want to stick with us."

"I'm not sure myself, but I will not continue to help colonize this planet, and I will not return to Fierz. Wherever it is you are going, it will be a better place than back with him."

Henry caught the fear in her voice. There was more to Fierz than a domineering father figure. He shuddered at the thought.

The sun rose over a distant ridge, outlining a translucent figure standing beside Anth. A warmth filled his breast, more than the sun's rays could explain. He said, "It's about time you showed up."

Anth followed Henry's gaze.

Seth said, "It's his wife, Elizabeth."

Anth said, "I see no one there."

"Oh, she's there. Where to, sir?"

Henry smiled. "You picked a good direction, Seth. We're going to keep going south." He patted Anth on her shoulder. "And you're welcome to stay with us for as long as you wish."

Chapter 22

"**W**hat do you see, sir?"

Henry lowered his binoculars. "Remember those buzzards about ten miles back?"

"I do, sir. They were feasting on a deer's carcass."

"Remember how they flew up, kind of circled over us as we passed?"

"It's a natural reaction. Why do you ask, sir?"

"They're doing it again."

"Meaning—"

"I have no idea what it means, but I'm sure it's not good."

Anth said, "There is a town ahead. Perhaps we can find shelter."

Henry wondered if the hike was having an effect on the reptilian. Aside from the thin tunic she had little else to protect her from the constant wind. "Are you okay, Anth? It's been cold and—"

"I am fine."

Her conversations had grown short, almost curt. Something was eating at her, and she would decide when to talk about it.

The road sloped down through a shallow valley and led to a small town about a mile distant. He stared at its outskirts, willing his eyes to focus on details so far away. Seth said, "School buses, sir." Little yellow rectangles morphed into buses.

"Great eyesight, Seth."

"20-20 slits, sir."

The three reached the edge of town and stopped at a welcome sign. Two traffic lights jutted up along the main thoroughfare before the street emptied out into a grassy plain and mountains beyond. The name of the town had peeled off the sign years ago.

Henry said, "Maybe there's something here we can use."

"Five buses, sir."

Henry focused on the one-story brick school building about a quarter mile off and then back to the buses. "All yellow, except for the small one with a blue streak."

Anth stepped up next to Henry. "What is the meaning of the blue color?"

"That's a code for—" Henry ran to the school's parking lot. When the other two caught up, he said, "Propane. Son-of-a-gun, it runs on propane."

Seth waddled over to the smaller blue-colored bus and opened the side panel. He twiddled a knob and said, "There appears to be fuel in the tank, sir."

"Great!"

Anth said, "Why the excitement?"

Seth said, "Vehicles powered by gasoline would be a problem to start. The hydrocarbon fuel is apt to undergo oxidative degradation, which over a period of so many years would result in polymeric impurities which would interfere with proper engine performance."

"What Seth is trying to say is that gasoline goes bad, and after some time, it's sludge, and that would clog up the lines and the engine."

"My words exactly, sir."

Henry pointed out several rusty hulks in the street. "We'll never get those to start, much less to run." He walked over to the front of the bus. "Body's not too bad. Only one cracked window."

Anth asked, "Why the interest in this bus?"

"Buzzards." Henry smirked at his own joke. "The birds flying in a circle on the other side of the valley—where we came from."

Anth said, "Meaning?"

"Something's coming this way."

The window at the driver's seat slid back, and Seth's dome loomed at its rim.

"Pop the hood, Seth."

A moment later, Henry had his head in the engine compartment. "It's damn filthy in here. Battery's a mess. Corrosion almost took out the fuel lines. The oil has turned into tar." He jumped down. "And the radiator's empty."

Seth said, "Standard transmission, sir."

"This could be a good day."

Henry kicked at the crumbling rubber clinging to a wheel rim. "Might last long enough for us to get going. With a little luck, all we'll need is some water and fresh oil."

"What is the plan?" asked Anth.

"The plan is to get this beast resurrected and outrun what's coming."

Anth asked, "Bring back from the dead?" Her head tilted in a very human way.

Henry said, "An idiomatic phrase, Anth."

"Sounds idiotic to me."

"A pun, Anth?"

"Unintentional."

Henry waved his arm at the bus. "Riding in a vehicle is better than hiking. Besides, it would keep you a bit warmer."

"Sir, we will be spotted much easier in this bus."

"True enough, Seth. Being spotted is not something we need fear. It's been a week since our last encounter with the Soofysh. I was hoping they'd have lost interest in us." Henry looked out over the valley. "Maybe they haven't."

Anth asked, "You think they are coming?"

"Yeah, but you'd think they'd be spread thin, what with taking over the world and all."

Anth said, "I do not know their number."

Henry nodded. "I'll be right back." He ran across the street to a gas station and called back. "We're going to need some tools and supplies."

<>

Henry lifted himself out of the engine compartment and tossed away an empty plastic bottle along with the air filter. "So far, so good. Got my fingers crossed on the wiring, on the engine and the ignition—and the alternator—and the radiator. I'm not betting much on the belts." He chanced a look down the valley. "I don't think we have much time left." An internal alarm tolled in his mind. They were down to minutes.

The station had yielded foul-smelling water, several cases of motor oil, and transmission fluid. Seth poured the fluids in, while Henry checked to see what came out the bottom. The lighter transmission oil was no problem, but the heavier goo that passed for motor oil took its time to ooze out of the crankcase.

"That's it, Seth. I'm closing the drain. Top it off." Henry rolled out from beneath the bus and wiped himself down with a rag. "It's going to have to do. No telling how bad the gunk inside the engine is, but what the hell."

Anth asked, "What about the tires?"

Henry laughed and wiped his hands on a tuft of grass. "That's the least of our problems. This old bus runs on propane. The thing I'm worried about is getting the damn thing started."

"Does that not require electricity?"

"Push-started is what I meant."

Anth said, "Push-started?"

Henry gave her a top to bottom look. "Yeah. We'll need to get it into the street." He pointed toward the center of town. "Someone has to push it down that hill." He slapped her back. "And I think you can do it."

Seeing that Anth looked confused, Henry pointed at the other buses. "Come on. At least it's not one of those big ones." He glanced past Anth. The empty road and the thick forest beyond belied their tranquility. Nothing stirred as yet, and that fact alone set his teeth to chatter.

"Seth, you stay up there and steer into the street. Go downhill, and keep the doors open. Once we get this thing moving, we'll be joining you. Anth, you and I have some work to do."

The bus faced the street, so the plan was simple, assuming they had the strength to move it, and Seth could steer it, and a thousand other things went right.

Henry joined Anth at the rear. They pushed. Nothing. They pushed again. Nothing. The wheels might have been seized, metal fused to metal. Henry started thinking about ancient axle grease turned to solid wax, when another thought percolated up.

"Seth. Is the gearshift in neutral?"

A metallic screech rumbled through the old bus's carcass.

"It is now, sir."

Anth shook her head. "Shall we try again?"

"Sir, you're right."

"About what?"

"There is something coming."

Henry's stomach leaped to his throat. He leaned to the side to get a view of the valley, back along the road. At a mile away, the object could have been a truck, a big one. White and shimmering in the dying afternoon light, it sat unmoving, giving the impression that it had paused to survey the valley, perhaps to locate its quarry.

Anth said, "It is not one of our vehicles."

"Seth, grab the steering wheel. Anth, give me everything you've got."

Henry pressed his shoulder to the bus and they pushed. The bus groaned and lurched several inches. "Again." A foot. Then several feet, and the blue heap heaved forward on its own, leaving behind black rubber shreds as the steel rims sliced through rotten tires.

Henry motioned for Anth to follow while Seth turned the bus into the street. He leaped up the stairwell and into the driver's seat. The little robot sprung into the seat behind as they picked up speed. The bottom of the hill was a mere hundred yards ahead.

"Where's Anth?"

"I believe she's pushing the bus, sir."

"Damn it. Anth, get the hell in here."

Henry looked to the rear of the bus. If he had actual blood coursing through his body, it would have turned icy cold. The object that had been sitting at the entrance to the valley was streaking toward them, kicking up a whirlwind of dust as it drew nearer.

Anth clambered through the open doorway.

Henry seized the steering wheel with one hand and the gear shift with the other. "Time to pray." The bus picked up a little speed as they reached the bottom of the hill. He eased the shift to second and nudged the clutch. The gearing caught with a deep-throated growl, but the engine refused to come alive. Henry backed off for a few more seconds as the bus rumbled across the flat bottom of the hill and once again shifted into second gear. The engine sputtered a moment before dying.

"This is our last chance."

The bus coasted to a crawl, threatening to grind to a stop. Henry eased the shifter into first and popped the clutch. The engine coughed and the bus jerked forward. Slipping into second, he stomped on the gas pedal. The engine roared and the wheel rims screeched on the asphalt.

Henry shouted, "Woooo! We got ourselves a bus!"

Seth yelled back. "I suggest you increase the speed, sir. That rather troubling object is right behind us."

The rear-view mirror reflected an image of an undulating white mass, writhing like a half-filled hot air balloon. A featureless arm extended out to the back door like an amoeba groping for food. Henry jammed the shift into fourth, and fifth, and then things got confusing.

Chapter 23

"Henry, are you all right?"

He recognized the voice.

"Liz?"

The lights came on. Had he passed out?

"Who did you expect?"

He shook his head and tried to focus. Across from him, seated at the dinner table, Liz propped her hands beneath her chin and smiled back. "Too much to drink?"

Nausea flooded Henry's senses. A wine glass slipped through his fingers and crashed on the floor. He focused on the sparkle of the glass shards, little islands jutting up from a crimson sea.

"I think—maybe—"

"There's no maybe about it. Let's get you to the sofa."

Henry felt her hands gripping his armpits. The two staggered through a doorway. The sweet musty odor of the couch folded over him. The springs of the old settee shifted as she sat next to him.

"How?"

He had trouble opening his mouth, controlling his lips. His head became heavy. Was he drunk?

"It's okay, Henry. Relax."

"But—"

A pillow slipped in under his neck, and his eyelids lowered to half-mast.

"Shhh. Get some sleep. We'll talk in the morning."

<>

The smell of coffee lured him up from the dark. Henry rolled and fell to the floor. His elbow found the couch and he hoisted himself up on shaky legs. After waiting a moment for the room to slow down, he found the courage to raise his head. He was in his den, in his cabin. He recalled that much the night before, *when Liz—when Liz—*.

"Up already, Henry? Ready for breakfast?"

Her lilting voice came across as a siren song—an aria of wind chimes. Each inflection was music to his ears, filling him with a joy he had relegated as long passed, consumed by a dark and fearful nightmare. A spoon clinked and ran its tiny metal body up against smooth ceramic—a mundane sound, which this morning had become a thing of wonder. For some reason, he kept thinking that Liz had been gone for a long while.

Henry staggered to the kitchen doorway. Liz held two mugs of steaming coffee and laid them out by a plate of freshly-baked rolls. Was it their aroma that made his eyes tear?

"Liz."

"How are we feeling this morning? You sure outdid yourself last night."

He slipped into a chair. Yesterday was in tatters. He had trouble remembering. "I feel like crap."

"That's all right, honey. It's not every day we get to celebrate our anniversary. And I warned you about that wine. That stuff must've been a day shy of becoming pure vinegar."

She coughed, and the sound ran a knife through Henry.

Liz said, "The coffee's hot so be careful you don't spill it."

Henry sipped the brew and felt its heat run across his tongue.

"That cough. It doesn't sound good."

"That's why I've decided to go with you this afternoon."

"This afternoon?"

"Across the bay—you know, to the Systems people. You told me they set up a clinic. You do remember telling me we should go, and the sooner, the better?"

Henry's gut tightened. The Systems clinic. How could he forget? For some reason, he had trouble remembering that or anything else before last night. He took a deep gulp of the java and sighed. A tendril of recall arrived with the swallow. "Yeah. I remember the radio said it was the last call—that they plan to leave soon."

His words sounded familiar. He felt he was playing out a scene and shuffled to the kitchen window with mug in hand. For some reason his gaze strayed to the window and out to the forest edge.

"Henry, the rolls are getting cold."

"Need to stretch the legs, Liz. Be right there."

Leaves wafted down from stately elms. Their gray skeletons formed a muted backdrop for the deep green pines. Sallow needles graced the foot of the tree line. Something used to be there. Something important. He turned back to look at Liz with her blue sundress and her red hair shimmering in the reflected light from the window. An emptiness awoke within him. He yearned for her warm glow.

"What a doozy."

"My coffee?"

"No, no. Just a bad dream, I guess. I can't seem to shake it off."

"Tell me about it, honey."

"Ah … It's in pieces. You know how it is with dreams. There was this little robot—"

Liz chuckled, and said, "Go on. I didn't mean to interrupt. Any dream that starts with a little robot—"

"—and a giant reptile."

Liz snorted. "Sorry, please ignore me." She covered her mouth, failing to hide a smile. "Please go on."

"I know it sounds weird, but stay with me here. The reptile had arms and legs. She was an alien and there was an invasion going on—"

"A female reptile? And an invasion? Goodness, anything else?"

"You, Liz. I remember you."

"Finally. Something that makes sense. I'm touched. What was I doing?"

Henry sat back down. For some reason the question darkened his mood. Liz ran her fingers across his hand and said, "So what were you up to in this invasion dream of yours?"

"Like I said, I don't remember much."

"It's something out of a movie. If it was me, I'd remember all the good parts—you know, who invaded, and what I was doing about it."

"Right."

"I think you're holding back. There's something you're not telling me. Was there another woman?"

Henry thought about the backyard and the empty meadow. "No, no, nothing like that."

Liz washed her mug out in the sink. "If you don't want to tell me, that's fine. I thought it'd be fun to talk about it."

Henry chewed down the remains of his roll. "Honey, I just don't want to get you upset."

Liz glared at him from the sink. With arms akimbo, she raised her voice. "It was a dream, you dummy. How can it get me upset?"

"See what I mean?"

Henry's grin froze as she hung her mug on a dowel over the sink. He looked down at his own cup. Dread gripped his heart. An icy feeling crept up his back. His free hand slipped into a jacket pocket and his fingers curled over something sharp-edged. The kitchen looked like it always did. The counter, the floor, the blackened oven door—they all looked normal. "Henry, you look terrible. Come and sit on the porch and get some fresh air." Liz led him by the arm. "I'm sure you'll feel much better if you tell me about your nightmare before we go to that clinic. Who knows what'll happen there."

Henry sucked in the cool air, hoping his mind would clear. A lark few across the meadow. Leaves rustled as a mild breeze passed by. He settled into the Adirondack chair with Liz seated next to him. For some reason he felt stiff and cold.

"I don't know how to begin."

"At the beginning, silly." Liz smiled and wrapped an arm around his shoulders.

"Trouble is—the beginning has you dying. I didn't like that part."

"No kidding. How did I die?"

"The Yellowstone. That cough—they couldn't save you." Henry took a sip. The coffee had grown bitter. He stared into Liz's eyes. "It was terrible. Maybe we shouldn't go today."

"I'm sure it's a stupid cold, maybe the flu." Liz turned away for a moment and sniffled. "So, what happened after I died?"

"I hated everything. I couldn't stand living in a world without you. I think I lived alone for a time—years maybe. After a while I came across a little servant robot. His name was Seth."

"Cute. So that's the little robot. And you were alone for what … fifty years? Must've been hard for you." Liz's eyebrows arched in a show of empathy.

Henry wondered how she knew that it was fifty years. "You get used to it. I mean being alone."

"What about the invasion—you know, those reptiles?"
"Yeah, as it turns out, the Earth wasn't hit by an asteroid, or maybe it was. I'm not sure. Anyway, something else caused the destruction, and that

something else was what killed all the people, including you."

"I don't follow."

"The reptiles weren't the actual invaders."

"Now I'm more confused."

Bits and pieces of his memory knitted together as Henry went on. "There was a third party. We figured out they wiped out human life and convinced the reptiles to settle here—I think for quite a price."

"We?"

"Oh, I forgot. One of the reptiles, a female—I think she was a teenager. We worked together for a while."

"So there *was* another woman. You're making me jealous." Liz laughed out loud, perhaps a little too loud. "You've got some imagination—reptile invaders, a mysterious third party. So you and she were going to save the planet?"

"Too late for that. Ouch."

"What's the matter? Did you sit on a pine needle?"

Henry brought up his hand. A white chunk of ceramic covered with a blue stain hung between his two fingers.

"What have you got there? Oh my, you've cut yourself."

"Yeah, blood. Don't you think it should be red?"

Liz stared and said nothing.

"And this—a chip from a mug. Does it look familiar?"

"No. Should it?"

He turned it over. "See the letter 'L'?"

Liz withdrew her arm from Henry's shoulders. Her smile faded and her complexion turned ashen.

Henry said, "I guess you people aren't all that clever after all."

<>

Henry's back arched, and his body slammed forward into something hard.

"Look out, sir."

He lifted his head from the steering wheel. The world shook and screamed. A corner building at an intersection ahead grew to an alarming size. Instinct guided his feet to the brake and clutch, and a hard turn which sent the bus into a sideways skid, screeching metal-on-asphalt. When they slammed into the curb, Seth landed in Henry's lap. "I am quite all right, sir."

"Me, too, Seth." The undulating voice from the rear of the bus sounded anything but.

Henry shook his head. Moments ago, he had been with Liz. Or

had he? "The white balloon thing—did you see it?"

Seth said, "I did, sir. It covered the bus."

Henry leaned into the aisle. "Anth, how about you? What did you see?"

The reptilian dislodged herself from a pair of seats. "I saw the white object through the rear window. It reached out, and then it disappeared and you stopped the bus."

"What about you, Seth?"

"The object seemed to fold over us, sir. And when it did, it vanished."

Henry shook his head. "Seth, in your estimation, how much time elapsed between then and now?"

"Seconds, sir."

"Anth, have you ever seen anything like this happen before?"

"The technology is foreign to me."

"You didn't have any dreams? Nightmares?"

"Visions while sleeping? We do not dream."

"It's a fair bet that we just encountered Soofysh technology. I think they want to know where I was going and why." The bus shook and squealed. Henry applied gentle pressure on the gas pedal. "They made me think it was a half-century ago, when Liz was still alive."

His wife sat on the hood of the bus. She looked back at Henry with a serene, undisturbed look, as if nothing had happened.

"Sir, what did you tell them?"

"Couldn't tell them what I don't know. In a way, the big secret is with Liz." He guided the derelict bus back into the street. "We'll see how far this wreck can take us. We're headed south and I don't give a damn if the Soofysh know where we are."

Anth said, "Henry, do not forget what they are capable of. They will not treat you or us with kindness."

Henry licked his injured finger tip. "One thing I know—they're not perfect. They don't know everything, and we must be making them a little nervous. I'm betting we're worth more alive to them than dead. I'm just not sure why."

Chapter 24

Fifty-six miles—that was how far they had gone according to the speedometer, but of course, it was an estimate. Wheels without tires had a smaller circumference, so the actual distance had to be something less. Add to that the incessant skidding and infernal screeching. In any event, a broken front axle had a kind of finality to it.

Henry stepped off the bus with Seth close behind and swung his sack over a shoulder. "Looks like we're walking again."

"The noise was getting a bit tiresome, sir."

Henry laughed. "It's a wonder we didn't go deaf. At least we got some rest. All set?"

"Anth may not be, sir."

He leaned back into the door. "Hey, are you coming?"

Anth sat across several seats and stared out a window, as if making it a point to ignore Henry.

"What's up?"

"I'm tired of this, this quest of yours. It is nonsense, a waste of time. The Soofysh know where we are and will arrive any moment with something more than a balloon. They will capture us and if we are fortunate, kill us with some efficiency. So, what is the point of continuing?"

"Kill us? Maybe. They might want to get you back to your home. Maybe that's what you fear."

"There is no purpose in going on. You said so yourself."

"I said I don't know where we're going, but there *is* a purpose—I know it."

"And that is?"

Liz no longer sat on the hood. Transparent as ever, she appeared a few yards up the road and motioned for Henry to follow.

"Okay, I don't know it, but trust me, there is one." Henry fought to keep his growing doubt hidden. He looked once again at Liz. *You have to be real. You have to be.*

"An unknown destination with an unknown purpose—I'm tired of this foolishness."

"Aren't we all in the same boat?"

She lowered her head. "Go on without me. Chase your delusion. I do not care if it is your dead wife, just leave me alone. I deserve whatever happens."

"You and I are on the same mission. Do *you* really know where you're going, and *why*? Your people set about to colonize my planet. What happens after that? More will arrive and grow your population. What then? What's your purpose, Anth? Are you so different than me?"

"We came here for a new beginning. Our purpose is noble. It is one of survival of our people, exploration, and discovery. It is the way of all sentient species. That is our purpose with real meaning."

"Yeah, survival. And you and your people don't appear to mind how you go about it. It's fine to let some damned Soofysh enterprise prepare the way for you. Goddamn murdering assholes. You must feel kind of special with them as your friends."

"They are not my friends. We were misled."

"And now that you know better, if you don't at least try and do something about it, you're no better than they are. Hell, weren't you wearing their emblem?"

Seth said, "It's getting dark, sir. If we hope to avoid immediate capture, perhaps we should be on our way?"

Henry slammed his hand against the folding door. "Sounds to me, that you're giving up *your* purpose. Good luck, Anth. I doubt we'll ever see each other again." Henry stepped away and walked toward Liz with Seth at his heels.

Anth's voice roared from the bus. "You're insane! Following some spirit guide—do you know what that sounds like? You and that little mechanical idiot of yours are both deranged!"
"Come on, Seth. The insane are going to hit the trail."

<>

Henry approached the campfire, naked and wet. He extended his hands to soak in some heat. "It's funny how this mechanical body feels so cold when it's wet."

"Basic thermodynamics, sir. Evaporation is an endothermic process."

"It's still funny."

"A wash in the stream *was* a good idea, sir."

Henry gave his buddy the raised eyebrow query.

Seth added, "I was speaking of your clothing, sir. Your jacket was beginning to emit an odor that would be easy to track."

Henry ran his fingers over the side of his head. "At least the ear patch is still intact."

"Here, sir. Your fish is ready."

Henry chomped down on the braised trout. "It's funny how something cooked in the wild always tastes better."

"You've experienced many funny things on this trip, sir."

"You're quite the comedian, Seth."

"I try, sir."

The evening sky had turned into a thin sallow line along the western horizon. Henry listened to the high-pitched chirping of frogs from the nearby stream and the rhythmic thrum of crickets—survivors of the apocalypse and a reminder of a time that was never to be again.

Henry knew the next hundred miles would offer scant forest cover. He scrutinized the nearly invisible horizon, something he did each evening, letting his imagination dot the darkening expanse with the glow of cities and towns. He shrugged off the wistful scan and instead focused on the prairie surrounding their campsite, hopeful of spotting a large reptilian skulking through the tall grass. His heart went out to her. Anth had abandoned her people and her parents. She was alone and must feel lost, much as he had been for half a century. And she was right—he had no purpose.

Something brushed his shoulder. He turned to see Liz standing alongside. "Did you do that? Did I feel you touch me?"

She faded into the guttering light show cast by the campfire against trees nearby.

Seth said, "I cannot reach you from here, sir."

"No, Seth. It's not you … it's …" Henry blinked and shook his head. Liz was gone, and in her place stood Anth.

"Damn, where did you come from?" asked Henry. "How did you—"

"I'm sorry if I surprised you."

"Surprise me? No way. I come from a long line of trackers and hunters. No, no … We knew you were following us. Right, Seth?"

"Indeed, sir."

Chapter 25

Several days later, as the late afternoon sun melted into a haze, the trio sighted a landmark Henry knew well—the twin buttes of the Pawnee National Grasslands. Ancient 300-foot tall mesas reared up from a sea of buffalo grass speckled with prickly pear cactus and soapweed yucca. Henry was surprised to see that the buttes each sprouted a wind turbine maybe 150 feet tall.

"Damn *wasicu*."

Seth said, "Greedy white man who takes fat?"

Henry laughed. "That's one meaning."

The turbine blades stood motionless. Their mottled white towers could have been mistaken for lighthouses erected on rocky outcroppings. To Henry's mind they were no more than scars on the land left by the European intrusion, triple-bladed eyesores frozen by time. He was surprised by the thought. He had never pictured himself so intolerant. Maybe he was depressed at possibly being the last human. He promised himself to be less brooding. After all, he represented what was left of the human race. He reached down, snapped up a beard of wheatgrass, and stuck it between his teeth. The apocalypse had at least one redeeming feature—Nature was taking back what was hers.

They had reached Colorado at the western edge of the Great Plains, and they accomplished this without once engaging in any meaningful dialogue. Just the same, Henry was happy to have her back. After all, she was like any conflicted human teenager with tons of self doubt. He hoped that she, and they, were making the right decisions on this odyssey.

Henry said, "We're going to do some climbing."

Anth said, "To what purpose?"

Finally, she talks. "There you go again. I have to admit, I don't know."

"Your wife?"

The tone of Anth's question made Henry cringe. He nodded and avoided her gaze. "There's a reason for everything. We'll have to find out what that is for ourselves."

Anth turned to Seth and shook her head. Henry wondered at the coincidence of body language. Maybe it was something she picked up while travelling with him. He wasn't about to tell her that Liz stared at them from about two paces away and pointed at the top of the nearest butte. He wished Liz would talk, to explain what she wanted from him.

The climb was treacherous. Loose siltstone coated by a thin layer of Yellowstone dust made for poor footing, which didn't seem to bother Anth with her three toes, but might as well have been marbles to Henry and his stiff cyborg feet.

He was half-way up when Seth called down from the cliff edge. "Sir, do you require assistance?" Anth's face appeared over the rim with an expression that Henry swore must have been a smirk. A half-hour later he angled up and over the sandstone brim, exhausted and covered in dirt.

<>

"These may taste better cooked, sir."

The evening wind picked up, carrying with it a crisp scent of pine. Henry shoved the turbine's access door shut, but its warped edge kept it slightly ajar. The dank interior reeked of death. Anything could have been trapped behind the corroded instrument panels lining the walls. Regardless, with the temperature dropping, Henry was glad of the shelter especially for Anth's sake.

"No fire tonight, Seth. It's bad enough the Soofysh might have an idea where we are. No sense in putting up a neon sign." Henry snatched up the roots Seth held out. "Damn. Prairie turnips. How did you find these? This time of year there are few left above ground." He shook out some clinging tufts of soil. "We used to call them Timpsula—good cooked or raw." An image of a family dinner at his grandfather's house flickered in Henry's mind—everyone gathered around an oak table, the sweet aroma of roasted deer and baked bread, his mother passing out the Timpsula—a century ago, or yesterday.

"Want some, Anth?"

The reptilian sat motionless against a center post, arms wrapped about her knees, her membranous wings folded over her body.

"Your loss." Henry bit off a hunk. "Not as bitter as I remember it." He savored each mouthful and sat back in the darkness to watch memories scoot by like a slideshow.

<>

A sliver of sunlight slipped through the door's seam and painted a bright green line across Anth's face. She remained motionless in the same fetal-like squat she had adopted the night before.

The door swung open and Seth leaned in. "I'm afraid there is no breakfast, sir." He pointed back to the rim of the butte and the expanse beyond. "But we may have company soon."

Henry fished out his binoculars and followed Seth to the cliff edge. "Damn. What the hell is it this time?"

At first Henry saw only the swells of tall grasses playing in the wind. Then his eye caught several golden pinpoints weaving through the yellow-green sea. They moved as fireflies in an early evening dusk—random, glittering arcs in the night air. The illusion was soon dispelled by their precise movement, each sparkle zig-zagged in a choreographed dance in sync with all the others. An occasional flash of bright blue joined the spreading chorus as if some of the entities below were taking flash pictures.

"Peculiar, sir."

"Little silver balls … quite beautiful with the reflected sunrise. They're moving over the grass and—there it is again—that flash. They're zapping things down there."

Seth said, "They are killing anything that moves."

Henry felt a touch at his shoulder. "Anth, so you're up. Do you have any idea what we're looking at?"

"Soofysh technology, not ours."

"That much I guessed. But what are they?"

She shook her head and remained silent.

Seth said, "Perhaps they will by-pass us, sir."

Henry edged closer to the rim. "Hope so, Seth. They're moving around the butte like some kind of probes."

Anth said, "If so, it is unlike the Soofysh to ignore this outcropping."

"Maybe they don't care."

"The Soofysh are deliberate. They never overlook anything."

Seth said, "Sir, Anth may have a point. Several of your beautiful globes are on their way up."

Their mini-plateau covered an area less than a football field with little more than several boulders and knee-high juniper trees jutting above the short grass. There was nowhere to hide— except one.

Henry said, "This way." He ran back to the tower, motioning the other two to follow. The wind turbine was built to last. The outer skin, made of stainless steel, appeared intact. The ladder within was another matter. Rust ran along its rungs and railings.

"What do you think, Seth?"

"I suggest letting Anth go up first, sir. If it holds, then—."

Anth needed no further convincing. She leaped onto a rung and soon disappeared into the pitch black above. The ladder shook and groaned, and when it settled, Henry pointed at Seth. "You're next."

"I beg your pardon, sir. I am but a mechanical construct, unlikely to interest the Soofysh."

"All right, Seth, but you better be right behind me."

A minute later the three jammed into a six-foot wide cylindrical room. The single source of light came from a small porthole set into a locked hatch midway up a wall. The ladder went no farther.

Henry focused his binoculars on the entry below and watched a silver ball ease into view.

Chapter 26

Anth wrapped her slender fingers around the hatch lever. She wasn't sure why she had rejoined Henry and his cryptic quest. Was it to spurn her father? Or was it that beneath her rebellion against authority ran a stronger current—one she was reluctant to acknowledge, one that was loyal to her people? Her feelings, her loyalty to family welled up, threatening to overcome a growing affection for the cyborg. Henry was a creature of great interest to both her father and to the Soofysh. Her father has an obsession with the creature and how it works. Too bad he had little such interest in his so-called daughter. To Fierz, she was but a means to an end. At times Fierz's intensity terrified her. Then there were the Soofysh—inscrutable and even more frightening than her father. They also appeared to be obsessed with the cyborg. What was it about Henry that drew so much attention?

Henry asked, "Can you open it?"

The lever moved with a dull groan. She tugged, but the hatch remained closed. "I need to tell you something."

"Sir, I think we must hasten. That beautiful globe of yours is rising swiftly."

"How about it, Anth?"

Anth heaved a shoulder against the hatch, but to no avail. At the same moment, the room brightened. A metallic ball, about a foot in diameter, bobbed in the air between them, emitting a high-pitched static hiss. Anth swatted it with her free hand. For a moment it seemed disoriented, pausing in front of the reptilian. She slammed it again, sending it reeling into the wall where it exploded as if made of glass. Several wiry components jiggled on the floor among the silvery shards.

Henry said, "What did you do? I bet the rest of those buggers will know we're here."

"I have a confession. These balls are Soofysh technology, but are not designed to hunt you down. I think the Soofysh used them to clear areas for settlement. I remember seeing them in action when my people arrived."

"Why didn't you say so before?"

"Henry, my actions have been part of a greater lie. Your escape from our colony was a trick, a ruse. I joined you in deceit."

"What trick? You've been with us for quite a while now. You even saved my life."

She exhaled, wishing all her troubles would follow that breath and ride on the wind to be forgotten. "Once I discovered your purpose and whether there were others like you, I was supposed to bring you back—back to Fierz." She sagged as her body became limp.

"And you're telling me this because—"

Anth leaned back against the frozen hatch. "I do not know. Thinking back, at first I wanted to please my father, but as we travelled farther away from our settlement, and I saw more of this world … I thought of the terrible thing the Soofysh had done—and you—a wondrous human cyborg—to me, you became more than a textbook human being. You became a friend."

Seth said, "Sir, there is another globe on its way up."

Henry said, "We can talk about this later." He grasped Anth by a shoulder. "You claim these things are supposed to what … sterilize an area for your people?"

Anth slammed an elbow into the hatch, snapping the hinges. A second blow launched the door outward. She squeezed through and swung her legs onto an external ladder. "Come. I have an idea."

Henry and Seth scrambled through the opening.

"Why don't you just smash the orbs as they come up?"

"I was lucky. The orb must have been confused. If it had not hesitated, that Soofysh technology would burn through me in a second, and the next one may not be so mystified."

The ladder ended beneath the generator nacelle of the wind turbine. Three 60-foot blades extended from its other end. Despite the winds, the assembly remained fixed, unmoving and creaking with each gust. There was nowhere else to go.

Henry asked, "Now what?"

Anth looked down to see a silvery sphere emerge from the hatch. "We jump." Without warning she locked her legs about Henry and Seth, and leaped into the wind. Her wings caught an updraft and for a moment they rose into the air. The extra weight meant her descent would be faster than usual. She aimed at a point where the sterilization spheres had already done their work.

The landing was rough, sending Henry and Seth tumbling. Anth arched up on her toes and looked back at the butte. The shiny pinpoints continued their mesmerizing march away, content with their single-minded task of ridding the area of any unwanted life forms.

Henry crawled over and said, "You saved us."

Anth said, "It would appear your wife misled you."

Henry pointed to the butte. "But she knew we had to get up there. Otherwise, that miniature Soofysh death squad would have toasted us here on the ground."

"Perhaps your mind was playing tricks on you."

"Playing tricks? That's a funny thing for you to say."

"Our minds are not as different as our outward appearances would suggest."

Henry said, "Then how did I know that those nasty little balls were coming?"

Anth shook her head. "That is a puzzle. As far as I know, we are the only colonists, with more of our people to arrive a year from now."

Henry smiled. "Isn't that great? More guests on the way. Reminds me of a time when we welcomed visitors from Europe. We were naïve enough to call them guests, not thinking about the consequences. Those guests thanked us by taking our lands, stealing our treasures, and wiping us out with murder and disease."

Seth said, "The day is still young." Henry gave both the robot and Anth a look as Seth continued. "Which direction do we take, sir?"

"I'd say the route that gets us something to eat, and soon." Henry walked off, heading south, no doubt following his dead wife. Given no other obvious options, south was as good as any direction. At least it was getting warmer.

Seth said, "I wish to thank you, Anth."

The comment broke her stride. Seth had never talked to anyone but Henry.

She said, "There was no other choice to be made."

"You had many choices. Leaving us on the turbine was one."

She marveled at the robot's insight. "That is true." Seth's eyeless head was poised as if expecting more. She said, "You are welcome."

The robot nodded and remained by her side, taking two steps to every one of hers. In all her research of human technology, Anth had not come across such a one as Seth. The same was true of Henry.

<>

Hours later the sun touched the horizon. Frigid evening gusts sent the golden grasses recoiling. They paused at the crest of a modest rise, beyond which a narrow creek ran alongside several knobby stands of pines. The cold air was a worry.

Anth said, "Henry, I cannot go much farther."

"Is there a problem?"

"The temperature. My limbs have become sluggish. I need to warm up."

"The day's about done." Henry nodded at a depression ahead. "We'll setup for the night by those pinion trees. There's water there, and with some luck, we'll have pine nuts for dinner."

Seth was quick to build a fire using dead branches and his infrared eye slit. He topped off the construction with several flat stones, creating a makeshift oven. Anth squatted nearby. Her membranous wings cupped the warmth to her torso. She watched Henry spread handfuls of pine nuts over one of the stones and in minutes their exotic scent filled her nostrils.

"Are you not concerned about being spotted by some Soofysh drone or one of my father's underlings?"

"At this point, I just don't care."

Anth held out several rodent carcasses she had picked up along the way—victims of the sterilization orbs. "I think you prefer these cooked."

Henry said, "I'll have one if you try these nuts."

"Fair bargain."

After dinner, they settled in for the night with Seth tending the fire. Anth allowed Henry to lie alongside her to help stave off the growing chill—a human cyborg and a reptilian from light years away huddled together on an empty planet. The thought threatened to undo her mind.

She awoke to blinding white. The snow had arrived.

Chapter 27

The cyborg stirred and Anth's wings crackled in protest as she pulled her arms back. Ice needles stung her eyes. Seth must have tended the fire through the night, explaining the lack of any appreciable snow cover on her or on the cyborg. The prairie winds had picked up since yesterday. Although she had experienced snow before, she always had shelter. The thought of prolonged exposure had her worried.

Henry shifted nearer to the sputtering campfire. "We've got ourselves the first snowstorm of the season coming in and it's a doozy."

Seth stoked the dying fire with a finger. "Travelling today may be a challenge, sir."

"Not for you or me, Seth. But Anth may be a different matter."

Anth faced away from the wind, bringing up her wings to cover her head. She said, "I will try and keep up"

Henry said, "I know you will."

"However, I fear that the cold will slow me down. Without heat, it is possible I will cease to function."

"Cease to function?"

"My muscles will weaken. Our kind cannot function in the cold. At some point, I will fall into a sleep. Death will follow."

"You're too big to carry. Seth, any ideas?"

The robot lifted one of the flat rocks near the fire. "We can keep Anth warm enough using this." A red beam shot out from his slit and struck the rock. Seconds later Seth handed the slab to Anth.

She held it to her bosom, absorbing its life-giving warmth. "This may work. Very clever."

Seth said, "Whenever you need it heated up again, let me know."

Anth folded her wings over the rock, retaining the heat as best as she could manage. Once again she marveled at the little robot's intelligence and resourcefulness, a thought which added weight to her misgivings about the little creature's origins.

Henry swung up his backpack. "We're heading out."

Anth snorted snowflakes out of her nostrils. "There are no landmarks. The snow is so dense that we cannot see anything. How can you judge which way to go?" She knew before she finished the question, what Henry would say.

"I know."

And if the cyborg's ghost is merely an illusion, a trick of a damaged brain, they would be marching off to oblivion and a lonely, frigid end. Anth steeled herself against argument, and focused instead on staying warm.

<>

The storm ended three days later.

They had trudged through ice, sleet, and snow drifts several feet high, stopping every hour or so to warm up with Seth's help. Henry's roasted pine nuts ran out the day before. Anth felt weaker than she ever remembered. Sleep, an eternal sleep, cloyed at the edges of her perception, taunting her, imploring her to lie down and rest.

Seth's rock trick did a great job keeping her core warm, but it had its limitations. She had lost feeling in her extremities, especially her feet. She knew that each step brought her closer to a dull and pitiful end. She would not succumb, she would not complain.

It was mid-morning when Henry exclaimed, "I think we're in luck."

The snow continued to fall, coming down in stinging bursts, pausing at times as if to catch its breath. The landscape had changed from a featureless prairie to a series of low hills. The shallow valleys provided little relief from the constant winds which threw up clouds of sharp, biting snow loosened from drifts. Anth had become disconnected from her body. The cold, the relentless howling—the world of pain had faded, replaced by a hazy, drifting sensation, which alarmed some deep part of her mind. Survival had morphed into an abstract concept, scarcely worth considering. She strained to focus. A dark rectangular outline drifted into view, embedded among a sparse stand of pines. Henry became a ghost, floating over the snow. She imagined his wife must look much the same to him. He waved his arms and yelled out something obscured by the distance. Anth pushed on.

Henry reached the door of the structure and jarred it open. Anth staggered through the entrance and collapsed on the floor. She heard the door slam shut and closed her eyes, yielding to siren call of the abyss.

<>

Her face felt warm. An orange, flickering glow danced across her eyelids.

"She's awakening, sir."

The flames of a fire licked at a blackened stone hearth. Several logs within sizzled and spat. She stretched out her arms and legs to soak in the heat, a simple action which fatigued her to the point of near unconsciousness. A blanket draped about her shoulders fell away.

"Not too close, Anth. You'll burn yourself." Henry squatted near the fire and poked the logs with a stick, releasing a gush of embers. "Feeling better?"

Anth pulled the blanket over her back. With Henry's help, she raised herself to a sitting position. "Better."

Seth waddled to her side. "Would you like some soup?" He held out a bowl with a most pleasing aroma. "It's chicken soup."

Anth cupped the bowl in both hands and slurped at the strange brew. She relished the sweet, meaty taste and lifted the bowl to permit the warm golden nectar to run down her throat. As she lowered her head for a second mouthful, a shadow passed across the floor. She looked to the window by the entrance. Dusty glass reflected daylight into an opalescent blur. Occasional white flecks danced across its frame. Something much larger than a snow flake must have cast the shadow.

Henry said, "We may be getting some more snow. Maybe that's a good thing. It'll be a little harder for the Soofysh to see our smoke, or to track us. So, do you like it?"

She nodded and repositioned herself to face the window. "Chicken—what manner of beast is that?"

Henry said, "Just a bird. I think it's a bit stale with being in a can for many years, but to me it's heaven."

Seth held up a glass bottle containing a white powder. "The secret is in the seasoning—salt."

Anth much preferred live fare and worried that she might develop a reaction as she often did when consuming strange foods. Nonetheless, she finished off the soup, trusting its short-term benefits outweighed the risk.

Henry got up from the fireplace and ambled to the front door. "You saw it, too?"

Anth put the empty bowl down. She tried to stand, but lost her balance and fell back down, landing on her rump. "Something passed by. I did not see what."

She heard a creak from outside, maybe from a loose floorboard.

Henry said, "Whatever it is, it's heavy and on the porch."

Seth took up his bat and joined Henry at the door.

Chapter 28

An escalating feeling of dread threatened to reduce Genz to a quivering jelly. He paused at the door and was about to knock when Fierz's gravelly voice erupted from within. "Are you going to stand out there all day? Get in here."

His hands flew to the handle, while his gaze brushed by the hallway camera. With the door held ajar, he peeked in. "Is this a good time?"

"Shut the door and sit down." Fierz was taller and broader than most, a combination that instilled a palpable fear, if not sheer terror, in all he addressed. The commander's physicality lent great weight to his position as head of the colony. Charm and empathy were not his strong suits. In fact, Genz couldn't recall any past instances where such qualities might have been displayed, even accidentally.

Fierz sat at a narrow and wide desk with his head hidden behind a large monitor. Genz slipped into the only other chair in the room. Facing the back of the monitor, he was grateful for the temporary lack of eye-to-eye contact. He wasn't sure what to say, or even if he should speak.

Fierz said, "Well?"

His mind spun. "Sir, I have not—"

"I know you have *not*. Your girlfriend has *not* reported and you don't know where they are." After a pause, Fierz spoke again, but with a lower, more menacing tone. "You and I are going on a trip."

"But my work here—"

"Can wait. Your damn girlfriend took off with a valuable item, and I am going to get it back, and you are going to help me."

"But, but—how do we know where to look?"

The monitor swung round to face Genz. It displayed a map of their immediate territory and several lines, all converging in a single direction. Fierz leaned over the screen and ran a finger along the lines. "I know where they are going."

"But how?"

"From Custer town they headed here." Fierz pointed lower on the screen. He looked up at Genz. "I know this—the Soofysh told me so."

The reference to the Soofysh was typical of Fierz. He took every opportunity to elevate his status. The trick always worked. Bringing up the Soofysh chilled Genz's bones as if he was standing outside in the frosty wind. He didn't think that anyone had ever seen one, and that Fierz communicated with them set his mind spinning.

Fierz toggled a switch and the display rolled up. "The next sighting was here." The commander's finger pointed lower still, to a set of small plateaus.

"How do I know this? The Soofysh reported a problem with several of their sterilization modules … right there."

Genz knew about the modules. He tried thinking of something else, but his mind filled with images of robotic spheres chasing him down, cutting though his flesh with their beams.

"Do you see it?"

Genz leaned forward as if getting closer to the monitor would enlighten his rattled brain. "I'm not sure, sir."

"Fool. It's a straight line."

He looked again, following the line's trajectory to where it intersected a mountain.

"It's as obvious to me as the dull pallor of your skin. This is no coincidence. They know."

"Know what, sir?"

"Assemble several days' provisions for the two of us. Don't tell anyone what you are doing, not even my wife. This is between you and me. Understand?"

Genz nodded. Eager to leave, he backed away.

"Go."

Once out in the hall, he managed to settle his nerves enough to think. Commander Fierz was in contact with the invisible Soofysh. And then there was the matter of the cyborg. Why was Fierz so single-minded about getting that creature back? For that matter, why was Anth intent upon staying with it?

Genz entered the kitchen and the smell of fresh meat filled his nostrils. A female looked up at him from the counter and set down her knife. "Genz, how nice to see you. I'm afraid Anth has stepped out."

"Good day, Ma'am. Oh, no, no … I'm not here for her. Your husband, I mean Commander Fierz, asked me to obtain provisions for several days."

The female seemed taken aback and paused before replying. "I see. Fierz is up to one of his adventures, and he told you to say nothing about it."

"Yes, Ma'am."

"No problem. I'm finished with this. I'll wrap it up into portions. Several days, you say?"

"Yes, Ma'am. It's kind of a field trip. I'm not supposed to talk about it."

"I can see that."

"I need to tell my folks. I'll be back in a moment."

Genz closed the door behind him, glad he wasn't asked for more details. The next few days were certain to be harrowing—alone with Commander Fierz. And then there was something the Commander had said. *Somehow they know?*

Chapter 29

Henry placed his finger on the dead bolt. "Did you hear that, Seth?"

"It sounds like a bear, sir."

The aroma of chicken soup lingered in Henry's nostrils. "I wouldn't be surprised." He stepped back, grabbed his revolver, and flipped open its cylinder. He ran a hand over this jacket. "Six in the cylinder, and two in the pocket."

Anth whispered, "I wouldn't mind some meat."

Henry shook his head. "I think the bear has the same thing in mind."

A floorboard creaked, sounding louder. A roar erupted from behind the door and Henry stepped back, half-expecting it to implode, perhaps even carrying with it a giant furry beast armed with massive teeth and claws.

The disquieting silence which followed prompted Henry to chance sliding the bolt back and easing the door open a crack. A waft of cold air met his face, carrying with it tiny snowflakes dancing in the air.

Seth said, "Perhaps it has gone, sir."

The slight snow cover on the porch betrayed a set of prints climbing the two steps and then wandering off to the side. Henry had seen such tracks before. He whispered, "Grizzly," cocked his revolver, and nudged the door open a bit more. He was about to lean out to sneak a look when the bright snow-covered firs beyond the porch disappeared. A bear filled up the entire doorframe. The beast reared up on its hind legs and paused a moment. Its mouth sprung open releasing a thunderous growl as it swung a paw through the air. Henry fell backwards over Seth, and reeled at the gagging plume of rancid exhale.

Seth untangled himself from Henry's legs and smashed his bat against the grizzly's outstretched paw. Henry caught Anth's movement behind him. She raised herself and the bear arched backwards at the sight of the tall reptilian. Anth staggered to the door jamb. At the same moment, something dark and furry appeared at the bear's shoulder. The grizzly lurched backwards and clawed at its neck.

A curved line of spittle and blood spattered on the bright snow coating the porch. Henry caught sight of a pair of wide, yellow eyes. An oversized wolf dangled from the bear's neck. Its gaze locked on him for a moment. *The Custer town beast.* The grizzly howled and twisted. The pair fell to the porch and rolled to the base of the steps, leaving a jagged crimson trail behind.

Henry lunged outside and raised his gun, screaming back to the cabin. "You two stay inside."

Seth said, "Which will you shoot, sir?"

Good question.

Henry slammed the door behind him. The tangle of black and brown fur continued to thrash. The grizzly's growls came in short bursts and its mammoth paws slowed their swiping. Blood spurted through the wolf's jaws and seeped out of several wide gashes in its haunches.

All of a sudden, the bear raised itself on its hind legs and whipped the wolf over its head, sending it cart-wheeling onto the blood-streaked snow. The wolf rolled onto its side, writhing, and gasping. The grizzly coughed up more blood. It roared again—emitting a wet and wheezing sound.

When it lunged at the wolf, Henry fired. The mammoth head jerked to the side as if it was annoyed by some pesky insect. It straightened up on its hind quarters and turned toward Henry. A mortally wounded animal might follow its last steps in a blind effort to escape danger. Those tracks ran beneath Henry's feet. He fired again. The behemoth clasped its face with both paws and dropped to its knees. Henry drew nearer and aimed, but before he pulled the trigger, the grizzly keeled over and slumped to the ground. It heaved a protracted, gurgling sigh. Blood seeped from its neck and ran in rivulets along its shoulders, pooling beneath its body.

A second, weaker growl caught Henry's attention.

The wolf hunched up onto its forepaws and snarled. Despite his instincts screaming for him to run, Henry lowered his revolver and took a step nearer the wounded animal. The wolf pulled up a hind leg, steadied itself for a moment as if preparing to attack, and then fell over on its side.

Its eyes, bright yellow globes, remained focused on Henry as he neared.

"Seth, I'm going to need your help here."

<>

"No infection, sir." Seth carried a wet rag and a pan filled with water. Behind him, a furry four-legged killing machine curled up in a corner of the one-room cabin. The wolf's head bobbed up, following Seth with its nostrils flaring and pink tongue dangling from its mouth.

Henry said, "I think you've made a new friend."

"I am fond of animals, sir."

Henry skewered a chunk of bear meat with a poker and propped it over the fireplace. He handed a raw strip to Seth. "Here, I think your buddy might like this."

Anth wiped her mouth with the back of her hand. "I do not understand why you humans prefer heating your food."

"We don't have your sharp teeth. We need to chew, and that goes for meat in particular."

"That may be, but the heat ruins the taste."

Henry rotated the poker. The heady aroma of seared meat filled the cabin. Three days had gone by since the grizzly's visit. Three days of rest. Three days for the Soofysh to locate them.

Henry said, "I wonder about your Soofysh. Wouldn't they have come for us by now?"

Anth stood up and stretched her membranous arms. "There may not be many Soofysh yet present. They may have left, or considered us a low priority."

"I doubt it. And then there's your father—or whatever you call him."

"Fierz. Commander Fierz."

"Why is he so interested in me?"

"A human cyborg is an unexpected find. My studies of your sciences did not reveal such a level of technology."

Henry glanced at Seth while biting off a juicy morsel. "There's a lot here that's a mystery." At that moment Liz appeared between them and pointed to the door.

Henry said, "We need to get going first thing tomorrow." As he brought up the poker for another bite, a nudge to his elbow gave him pause. A wolf's snout emerged from beneath his arm and a long tongue lapped at the juicy meat.

133

Seth said, "It appears, sir, that you too have a new friend."

Chapter 30

Henry said, "Sorry about the smell."

Anth pulled the bear skin about her shoulders and inhaled through her wide nares. "I detect nothing repulsive."

"That's fortunate. I left a little fat on it for more insulation. Doing it right would take a few weeks for the skin to dry out, but we don't have that luxury."

Despite the wolf's aversion to Anth, it chose to trot behind her. Henry was sure it was due to the odor of the hide more than a growing fondness for an eight-foot reptilian. Maybe it saw Anth as possible snack food. Wolves were dangerous enough as pack animals and, as loners, the jury was out. One thing for sure, they were never happy with humans. Henry expected it would take off on its own as soon as the bear meat ran out, or when it felt better.

The weather had grown a bit warmer in spite of the higher elevations, but not warm enough to melt the frozen strips of bear meat in Henry's backpack. With winter about to descend from the north, he welcomed the temporary respite. The plains had long ago given way to rolling hills and several snow-capped mountains jutted up from the blue-gray horizon beyond. They were doubly-blessed as the snow cover had thinned to a few inches, parts of which succumbed to the waning sunlight, exposing foot-high yellow grass.

Liz maintained a steady pace, leading the group west. Henry longed for her to talk. The thought was a constant nag but had him even more hopeful that Liz was still alive. He didn't think it was his imagination when she warned him back at the cabin. Perhaps it was better this way. Hearing voices was a clear symptom of derangement, and he hadn't yet decided if he was crazy.

"Sir." Seth had positioned himself atop the next rise and pointed at something in the valley ahead. For a moment Henry thought the robot had seen Liz.

"Whew." A huge table of ice filled the shallow valley before them—a winding shape running north and south. Henry guessed it to be a frozen river maybe a mile wide.

Anth caught up. "Is there a problem?"

"This wasn't here the last time I visited this part of the country."

"Sir, that was a while ago."

"Yeah, before the asteroid, or should I say, the invasion."

"Some tectonic shifting might explain it."

Liz floated over the half-thawed shoreline and waved back at Henry. It made Henry crazy to think she saw him.

"However it got here, it's something we need to get past."

A few minutes later, the group walked along the river's edge. A narrow strip of water separated the ice from the shore. Henry leaped over it and slid onto the frozen surface. The sounds of cracking ice obliged him to shuffle farther away from the shore. Bright crooked lines marked his movements. Once the river ice settled down, he took several more steps away and said, "It's much thicker toward the middle." At least, he hoped so.

Anth picked up Seth and wended along the frozen mud to a different spot.

"It's okay, Anth. When you jump, keep going. Hold up when the cracking stops."

She loped onto the surface with one huge stride with her momentum sending her sliding and falling on her butt, all the while embracing Seth with her bearskin. When they came to a stop, the robot rolled off to his feet and said, "I am undamaged, sir."

Anth pulled herself up, struggling to maintain her balance. Her three-toed feet left behind thin scratches in the ice as she skidded. For a moment she reminded him of a scrawny bright green chicken—an image he would never share with her.

A whine echoed across the valley. The wolf remained at the shore, likely unhappy about the potential to get wet.

"Come on, boy. It's all right." Maybe this was goodbye. Wolves and cold water rarely mixed.

Instead of retreating, the wolf brought its forepaws to the water. It flinched, shaking each paw in turn. Falling in could prove to be a one-way trip. Henry shuffled closer and lowered himself to all fours. "You can do it. Jump. I'll catch you." He extended a hand, and at the same moment, the wolf leaped.

Its hind legs caught the water, while Henry grabbed its barrel-sized torso. With forepaws curled around his neck and slavering jaws snapping at his ear, the wolf's landing slid them backwards. In the next instant, it was on its feet and shaking out its hind legs. When it finished, rather than the expected growl, the wolf yelped as a dog might. Henry swore it wagged its tail as well.

Anth asked, "What do you think happened to the other ones—the wolves back in Custer town?"

Henry said, "Maybe they wandered off."

"I thought wolf packs were family."

Henry gave Anth a second look. Her level of understanding of human culture was impressive enough. "More from your studies?"

"We were taught to be thorough. Since we did not expect to encounter any humans, other significant life forms, especially dangerous ones, became part of our curriculum."

"Hmm, if his buddies didn't wander off, then this badass either left them, or—"

"Ate them."

The wolf lapped at its fur.

"That's an encouraging thought."

A crack reverberated across the icy expanse in protest to the sun's rays breaking out from the clouds. Henry scanned the blinding white landscape. A mild breeze tickled the undulating lines of snow running along fissures. No major gaps were visible. "Not to worry. That's normal. It's ice expanding. Keep moving. I don't like being exposed like this."

When the group reached the midpoint, Henry motioned for all to stop.

Anth said, "The ice is different here."

He lowered himself to a knee at an uneven line in the ice. When he wiped off the snow, the deep blue translucence sent a shudder through him.

Anth said, "Is there a problem?"

"Two problems. This ice is newer—thinner than what we're standing on."

Seth said, "Perhaps it is the result of a faster current in the middle of the river."

"I don't think so, Seth."

Anth said, "And the second problem?"

"Something passed through here recently."

Anth said, "Passed through?"

"Something broke this ice."

Seth said, "The width of the disturbance suggests the object was small—maybe a foot wide."

"I agree, Seth. Can you estimate when it was made?"

"Based on the average temperatures for the past several days, the thinner snow cover, and the thickness of the new ice, I would say sometime in the past 24 hours."

Henry chipped off a protruding edge at the rim of the disturbance. "And it's not the first time. Something seems to be coming through here at regular intervals."

He no sooner finished the thought, when the wolf let loose a growl. It stared northward along the mysterious line in the ice. A distant rumbling perked up Henry's ears.

Seth said, "We may find out what is causing this phenomenon quite soon"

Henry asked, "Can you see anything, Seth?"

"My sensors indicate a pointed black object protruding from the ice—perhaps indicative of something larger beneath, sir. It's coming this way."

Henry broke into a trot. Anth caught on and lifted Seth to her shoulders. As if sensing the impending danger, the wolf out-paced the group, and sprinted toward the shadowy image of Liz, hovering over the shoreline. Beyond her, the land rose into a series of fir thickets.

Minutes later, they splashed through the few feet of open water at the shore and dived into a bed of dried grass and low-lying juniper brambles. Henry lifted his head and swung a branch to the side.

The object continued its movement through the middle of the river. Its size and shape reminded Henry of a submarine periscope, an image brought home by a thin pipe-like projection which rotated as it tore through the thin ice. The wolf stood its ground at the shore and howled.

"That wolf certainly doesn't back down, does it, sir?"

"Maybe it'll scare off that thing in the river."

The crackling sound stopped, and the wolf ceased wailing. A feeling of impending doom rode atop the dead silence which followed. The wolf must have felt it too, for it backed away from the water, tail tucked between its rear legs. The black projection grew to twice its original height.

"Sir, do you think it spotted us?"

"No doubt about it. It probably saw us while we were crossing."

Anth said, "My ears. The pain."

The wolf whined and galloped away from the river.

Seth said, "The object is emitting a high frequency sound."

Henry said, "That can't be good. Wolf!" and began the climb through the woods. To his surprise, the wolf was quick to take the lead again, no doubt more than happy to get as far as possible from the monster in the river. It took a few minutes to reach the summit.

Seth said, "There is something coming, sir."

Henry brought out his binoculars. "I don't see anything."

"Take a closer look, sir."

Henry searched the trail they left behind in the light snow. Midway up the slope, a tree branch moved. He refocused his scope. "Damn. I still don't see anything, Seth."

Anth said, "It must be Soofysh. They are coming for us." The pitch of her voice belied a fright Henry had not heard before. The terrain ahead consisted of hill after hill, wooded and rising to meet the mountains miles away. The going would be slow.

"Are you sure there's something there, Seth?"

"Look again, sir."

A cascade of powder snow fell from a branch closer than the previous. Still, there was nothing to see. This time Henry scanned the ground where they had left their prints in the snow. New ones appeared.

"Damn it all. There *is* something there, but I don't see a damn thing."

"Agreed, sir."

"We're not going to outrun it. Split up. Each of us takes a different route. Keep in sight of one another. Find a tree or something to climb. Go."

"What is the plan, sir?"

"Ask me later, Seth."

The three set out on parallel paths. The wolf was gone and Liz was nowhere to be seen. About a quarter mile later, up another slope, Henry signaled to the other two to spread out and scrambled over an outcrop of rocks. He spread himself out on a thrust of granite which overlooked the positions of the other two—both had scurried up trees.

Seconds later, several low-lying pine branches about twenty yards off trembled and released snow showers, The dusting of snow outlined a rectangular object, standing about as tall as a human. A gust of wind blew off the powder snow and the object vanished once again. Henry followed its emerging imprints in the snow. The impressions reminded him of Loggerhead turtle tracks in the sand, regular and mechanical. The tracks seem to head toward Anth's tree.

Henry threw off his bow and quiver, and rummaged in his sack for the revolver. When he looked again, smoke rose from the base of Anth's tree. He was about to fire off a round at the unseen automaton when a nearby medium-sized boulder gave him a better idea.

It was heavy. He was sure that as a human it would have been impossible to lift, much less carry. He staggered to the edge of the rocky cliff. Anth's tree sagged to the side. He dropped the boulder, hoping it would at least distract the thing.

The stone landed with a loud thud. The crunching metal-on-metal sound of a car crash gave Henry a sense of satisfaction however uncalled for. An oblong vaguely human silhouette materialized—gray and resembling a Hollywood robot from a century ago. An unnerving series of squawks reminded Henry of finger nails dragged across a chalk board. A square head appeared, sporting a concave dent, and a device at its midsection spewed a fiery arc as it twisted in an effort to remain standing. The tree snapped a final time, sending Anth tumbling into the snow.

Seth appeared behind the mechanical enigma and smashed off its blowtorch nozzle with his bat. By the time Henry clambered down from the rock pile, the thing had ceased caterwauling and had come to a complete standstill.

Anth said, "What manner of creature is this?"

Henry said, "I was going to ask you the same thing."

Seth said, "It is likely to be a Soofysh construct."

"Yeah. That might make sense with the river and all. I mean, that river … it's artificial, maybe a border protecting something, and this thing—"

"A border guard," added Seth.

Anth said, "Which must mean the Soofysh know where we are."

"My guess is that they've known that for a while."

Seth said, "What do we do, sir? Wait for them to arrive?"

"I think they're waiting for *us* to arrive."

<>

After traipsing across several more hills, they settled on a campsite with a western view. The sunset provided no more than a hint of warmth. Seth tended to a fire and heated up some of the frozen meat.

Henry fiddled with the remains of the Soofysh robot while Anth's strength was put to good use in tearing apart its metallic torso. With her help and his mechanical instinct, Henry lifted out a mechanism that sprouted tendrils resembling wires. These led to many other internal parts, suggesting its likely role as a source of power.

"The meat is ready, sir."

"Be right there, Seth." Henry yanked out a separate, plate-shaped component which had been loosened by the boulder. He dangled it over the presumed power supply and disappeared.

Seth continued to hold out the broiled chunk toward where Henry had squatted a moment before. The meat lifted from his hand, floated for a second, and also disappeared.

Chapter 31

Henry awoke to a curious sound he last heard back at Anth's menagerie.

Seth nudged him. "We have a guest, sir."

Anth grunted and hissed while she dragged something to the dying campfire. For a moment, Henry thought the wolf was back. Instead of dark fur, he saw Anth stroking green scales. A second reptilian lay stretched out at her feet, arms splayed. Seth was quick to stoke the fire and renew the blaze as Anth drew the creature closer to the rising warmth.

Henry said, "One of yours?"

Her response sobered his half-jest. "It's Genz. I'm sorry to say, he is a friend."

The unconscious reptilian's breathing changed, becoming shallow and labored. Several gashes across his arms and legs caught Henry's attention. Dark streaks of what looked like blood ran across his chest. "He looks hurt."

"The wounds are superficial. We need to warm him up."

Henry stepped away and followed the creature's unique, three-toed trail in the snow beyond their campsite. "Don't you guys use shoes?"

"There is no need. Our soles are thick, much like the leather you use to cover your feet."

Henry extended his leg, displaying a weather-worn moccasin. "Not like *my* leather shoes. I don't see a vehicle. He must have walked here."

Anth turned back to her colleague. "Genz, can you hear me?"

Their guest remained unresponsive.

Henry asked, "What can we do to help?"

"It is the cold. We cannot survive without an external source of heat."

"Seth, think you can do that rock trick of yours?"

While Seth scurried away, Henry kneeled down next to Anth. "Is Genz here ... you know, from your outpost back in South Dakota?"

"We worked together."

"So how the hell did he find us? He can't have walked all the way."

"I do not know. We need to get him awake."

Henry watched Anth cradle Genz's head. Their relationship was more than casual.

Anth said, "He was in charge of the ... warehouse, where we stored artifacts of interest."

"Be right back." Henry loped over to Seth who carried several selections of slate rock and took hold of one. He whispered to his diminutive friend. "What do you think?"

"Anth is correct that her companion's wounds are superficial."

"Anything else?"

"A troubling aspect, sir—the reptilian's body temperature appears to be similar to Anth's."

"Ah, so hyperthermia can be ruled out."

"It is more serious than that, sir."

"Internal wounds?"

"I think he is faking, sir."

<>

Genz stirred. His head swung round and focused on Anth. "Is it safe?"

When Henry and Seth were some steps away, she said, "Talk fast."

"It's Fierz. He's watching us from the next hill."

"He's here?"

"He wants your cyborg."

"He's not mine."

"Yours or not, he's determined to get it."

"So why are *you* here?"

Genz looked away, as if ashamed. "I was worried about you."

The other two approached.

She whispered, "Don't do anything stupid."

Henry said, "How's he doing?"

"I think he will recover."

While Seth placed two slates on Genz's chest and heated them,

Henry reached below the reptilian's arm to a soft spot and pinched. Genz jerked upright with eyes wide open.

Henry brought up his revolver and said, "Did you think your act would fool us?"

Anth said, "What are you doing?"

"Your guest is a liar."

"It is true. He is not injured."

Genz seemed to glare at Anth, as if perplexed that she would betray him.

She spoke to Genz in their native language. "Time to share, Genz. Tell us why Fierz sent you here."

Genz said, "I thought you—you—"

"You thought wrong. This is my family now. Talk."

Genz sat upright, tossing off the slate stones. "Damn it all, Anth. Fierz made me do this—to find out about the cyborg—"

"His name is Henry."

"Whatever."

"Go on."

"If you don't help us, he'll kill you—I couldn't let that happen." Genz's words stabbed at her heart. "My father—kill me?"

"He is obsessed with the cyborg. He'll do anything to get his hands on it before the Soofysh do. You were supposed to help."

While Anth translated for Henry, her mind raced ahead. Commander Fierz was insane. He expected Genz to return with news—that Henry was here, that she was with or against him. Then what?

Henry asked, "How did they track us down?"

After more discussion with Genz, Anth said, "Fierz is convinced he knows where you are headed, and he intends to stop you before you get there."

Henry turned to face the mountain range to the west. Liz appeared at the edge of the clearing facing the same way. "That's really funny. I'm the only one who doesn't know where we're going."

Anth appeared at his side. "They have a vehicle."

"What's his plan? Swoop down the hillside and snatch me up?"

"I'm sorry, but even Genz does not know. He was to convince me to help and together we would secure you."

"Sounds like a good plan."

"Not without me. I took on this journey to free myself from Fierz. I was impressed by your quest for answers—answers to the same questions that ran through my mind. I think we can agree that Soofysh are evil. I will not be a part of a colonization based on lies and murder."

"What about your friend—Genz? Will he see things the same way?"

Anth had never imagined that her father, her commander, was filled with so much hate. He would kill her to get his hands on a human cyborg. The pain in her bosom swelled. Fierz was a monster.

"Once I explain the way of things, he will."

Chapter 32

Bookended between **Anth and Seth**, as they made their way up the slope, Henry's feet left behind two raggedy lines in the thin snow. Anth noted Henry's attention to detail as his chin bounced on his chest, lolling from side to side with each step. The cyborg played his part well.

She said, "How much farther?"

Genz pointed with his free hand. "Over the next hill. We should see the rover soon."

After several minutes, a distinct metallic click stopped them cold. A figure emerged from behind a tree holding something in its hand.

"I see you have come to your senses, daughter."

The way Fierz said 'daughter' was like he was clearing his throat. Anth fought back the urge to pummel him to the ground. The weapon in his hand commanded her attention and her body trembled with an unhappy alliance of anger and fear. She forced the words out, using the right fawning intonation. "I have, father. It was wrong of me to run away. I hope you can forgive me."

Fierz lowered the weapon. She recognized the device. It looked much like a rifle and was equipped with a large muzzle designed to unleash a most unpleasant fiery death. "You haven't damaged the cyborg, have you?"

Genz said, "No sir. A light tap on the head and it succumbed."

"It is good that I intercepted you before you reached your destination." Fierz shrugged in the direction of a mountain in the distance.

"What do you know of our intentions?"

"Once again, you underestimate me, daughter." Fierz stepped closer. "You idiot. A light tap?" He ran a finger over Henry's bruised ear flap. "If this thing fails to revive, I'll have you flayed."

"Father, not to worry. He is still in working order. Perhaps we should bind him before he awakens."

"Your girlfriend uses her head, Genz. Maybe you can learn something from her." Fierz sauntered behind the two and said, "Straight ahead and to the right. We'll secure it in the rover."

Fierz remained several paces behind, as if he was not quite ready to trust either of them.

Genz lowered his voice. "What do we do?"

"Patience."

When they reached a small clearing, Anth spied the rover at its far end. It was one of several they had brought with them on their voyage to Earth. Large enough for a half-dozen reptilians, its dual tracks were designed for exploration over a wide variety of terrain.

They lowered Henry to the ground near the vehicle.

Fierz said, "Genz, retrieve the cable from within."

While Genz scrambled inside, Fierz approached Anth. "You must think me the fool."

A blue plume erupted from his weapon and the air filled with a low hum. Anth stared at its bulbous barrel, mesmerized by the incandescent jet, as Fierz waved it at the sky. She asked, "What are you doing?"

"The cyborg put on a good show, but it was not good enough." Fierz stepped back and kicked Henry in the side, forcing out a groan. "See?"

Genz reappeared with a coil of wire in hand.

"Come join the party."

Anth said, "Father, we brought you the cyborg. I told you—he was stunned, not unconscious."

Fierz motioned for Genz to approach Henry, who struggled to sit up. "Tie up that creature and stow it in the rover. Tie it up tight, or you'll join it."

While Genz looped the cable about Henry's chest and arms, Fierz wheeled about and struck Anth in the head with the butt of the weapon. She fell backwards and landed on her haunches. The world turned a blurry shade of gray.

"You made a mistake, dear daughter." The words slithered through Fierz's teeth and lingered in the air like some putrid stench. "The cyborg's ear was damaged, but a slight tap wouldn't leave behind scorch marks. Details, Anth—you were always weak on details."

Genz exploded from Henry's prone position and raced at Fierz.

Anth saw but a blur and then heard a thud. The blur collapsed to the ground. She tried to stand, to help, but the ground quivered beneath her feet, sending her to her knees.

"Fools, both of you. It's a shame—two young colonists lost while exploring a dangerous new world. A tragedy. We'll remember you back at the settlement. It will be quite the ceremony. You'll be hailed as heroes—the first brave colonists who sacrificed their lives for the good of our race."

Another click and a blue flame emerged. Anth raised her hands in a vain attempt to shield herself. She closed her eyes and resolved herself for the end, but it refused to arrive. Her eyes cleared enough to focus. A bright blue column of scorching energy shot straight up and cast enough light to illuminate the clearing. Nearby pine branches caught fire.

Henry cast off the loose cabling and approached her, waving both hands. He may have been talking, but all she heard was the roar of the weapon still caught in the crook of Fierz's arm. The monstrous reptilian was on his back, motionless.

Genz sat up and smiled back at her.

"Are you okay, Anth?" Henry offered his hand as she staggered to her feet.

"What happened?"

Henry said, "Seth happened."

She blinked her eyes, using both inner and outer lids. A wooden implement she recognized as Seth's bat floated above Fierz. In the next instant, the little robot appeared below it, holding the bat in one hand and a metal box in the other—the invisibility device.

Henry said, "That was cutting it a little close, Seth."

"On time service is my motto, sir."

"I wouldn't mind if you were a bit early."

An arm cupped Anth's shoulder. She asked, "Genz, are you all right?"

"I was about to ask you the same question."

"I'll survive."

"Like me."

Henry raised his chin at the rover. "Do either of you know how to operate that thing?"

Anth said, "Genz is trained. He can drive."

"Then it's time for part two. Secure your boss and load him inside. We'll stop by our campsite to pick up our gear."

Anth asked, "Do we know yet where we are going?"

Henry looked about the clearing as if seeking out guidance.

Anth said, "Looking for your ghost?"

"No. Just checking out the mountain Fierz pointed to."

Chapter 33

The rover reminded Henry of armored personnel carriers of a century ago. He recalled the black and white illustrations in one of his history books back home. The thought brought up the sweet aroma of the moldering old tomes in his library, their leather bindings and yellowed pages. Liz sat across from him in the den, thumbing through a Mark Twain treatise on heaven and hell. Without looking up, he knew she was smiling. She always smiled.

"Look out!"

Henry's shoulder abutted Anth, who wedged in next to him. Genz occupied the driver's seat to his left. Designed for reptilians, the front row of seats was wide enough for Henry to sit between the two. It was a good thing his buttocks were designed for endurance.

Genz said, "Sorry. Rock."

His broken English was impressive compared to Henry's negligible command of the reptilian tongue. He justified his lingual incompetence by the lack of a forked tongue and sharp teeth.

"No problem, Genz. Slow and steady."

Genz nodded, but in no convincing manner.

"Everything is fine here, sir."

Seth had a way of anticipating a question, a quality which Henry had grown fond of. The robot sat behind them with Fierz bound and gagged in the rearmost row of seats. The reptilian was awake. His wide eyes spoke volumes and their content was anything but amusing.

Beyond the last row, the rear storage area held their gear and the few items they had scavenged along the way. Henry didn't need to look to know that Liz was lurking in its shadows.

Anth asked, "Are we going the right way?"

Henry said, "For sure. When you think about it, it's obvious. I suppose you've never heard of Cheyenne Mountain?" Henry paused long enough for Anth to swing her head around. "The Cheyenne Mountain Complex—the biggest little secret that everyone knew about. The Complex is supposed to be designed to survive anything short of a direct hit by a nuclear weapon—even the apocalypse, which is what we have here right now."

Genz interrupted. "Go on road?"

They had come up an embankment which flattened onto a highway. Henry knew the road—Interstate 76, which ran straight into Denver some fifty miles to the southwest. Colorado Springs was another fifty miles south. They were a few hours away.

He nodded. Driving on the flat macadam was a relief. "It's all underground with its own air, food and water. Maybe some of our folks are still alive." Henry's words felt flat. He was almost certain that would not be the case.

Anth gazed out the front window as Genz swerved to avoid an ancient pile up. "How do you know about this place?"

Tufts of grass and an occasional tree sprouted from cracks in the highway. Henry was a child when his parents took the cross-country trip. He recalled the utter boredom of the road, maybe this very one. His mouth curved into a smile. "The tunnels. I'll never forget the tunnels." The road opened up to a broad valley. He pointed through the windshield. "That's the one. The snow-covered one."

Several mountains lined the horizon forming a ridge, with one peak standing out. The illusion was not new to Henry. Their gray slopes, rocky shoulders, jagged crags—all seemed within a day's walk. The one with a brilliant white snow cap held his attention and was miles distant.

"Soofysh!"

Although garbled by the cable strapped across his mouth, Fierz's back seat declaration sent a chill through Henry. Fierz shouted the name over and over again, sounding more frantic with each iteration. The cabling creaked as he heaved against his restraints.

Henry said, "Did he say Soofysh? Are they in there? Are we driving to a Soofysh encampment, or headquarters, or whatever?"

"Fierz appears to think so."

Henry said, "He looks a bit nervous."

"He is terrified."

The Soofysh must be something else to scare Fierz. They had no problem killing billions on this planet. I wonder what motivates such monsters."

Anth reached back and pulled down the binding from Fierz's mouth. "Tell me. What do the Soofysh get for their services?"

"You'll kill us all. Turn around before it's too late. We can start over back at our settlement. It'll be as if nothing has happened."

Anth slapped Fierz across the face. "You tried to kill us. Are you so stupid to think we can pretend nothing happened? You're nothing but a self-centered monster."

His mouth opened and a split tongue twisted through an opening between his needle-like teeth. "Scum. You are leading us to slaughter. The Soofysh have no interest in your idiotic quest, a quest that has blinded you. You think me a monster? Wait until you find them. They will squash you like insects … and you're about to take me with you." He paused to take a breath. "I'm being murdered by a naïve teenager and her dim-witted boyfriend."

"What's he saying?"

Anth sat back in her seat. "He says the Soofysh will kill us, and him, too."

"Fine choice—either we get killed by your father or by the Soofysh. What do you think, Seth?"

"Either choice can be classified as undesirable. It is a dilemma, sir."

"But, what would you do, Seth?"

"Hope that we are facing a false dilemma."

"Great answer."

Anth asked, "False dilemma?"

Henry chuckled. "It's a logical postulate. Seth is suggesting that there may be a third choice we haven't considered."

Anth said, "I'm sure there are many choices to consider. One that occurs to me is to run…get away from both the Soofysh and Fierz."

"The Soofysh know where we are, and it's a certainty they can follow us wherever we go. And we can assume the same for Fierz."

"Then we are doomed."

Henry eyed Seth for a moment and shook his head. "What does a cornered animal do?"

Anth said. "You do not mean—"

"I sure do."

Chapter 34

Denver was no longer the glowing city of Henry's youth. As a child, he recalled being thrilled by its tall buildings, soaring structures of concrete and glass. After half a century of neglect, those testaments to human achievement were nothing more than a dark pall on the landscape. Windows hollowed out by storms and black towers covered in ivy and mold, the once grand testaments to human achievement looked more like the products of elfin mischief, cursed by time, swallowed by Nature itself. The rover veered, jostling Henry back to the present. An increasing number of wrecks dotted the fractured cement surface of the interstate. Fortunately, the highway was wide enough for Genz to negotiate through even the worst of them. They had travelled about a hundred miles with little to see beyond faded exit signs and lifeless towns. Henry fought back an urge to give it all up. His mind insisted on seeking signs of life, only to be disappointed with every overturned truck and abandoned car. Thankfully, the monotony of the road had the expected sedative effect on him and the passengers, and on Fierz, who appeared to have passed out.

As they trundled past the weathered remains of a gas station, Henry roused himself enough to ask, "What fuel does this thing use?"

Anth jerked her head up. "Wh-What?"

"We've entered the city of Denver. I'm just wondering if we need fuel."

"The rover is nuclear-powered."

"That's a relief."

Genz spoke to Anth. "Problem ahead."

A partially collapsed overpass loomed ahead.

Anth said, "We cannot go through."

Seth leaned over from the rear seat. "Sir, we should take this turn-off. It's the best route to Colorado Springs."

Henry noted the sign. "I'm guessing that says Interstate 25." Jagged slabs of the overpass covered all three lanes. "Use the exit on the other side of the road."

Anth translated and Genz steered over the divider, underneath the still intact portion of the overpass, and up onto the exit on the opposite side.

The bumpy ride stirred Fierz awake. "Fools."

Henry said, "What did he say?"

Anth gave him a sidelong look and said, "How much farther? I'm getting hungry and I need a break."

"I get it. Tell Genz here to pull to the side. I think it's time for a break."

Genz said, "I understand."

Anth said, "Not bad, Genz. I see some of my language drills must have rubbed off."

"He might understand more than he can speak. It's the same for us with new languages."

Genz nodded, veered the rover to the shoulder, and jerked to a stop on an embankment bordering a forest. Henry stepped out and stretched. The shredded remains of a chain-linked fence reminded him of a time the dense canopy was no more than a manicured set of fir trees and shrubs—artificial beauty to mask the concrete scar across the land. A crow broke out of the gloom and soared away, crying out a single caw that Henry felt was directed at him—"What the hell did you do to this world?" It circled over the highway and disappeared into the late afternoon sun.

Anth emerged from the trees. "We can go."

"What about Genz?"

When Genz stepped out from the same section of the woods, the reptilian quickened his step and made it a point to avoid looking at Anth as he got back into the rover. Henry thought he saw a dark green blush flicker across both faces.

"And Fierz?"

"He can go to hell."

Henry said, "So you have a concept of hell similar to ours?"

"Identical."

Fierz was massive—taller than either Anth or Genz, maybe topping nine-feet. Worse than that, his girth was twice that of the other two, and it didn't seem to be all fat. If he wasn't strapped in, he would have easily overcome the three of them, including bat-wielding Seth. It was a wonder they had subdued him at all.

"He'll be a problem to unwrap, escort and rewrap."

Anth said, "Loosen him enough for his ass to stick out the door."

Henry suppressed a smile. Anth really hated the Commander. "It's better than messing up the seats," Anth said, "And stinking up our rover."

<>

By the time they reached the outskirts of Colorado Springs, the sun had slipped behind Cheyenne Mountain and left the underbellies of low-lying clouds colored a deep, demonic red—an appropriate color, Henry thought. Henry eased open the rover's door and stepped out with Anth and Genz close behind. "Time to set up camp. Seth, take a break from guard duty and see if you can rustle up some firewood. These two will look after Fierz while you're gone. It'll be cold tonight."

Anth said, "The rover has a heating system. We could rest inside."

"Your choice. As for me, I prefer the outdoors—you know, fresh air."

Genz walked back to the rover. Anth's nostrils flared as if seeking a scent. "Do you think the Soofysh are in that mountain?"

Henry half-hoped they were not—that instead there would be a division of the US Army in there who managed to survive the holocaust. They'd have plans to deal with the Soofysh, to reestablish civilization, to defend what was left of the country, and the Earth. Fifty damn years. No one waits that long to counterattack.

He shrugged. "And they haven't bothered to welcome us."

Sarcasm, Anth."

She tilted her head, something she tended to do when confused.

"Sometimes people say things that are exaggerated in order to make an opposite point."

Anth said, "Human sarcasm appears to be culture-specific. In our society we speak what we think. It is difficult for me to detect the difference between sarcasm and truth."

"That's the beauty of it. Don't worry, with time and practice you'll have it down." Henry realized that she might never have a chance for much practice. "At least, with me."

Genz cried out from the rover, waving his arms.
Anth said, "Fierz is gone."

In seconds, the two were at the rover's doorway. Strands of cabling lay strewn over the rear seat with no sign of their prisoner.

Henry asked, "How?"

Anth reached in and held up a cable end. "Bitten through."

"Are you serious?"

"Sarcasm?"

"You bet." Henry scanned the ground near the rover. "It's getting too dark. We'll have to wait until morning to track the bastard."

Anth said, "We could ignore him. I doubt that sack of shit can survive in the wild. Let him starve or freeze to death. Either way, we will be rid of him."

"Whoa. Such language. Where did you pick up that expression?"

"Did I use it wrongly?"

"Not at all. I guess your reading wasn't limited to textbooks."

"A culture is not defined by technology alone."

"Good point. Fierz may be a huge problem, but he may also be of some value. We don't know what's waiting for us at the Mountain. One of your leaders would be handy if we needed to bargain."

Genz cried out again.

"What did he say?"

Anth lowered her head. "It appears that Fierz took his weapon with him."

Chapter 35

Sleep came in fits. Seth took up the watch by the fire. Henry kept imagining Fierz sneaking up and roasting them with a flame-thrower. He got up and took a walk around the camp to work off the anxiety and check on the two in the rover. In a way, they had become his adopted children, at times prompting him to take on the role of a parent. He even found himself scanning the windows for signs of condensation, signs of youthful lust. That there was none told him little, since he knew nothing of their biology.

As usual, Liz came into view on the other side of the campfire—her face, expressionless—her eyes, distant.

He approached her ephemeral image. "Liz, you managed to talk to me back at the cabin. Can you try again? Why have you led us here? What's waiting for us in that Mountain?"

He was afraid to ask if she was dead, a ghost, or maybe a half-century-long hallucination. The prospect of an answer terrified him.

Liz continued to stare into the night as if he had not spoken to her at all. The flickering campfire glow danced across the woods to her rear, giving her the appearance of a translucent silk veil.

<>

A mist arrived with the morning light.

Seth broke down the fire, and Henry gathered up his things. "Thanks, Seth."

"It is my pleasure to serve, sir."

"I don't mean that. Last night, you were here when I spoke to Liz. Thanks for being there." What Henry meant to say was thanks for not calling him out as a psycho. The robot had become family, and family knew when to speak up and when to listen.

"It is not for me to interfere when you see her, sir. You need Liz to keep up your spirits, and I need you to keep up mine."

The statement, given so casually, challenged Henry's understanding of robotics. He had accepted that Seth was unique, but something about his claim to have worked for another family always bothered him. Anth had pointed out that Seth represented a technology far superior to anything in the human record. For that matter, his own body was another such example, and was likely manufactured by the Soofysh. The thought paralyzed him at times, making him wonder if his actions or thinking were guided in some way by the very creatures who murdered the human race.

The mist coalesced into drops. At the sounds of sizzling in the campfire's ashes, Henry directed everyone to board the rover.

Anth asked, "I thought we were going to track Fierz this morning."

Henry hunched up and closed the door behind him. "Not much of a chance of that with this rain." Even as Henry spoke, a gust of wind whistled through nearby trees, and the sky opened up, releasing an icy cold downpour.

They hit the road again. Silver sheets marched across the highway, morphing the road into a formless streak across the windscreen.

"Does this buggy have a windshield wiper?"

Anth pressed a square on the dash. Within seconds, the glass cleared up, leaving behind meandering rivulets of water with most of the surface crystal clear.

"Cute."

Anth said, "Careful. Do not touch."

"Why is that?" Henry reached out and a spark shot the gap between his finger and the glass. His body arched upright, landing his head against the rover's roof. "What the hell?"

"As you have discovered, we use a static charge to repel the water. More recent models have safeguards."

Henry sat back and rubbed his finger tip.

Anth widened her mouth almost appearing to smile and said, "Were all humans like you?"

"Is that supposed to be sarcastic?"

<>

160

A few hours later they arrived in Colorado Springs. The sun shone down on a bone-dry road, while crisp air drifted in from the west—mountain weather. Food and water were on Henry's mind as he walked out from beneath an overpass. He turned his back to the sun, absorbing its sweet warmth.

Anth jogged up the exit ramp to the road above. She stared north, back to the way they had come.

Henry said, "What're you doing up there? See something interesting?"

Genz said, "She nervous."

"About what? Fierz?"

Genz nodded.

"We've travelled quite a distance. There's no way that creep could follow us on foot." Henry wondered if Genz would understand such a long sentence.

The reptilian answered. "He strong."

"He will follow us, sir."

"What for? He's convinced the Soofysh will kill us all—him included."

"He wants you, sir."

A movement caught Henry's attention. A knobby shadow bobbed up and down beyond the rim of the raised roadway.

"I see it, too, sir."

"What is it?"

Henry pulled out his revolver and jogged over to the railing across the highway. Seth and Genz joined him in time to be greeted by a giraffe. Its round baby eyes widened, as if the creature was surprised. Perhaps too curious about the visitors to break into a run, it continued sauntering along the embankment while keeping its lolling head turned in their direction.

"What the hell?"

"The Colorado Springs Zoo, sir."

Henry looked past the animal. What must have been an enclosure at one time had evolved into an untamed forest. Signposts, blank and leaning, erupted alongside the hint of a winding asphalt trail nearly buried by tall grasses. Henry recalled that his parents had stopped here. He ran ahead of them, desperate to see what wild beasts lurked beyond the next turn, all the while pausing to grab handfuls of treats from dispensers along the way. It was a simpler time, a bright and colorful time filled with possibilities. He blinked and returned his gaze to the giraffe who continued sashaying away, apparently satisfied that the strangers posed no significant danger.

Anth asked, "Edible?"

"I suppose so, but it's too big even for the three of us. What were you doing on the overpass? Worried about Fierz?"

"He was angry enough before we captured him. He was humiliated. I expect now he is even more eager to return the favor. I'm sure he plans to kill Genz and me. Was that a giraffe?"

"Yeah. Maybe all that's left of the zoo."

"Sir, not quite."

Henry followed Seth's finger. A dark furry creature skittered through the grass below.

"A boar." Before it scurried away, Henry unshouldered his bow, nocked an arrow, and let it fly. "Dinner."

<>

The morning light silhouetted Cheyenne Mountain. No longer a bump on the horizon, its solid snow cover jutted out from the rest of the granite ridge.

Anth said, "Do we need to climb that?"

Henry sensed the reluctance in her voice. "Don't worry. The main entrance is at the base. The complex is mostly underground."

"Why was such an installation built?"

"Years ago our government directed the construction of an underground bunker that would house state of the art detection and surveillance systems in case of an attack. I think they even had some missiles stored down there."

"I've read about your wars, but the most recent data indicated no significant threats to your country. Who would attack you?"

"We were a little paranoid at the time. Some of the countries on this planet did not get along, and a few unstable ones had nuclear weapons. Trust was in short supply."

"Then it was possible for humans to destroy themselves … it's what the Soofysh claimed had happened."

Henry shook his head. "People can get angry, mad and selfish, but seldom are they crazy—at least not crazy enough to destroy the planet. There's no excuse for what the Soofysh did.

"I'm sick of this waiting. Why do they not come for us?"

Seth said, "Sir, perhaps Anth's query is about to be answered." The robot pointed up.

"Do you think it spotted us?"

A tiny dot drifted through the haze high above and hovered over their location.

"A definite possibility, sir."

"Quick, into the rover."

Genz was in his seat by the time Henry clambered in. Seth settled himself in the rear next to Anth. "Do we have a plan, sir?"

Henry had no clue. When he turned to answer, Liz sat on the last seat. She mouthed a single word over and over. Henry shouted, "Go," and Liz nodded with a smile.

Genz said, "Go where?"

"Into the mouth of the beast."

Chapter 36

Anth asked, "Are we there, yet?"

Henry stifled a laugh. The tension in the rover had everyone tongue-tied. He kept checking the sky for the UFO and hoped that it was coincidental—maybe some alien craft with more important things to do.

"Just about. Genz, take the next exit—Cheyenne Boulevard."

Seth said, "My calculations suggest our destination is no more than thirty minutes away, sir."

"Does that answer your question, Anth?"

Anth stared out her door window and said nothing. Henry worried about her. The reptilian had given up a whole lot, and for what? He shuddered to think what would happen if the whole trip was some mental aberration. Maybe they were about to meet the real invaders, and these monsters wouldn't hesitate to cut them all down.

Genz hissed something which spurred an animated conversation with Anth. When she settled down, Henry asked, "What was all that about?"

"He's afraid. You must understand—none of us have ever met a Soofysh. Even Fierz was terrified, and he had direct dealings with them. This plan of yours worries me."

"I don't get it. Why are you afraid of the Soofysh? Aren't they your partners?"

"Of course, Henry. But I do not know what they are—how they think. At the present, it looks like they are trying to kill you ... and me."

"I'm sure they've got the technology to eradicate us anytime. Why wait for us to come to them? I have to admit I hate them, and that's without ever meeting them." Maybe I did meet them. He thought back to San Francisco—the encounter with Mike, the fully-upgraded Mike, the psycho robot Mike. The Systems people wanted to upgrade him the same way.

He ran a hand over his torso, his thigh. His body was artificial. The thought made him feel empty inside.

"A helicopter on the road, sir"

Maybe the chopper would be filled with live human beings. Henry whipped his head around. The eviscerated remains of a military helicopter loomed into view along the side of the road. Farther on, more vehicles came into view—the vestiges of a convoy lined up along the shoulder, all pointed at the Cheyenne Complex—trucks and jeeps, trailers and heavy machinery, even a half-track that resembled their rover. A single boot at the foot of the half-track gave Henry pause. It conveyed an even deeper sense of loss than all the decomposed bodies he had seen throughout his journey. These were soldiers. Maybe it was the stark realization that it belonged to some young warrior with dreams not unlike his own—cut short by the Soofysh invasion.

The line of vehicles brought home a picture of GIs climbing out, stretching their legs, taking in the scenery. They would have been members of a reserve unit—maybe on a routine weekend of active-duty. Little did they know, it would be their last weekend on Earth.

"More victims. Whatever the Soofysh used, it sure worked fast." Henry thought about the countless bodies decomposing in towns and cities along the way and maybe around the world. Things happened so fast that many were caught in their cars, going to work, coming home.

Anth said, "It was not completely effective."

"You're right." Henry thought back to the Crazy Horse Monument. "Some did survive, didn't they?"

"At the time of our arrival, I did not think it through. What it meant. I was following the orders of my Commander."

Henry shook his head. "Yeah. I've heard that one before. Genz, pull over next to that vehicle."

Henry stepped out and leaped into the back of a truck. The two-and-a-half ton had lost its canvas canopy years ago. Dried out human remains, bones and skin turned into dark leather protruded from rags that might have been uniforms. The truck had been full—no less than ten men—reduced by time to a shallow pile of vague memories.

Anth appeared. "What are you seeking?"

"These." Henry lifted two rifles from the resinous debris."Some ammo, and this kit."

"A kit?"

"We can't be firing a weapon this old without cleaning it first."

<>

A half-hour later, they arrived at the north gate of the Complex. Several tour buses sat in the visitor's parking lot a few hundred yards beyond the gate. Henry's attention was drawn to the iconic tunnel entrance—featured in films, TV series and novels. Once the heart of America's defense systems, it grieved Henry that it was exposed and unprotected. The end did not turn out to be nuclear. It was much worse.

They drove past the gate and parked next to one of the buses. The main entrance was ensconced in the mountain's shadow—a dark maw carved out of granite.

Anth asked, "Why stop here? Why not go inside with the rover?" "It's bad enough that the Soofysh know we're here. With us stuffed in this little box, we would be a gift waiting to be unwrapped." Henry took up his backpack. "Take only what you can use to defend yourselves. There's no need to go in there unprepared."

Henry donned his bow and quiver. Seth stepped out of the rover with a bat in one hand and the cloaking device under his other arm. Genz and Anth each grabbed a rifle. Henry noted the odd way the reptilians held their weapons—by their muzzles. "Have either of you ever fired such weapons?"

Anth said, "We have seen them—back at our base."

"That wasn't the question. I've loaded them for you. The ammunition clips should contain about twenty rounds." Henry took hold of Anth's weapon and shouldered it. "Keep it tight against your armpit and cheek, aim using these protrusions as a guide, and then squeeze the trigger." The report made Anth jump, and Genz chuckle. When he handed the rifle back, Genz fired off his weapon without warning. This time it was Henry who jumped. "Good job, Genz. Remember, don't touch any of the little switches. One of those settings will change the weapon to a machine gun. You'll end up firing off all your ammunition in seconds."

"Sir."

"What is it, Seth?"

The robot pointed to Henry's rear.

"Don't you remember me, Henry?" The oily voice pierced Henry's chest. He turned back. Seth was nowhere to be seen. The silvery mechanical man standing before him was familiar.

"Which one are you, Sandra or Mike?"

The robot had no pink tunic like worn by the Techs back at the cabin and then later at the clinic. The two twinkling green eyes bore into him. The reptilians raised their weapons.

"Sandra could not be with us today. Are you going to introduce me to your new friends?"

"I see you've been repaired. That's what you'd call it, right Mike? Repaired, using replacement parts for a machine?"

"Speaking of machines, Henry, where's your feisty little midget?"

"What are you doing here, Mike?"

"Just an FYI, Henry. You're right, I've been repaired. More than that, actually upgraded. Your little dinosaurs and their toy guns won't even leave a scratch on me." Mike glided closer—a whisper in the wind. "Cool, heh? Part of the upgrade—aircar tech in my feet."

Henry tried to keep the terror welling up within him at bay. "Okay, so you're invincible and some kind of super mechanical man. Back to my question."

"It's all about you, my boy. We want you back."

"We?"

"Don't be so obtuse. You must have figured it out by now. You're a walking, talking example of Soofysh technology."

"Tell me something I don't know." Henry dropped to a knee as Mike's image wavered and tried to regain his focus. After a half-century as a hermit he had been certain he was one of the few lucky recipients of some clandestine government research. Although he had come to accept that the Soofysh and Systems were one and the same, having it pointed out by one of their constructs still hurt.

Mike drew nearer. "Don't take it so bad, Henry. You're still you. Wasn't that your big worry?"

The people at the clinic had to be all Soofysh, or created by the Soofysh. Why was he saved by what claimed itself to be the most powerful entity in the galaxy? *Am I just a Soofysh project?* Mike had said, he was still himself. *I am still me.*

"You're damn right. I am Henry Wind In Trees. A proud descendent of the Lakota people—still a member of the human race. The damn Soofysh giving me a new body doesn't mean crap. I didn't ask for this. I owe nothing to them or anyone else. My allegiance is to my people." Henry gave the two reptilians a quick glance.

"That may be what you think, Henry. But you're our property, and the time has come for you to come home."

Mike took another step closer. A thunderous burst of rifle fire erupted over Henry's head. Sparks danced across the robot's torso. Mike took a step back and seemed to grin, though Henry was sure the mouth wasn't designed to broadcast any human emotion. When the volley ceased, Mike made a show of brushing off its smooth, unmarked chest. "See? Not a scratch. I don't wish to harm your pets, Henry. Please tell them to stand down. This is just about you and me."

Mike seized Henry's arm and tossed him over its shoulder in one smooth motion. The robot rose a few inches into the air and glided to the tunnel entrance. Henry looked back in time to see Anth and Genz running toward him. When they landed on Mike, the robot teetered for a moment, throwing Henry to the ground. The two reptilians wrapped their oversized arms around Mike's chest. The macabre dance might have yielded a draw, but soon their grips failed and the two flew off in separate directions.

In that instant, Henry jumped onto Mike's back.

"Enjoy the ride, Henry. Soon you'll forget you were ever human, and the beautiful thing is that you won't even know you forgot." Mike ground out a metallic laugh through his motionless jaw and started to glide away.

When the pair reached the mouth of the tunnel entrance, Mike toppled head first to the gravel road bed. As they rolled Henry spotted Seth holding the cloaking device over his head.

Mike sat up on its knees. "You again, you little shit. I'm going to take you apart limb by—"

Henry jammed the barrel of his revolver into Mike's right eye socket and pulled the trigger. The back of the robot's head bulged outward and silvery strands of confetti-like material shot out an ear hole. Mike the robot collapsed—laid out like a discarded mannequin.

Henry said, "Slick move, Seth."

"You're welcome, sir. I'm glad you were able to find the robot's Achille's heel."

"Who would have thought the heel was in its head?" Henry waved to the other two, while staring at the inanimate silvery heap. Mike was a marvel of engineering. In some ways he was sorry to see it laying there. Were he and Mike really so different?

He said, "Ready to meet the Soofysh?"

Anth said, "With such technology, how can we hope to survive in there?"

The wide black mouth of the arched entrance stirred up a primordial fear of the unknown. Sown into human DNA millions of years ago, the feeling was impossible to ignore. An ephemeral Liz stepped out from the gloom and said, "The time has come."

Henry turned to Anth. "We have another weapon in our arsenal."

All three stared at Henry.

"Their arrogance."

Chapter 37

With each step the tunnel swallowed another morsel of fading light. Henry and Seth sidled along one wall, while the other two stayed opposite. The cavernous space muted their footfalls and the gloom added to a growing, sinister feel.

A hundred yards in, Henry's fingers ran up against a rough granite surface. "I think we've reached an opening—a cavern. I don't hear a thing. No hum, which means no power. I don't like it."

"I do not like it either, sir. The probability is low that we will encounter living humans here." Seth veered to the center of the expansive passageway and cast a dull, throbbing red light onto the way ahead.

"I suppose you can't crank up the wavelength to white?"

"I can emit the entire electromagnetic spectrum, sir, but only one wavelength at a time. Perhaps, yellow would be better?"

Henry blinked at the brighter hue. Seth swept the tunnel by moving his head to and fro. The effect was mesmerizing and the way ahead opened onto a larger space.

Anth said, "A door."

Her eyes must have been sharper than Henry's synthetic orbs. They continued forward, and the outline of an enormous metallic door loomed into view. When he was a child, he recalled the massive structure, infused with giant rods and gears. It was spectacular then, swung open to reveal its inner workings, which were lit up like an animated Fifth Avenue store window display. The door was wide open, but cast in muted yellow and deep blue—more somber than spectacular.

"That's the main blast door." Henry peered into the blackness beyond. "Someone must have left it open." A really bad sign..

Seth led the way through.

Henry said, "There should be a second door farther in—much the same as this one."

The tunnel curved, cutting off the lingering tendrils of light from their rear, and turning the cavern into an opaque abyss. The darkness gobbled up Seth's puny beam like it was some spectral entity hungry for photons. The air turned colder and seeped through Henry's deerskin.

As he moved along the wall, icy fingers caressed his chest. The feeling continued along the skin of his thighs and back. He lurched to the side, gasping. "Seth, is there anyone else in here with us?"

The robot came to a stop—his beacon frozen on the second door several yards ahead.

"Seth?"

Anth said, "The door appears to be closed."

Genz loped ahead, following Seth's beam.

Henry tried to shake off the unnerving sensation that someone else was in the tunnel with them. Anth "Don't you feel it? The cold … I swear there's somebody here … maybe standing right next to us."

"Sir, shall we proceed?" Seth was back.

"What happened to you, Seth?"

Genz yelled, "Door open!"

The second blast door swung outward with a slight whoosh of escaping air. Henry was sure the door needed power to move. It opened by itself—an action that would have made his skin crawl if he still had a human body. The gap between wall and door edge slowly widened. A soft vertical glow grew along with it.

Henry said, "Lights. They must have power in there."

Seth said, "Who do you suppose is in there, sir?"

"Right now, I don't want to think about it."

The group eased through. Henry cast a backward glance to assure himself no one followed them inside, then shook his head. He saw nothing.

Seth said, "If someone is expecting us and has not attacked, perhaps their intentions are not bad, sir."

"Remember what Mike said. I'm guessing that someone, or better yet, something is likely welcoming me home, but I don't think it's to meet mom and dad."

"Maybe it is, sir." Seth's reply had a disquieting ring of truth to it.

"What happened to you back there?"

"I'm not sure what you are referring to, sir."

The light within the cavern system brightened to reveal several two-story buildings. Henry's attention was drawn to the giant springs. He counted eight, each the size of a standing man. He guessed there were dozens beneath the nearest building. These were windowless and showed no signs of life. Nets made of chain, designed to protect the structures, sagged overhead with the weight of scattered rock debris that must have cleaved off the ceiling over the years.

Without Liz's ethereal guidance, Henry was at a loss as to next steps. Genz had become less fearful, more excited, behaving like a little child opening Christmas presents. He jogged from building to building, trying the doors to each.

"Open!"

"Easy, Genz. We don't know what's in there."

When the group caught up, Seth approached the door. "I will go in first, sir."

"No way, Seth. You're too valuable." Henry meant to say something more profound, something personal.

"Sir, I am the one, non-living entity here. Life is fragile, I am not."

Henry scarcely had time to open his mouth before Seth was through and in.

"What do you see?"

Although mere seconds passed, the silence fast became unbearable. Henry said, "You two wait out here," and slipped inside.

The single source of illumination, an emergency spotlight in a far corner, outlined an array of small metallic figures. Seth faced several rows of diminutive robots, each with a bronze dome and a slit for eyes.

"My god."

"My sentiments as well, sir."

"They're all you, Seth. There's a dozen here … your twins." Henry took a step back. His companion for almost half a century seemed an alien. "Are you one of these?"

"Sir, I am your friend. These constructs are as much a mystery to me as they must be to you."

Shamed by the response, Henry moved closer to the miniature sentinels who stood as if at attention. No doubt Seth had as much to say about his situation as he did. They were both likely creations of the Soofysh. "Can you tell if any of these are alive … I mean active?"

"They are dormant, sir."

Henry bent over one to get a better look. "Damn. These robots are your exact doubles." He checked the neck-torso connection. "Even the seams and the actuator switch are the same."

"It would be logical to assume I was made by the one who made these."

Henry said, "Maybe they were manufactured by our people, a secret military project of some kind here in the Complex."

Seth said, "Unlikely, sir. I must be a Soofysh construct."

"Do you remember when you were first—"

"Turned on?"

"Yeah. I didn't mean it to sound so impersonal."

"Quite all right, sir. My first recollection was seeing humans. I don't believe they were Soofysh. I was assigned to—"

"The ones who lived in the house where you found me and saved my life?"

"Exactly, sir."

"Is it possible your memory was tampered with? I mean, maybe the Soofysh wanted you to believe you were a domestic robot of human design."

"I have no way of knowing that, sir."

Henry's finger ran across the activation compartment of the nearest Seth clone.

"I would not advise such action, sir."

"You're right, Seth. We don't know what these robots might do." Henry looked about the murky room and its silent residents. "Whatever their origins, considering that this installation is military, I doubt they were created to be playmates by either our military or the Soofysh."

Something brushed past Henry's shoulder.

"Damn it. Did you see anything near me, Seth?"

"I assure you, sir, we are the only ones here."

"This place gives me the creeps. We need to check out the rest of the buildings."

Everything had an ominous feel to it. Unlike his previous visit a lifetime ago, the lights were distant, hushed. It was as if he was walking in a dream. Nothing seemed tangible. The total absence of human beings transformed the clipped sounds of distant ventilation blowers and relays to something dark and foreboding. He stared at Seth and wondered about his friend of so many years. What was he really?

After Genz confirmed the entrances to the other buildings were locked, the group moved on to the next cavern through a short access tunnel. When they entered the passageway, the lights ahead came on.

"I think someone's playing games with us."

Anth asked, "What kind of a game?"

Henry shook his head.

The tour he took as a child had gone no farther than the first cavern. Four more buildings, also on springs, spread out before them. This time, Liz appeared next to one. His stomach tightened. Gone was her ever-present smile. Her eyes were sunken, underscored by dark lines beneath, and her face, gaunt and pale, as if she were sick or dying. She motioned to Henry in an awkward, almost spastic manner. The structure behind her looked much the same as the others—a white-washed cinder block edifice the size of a modest one-family home. Its single door was open.

"That's where we go next."

Genz was first to reach the door and swung it wide.

Henry slowed his pace, fighting off a jittery feeling that would not cease. The rest of the group gathered about the entry. All appeared to move in slow motion.

Liz appeared at the doorway again. "You are here at last, Henry." She had on the same sun dress she always wore, but this time, her features were less transparent. Henry swore she was solid. Her cheeks were hollow and her sad eyes bore into him.

"I don't understand, Liz. Why have you brought us here?"

"I need your help."

"Am I going insane?"

"I am as real as you are … my darling." Every word parted her diaphanous lips with effort.

Henry looked to the rest of his group. They hadn't moved or said a word. He asked, "What's happening?"

"You must hurry. They know you are here."

"They? You mean the Soofysh?"

Liz nodded. Her body wavered as if her image was displayed on an old-time raster TV with the tuning slightly askew. Time was running out.

"What do you need me to do?"

<>

"Sorry about that."

Seth asked, "About what, sir?"

"How long was I standing there?"

"I noted no pause, sir."

"You didn't see me talking to someone?"

Anth shook her head.

Well, I suppose that's good news. I might not be schizophrenic after all." Henry wasn't completely convinced of that. "But I do know what we have to do, and we need to be quick." He slipped through the doorway. "Follow me."

Unlike the former building, this one was not stuffed with little robots. Instead, the entire floor space was open, and its ceiling encompassed the second story. A huge concrete cube stood in its center—a chamber of a sort, with dimensions a few feet shy of the surrounding walls and ceiling. A circle of light reflected onto one of the room's walls, as if emanating from an opening on the side of the cube. Henry angled into the narrow corridor and headed toward the glow.

Anth said, "There are instruments along here."

Henry said, "I know. Don't touch anything. It's what's in this cube that interests me the most."

Seth edged up to him. "Sometimes being this size has its limitations, sir."

Henry picked up the robot and they both stared through a round porthole in the cube's side.

"What do you think, Seth?"

"I count thirty-six containers, or perhaps, coffins." After a pause, Seth asked, "Which one holds Liz, sir?"

Chapter 38

Genz said, "What are they doing?"

Anth had no clue, and wasn't about to share her misgivings. She was certain of only a few things—the Soofysh were evil, she hated Fierz, and she would never return to her colony. As the other two entered the chamber, she said, "I think Henry has found his wife. I'm not sure what he will do next, but he claims to have been in contact with her for many years. I expect we are here to rescue her."

"Do you know what that sounds like? It's bad enough that the cyborg is delusional. You too?"

Anth pointed to the massive chamber. "What if they find her body inside there?"

"What does it matter? Maybe it'll be a coincidence. We don't even know she's really there."

"I don't expect you to understand. They were in love. They are still in love."

"Oh, right. Maybe I'm too naïve."

"You're not naïve, Genz. Henry and Elizabeth made the decision to live together for the rest of their lives, and that was a half-century ago. That's longer than we've been alive. He never gave up on her, or she on him, for that matter. We've known each other for a few months. You can't compare their relationship to ours."

"So, what are you saying, I don't love you? What was that back in the woods? Was that just a game to you?"

"Physical love—it's not the same."

"Damn it all, Anth. You know I have feelings for you, strong ones. Just because we've known each other for a short time, that doesn't mean a thing. There's no minimum time for love to happen. I can see it in your eyes. We are meant for each other."

Anth liked Genz. Perhaps with more time, she would even come to love him. "Why are you here with me?" The ensuing silence painted a depressing picture. She added, "It wasn't your idea to find us, was it? You went along with Fierz to save your own hide. Tell me, if that bastard didn't force you, would you have come here on your own? To look for me?"

Genz sputtered, as if his mouth needed to wait for his brain to deliver the right words. "Absolutely ... It was killing me ... that you took off with that ... human or whatever. When we found out you ran away, I was—"

"That human is the last true spirit of this world. He may be the sole survivor of a species the universe will never see again."

"So what? They did it to themselves. This planet is ours now."

"You fool. Fierz hasn't told you?"

"He doesn't talk to me unless it's something I screwed up."

"It's the Soofysh. They're the ones that killed off the humans. And they're the ones Fierz is scared of."

"And you know this how?"

"I know. And if you have anything more than rocks in that box between your ears, you could figure it out yourself."

Genz paused a second and then said, "It doesn't matter how it happened. What's important is the present and the future for us."

"Are you sure there is an 'us'?"

His silence spoke volumes.

"Henry is brave, unselfish and loyal to the love of his life. He didn't know if she was alive or dead, or if he was going mad, for that matter. Let me tell you ... I will follow him wherever he goes. Are you willing to do the same ... to be with me?"

"I'm here, aren't I?"

It wasn't the answer Anth had hoped for.

Henry and Seth emerged from a side door to the chamber carrying an oblong human-sized box. Henry said, "Anth, give me a hand." Anth was quick to take up Seth's end. The three staggered through the narrow corridor, and placed the container on the floor near the entryway. Its ebony surface shimmered under the overhead light, displaying no markings or glass panels to help identify the contents.

Anth asked, "What is inside?"

Henry said, "Liz."

The one-word answer carried a formidable weight—an intangible certainty built upon years of hope. Anth looked into the cubic chamber.

"There are so many such containers. How can you be sure this one holds your wife?"

When Henry smiled, she knew the answer. Liz spoke to you.

Genz whispered, "He's crazy. We still have a chance to get out of here before the Soofysh show up."

Anth nudged Genz in the ribs.

Henry ran his hands across the container's glossy surface, as if caressing its contents.

Seth said, "I detect no obvious way to open this box, sir."

"That's where you come in, my friend." Henry turned to the instrument panels along the wall. "See if you can decipher the proper combination of key strokes and dial turns it takes to spring this baby open. Anth will help you."

Anth lifted Seth for a closer look. Instead of a keyboard or dials, the faint glow of a several colored panels suggested a possible way forward. After a moment, Seth said, "These may be sensitive to touch. I can start with several sequences, and proceed to permute them."

"Go for it, Seth."

The little robot's hands flew across the colored display, tapping out a storm of sequences. Anth heard a hiss erupting from the chamber and said, "Something is happening."

Seth paused. Henry leaned through the chamber doorway and said, "One of the containers just opened. Hold on, I'll check it out."

Seconds later, he emerged with a distinct frown. "Your last series of taps popped the fourth container from the left along the second row down."

Anth asked, "Did you look inside?"

Henry lowered his voice. "A female human body … mummified … skin and bones. Thankfully, not Liz. I guess Soofysh technology isn't perfect."

"What is the purpose of these chambers?"

"No idea. But, if Liz is still alive, maybe she will tell us." Henry's voice wavered. His confidence ebbed.

"Hope for the best, Henry."

Henry turned to Seth, "Permute that last sequence … and take your time."

Seth resumed tapping. Another hiss and another container sprung. A few more taps and the one on the floor whispered as its lid released.

Anth backed up, letting Henry angle between her and the box. The naked body inside was that of a female, and based on what she knew of human anatomy, it looked emaciated, but not mummified. She eased out a breath, not having realized that she had been holding it since the box opened. "Is that your wife?"

Henry said, "Liz. It's Liz." He repeated the name and stared without moving.

Seth said, "Sir, we need to get her out."

Henry's voice was almost inaudible. "Is she dead?" Maybe she was a ghost after all.

Anth helped Henry lean into the container. "There's a lot of junk in here with her. Seth, I'm going to need your help."

The junk appeared to be Henry's description of unfamiliar instrumentation. The interior walls were covered in all manner of oddities—some with wired components resembling electronic devices, some with tubes entering the female's arms and legs.

Henry pressed his ear to her chest. Anth felt her own pulse throbbing, and after a tormented moment asked, "Is she dead?"

"Damn it, I don't hear anything." Henry pounded his fist against the wall. "Liz. All this way, and for what?"

Anth felt an urge she had rarely experienced—to embrace him, to provide some comfort. The human had become much more to her than a means to a rebellious flight, a teenage insurgency against her designated parents. Henry collapsed against the wall and closed his eyes.

Seth said, "Hold on, sir, all hope is not lost." The little robot withdrew his hand from Liz's chest. "I detect a slow and weak pulse. In my opinion your Liz is in a coma-like state. She may yet be revived."

Henry slid to the floor—his voice unsteady. "Are you sure, Seth?"

"The problem is not so much if she's alive, but what we need to do to get her restored, sir. Did she give you any clue?"

"I don't think she knows." Henry looked about the room, no doubt hoping that an image of Liz would spring forth.

"This technology is quite involved, sir. It's amazing that the Soofysh were able to keep her alive in such a state for half a century."

Henry crawled over to the container and patted Seth on his back.

"There are other working examples, Seth."

"Do you mean, me, sir?"

"The two of us—you and me—it would seem we were both created by what may be the most despicable intelligence in the galaxy. I still don't get why they saved me."

"And why they want you back, sir."

Anth had been puzzling over the conundrum for most of their

journey. She had never met the Soofysh, but she was sure they always had a logical reason for all they did. She recalled coming across a number of human corpses, some with their brains removed. At the time, she thought their odd state was a consequence of the poisons and disease the humans had inflicted upon themselves. The truth was a harsh reality. The Soofysh had been collecting. They were experimenting.

She looked into the chamber—boxes with whole humans inside, wired and infiltrated with tubing. "What if you and your wife were an experiment, Henry? I am sure the Soofysh have the means to study humans, more specifically, human brains. When they first arrived, they collected a number of specimens. Some might have been investigated … like those in this chamber. Others, like you … modified … perhaps even constructed in their image."

"You know this for a fact?"

"It is a feeling. Think about it Henry. Didn't humans try to build robots that could think?"

"Yeah, that's a normal progression for any advanced culture."

"And what did you humans want your robots to resemble?"

"Point taken. So, you're saying I might've been created in the image of my creator."

Seth said, "Sir, I've back-traced to what appears to be a section of control circuitry. I think I've found a means of disconnecting Liz. The trouble is that I'm not sure if she will survive the procedure."

Anth said, "All that circuitry … Seth, is it limited to keeping the body alive?"

"Sir, Anth has a point. I cannot be sure, but its complexity suggests a monitoring function as well. If I disconnect Liz, not only would her life support be cut off, but the Soofysh may be alerted."

"They have been." The hollow voice erupted from the entryway. Its melodic undertones echoed in the room as if reflected from mountain to mountain in some vast alpine valley.

Chapter 39

"**Y**ou may wish to reconsider interfering with her stasis. You are likely to kill her."

Henry gasped. "Who said that?"

"Who said what, sir?"

Henry turned to Anth and Genz. "That voice. It sounded like the damn Wizard of Oz."

Anth said, "I heard nothing." She motioned to Genz to step out of the building, to check if anyone might be there.

"I am speaking only to you, Henry Wind In Trees."

The resonant voice made it difficult to pinpoint its source. Henry darted to the other side of the chamber.

Seth asked, "Is it Liz, sir?"

"Seth, stay right there and don't do anything." Henry leaned his head out of the building's entrance. "Genz, back inside."

He stepped into the half-lit outer hallway and beneath the building. Rows of gun-metal springs, each as thick as an arm, disappeared into its gloomy underbelly. "Who or what are you? And why am I the only one that can hear you?"

"We are Soofysh—a meaningless term to you. Perhaps your colleagues have mentioned us."

"Yeah, they did. You're the ones that murdered the people on my planet."

"An over-simplified assessment. We represent change, Henry. Something you appear to fear."

"I don't fear killers of innocents. Hatred is what I feel for you. Maybe it's you who should fear me." Henry forced himself to remain steady, his voice, measured.

"Killers of innocents? A narrow view. We are the inevitable instruments of change."

Henry looked along the walkway, but saw nothing.

"A few billion years ago your atmosphere became oxygen-enriched and a vast number of life forms were made extinct so that your ancestors might flourish. Was climate change a cold-blooded killer? Sixty-six million years ago an asteroid struck your planet and signaled the end of the dinosaur era. A shame—they were the single most successful species ever to have evolved here. Was the asteroid a murderer? Now it is the humans' turn to give way to another species. Death and rebirth. It happens all the time, all over the galaxy—humans are far from special."

Henry was taken aback by the cold eloquence of the argument. The long view had its logical merits. "A logical argument, but those events were due to the vagaries of Fate. Premeditated slaughter is your doing, your decision—a conscious act of brutality."

"Fate? Do you really believe the extinction of the dinosaurs was an accident?"

The implied revelation was beyond frightening. *It's trying to get under my skin.* The Soofysh seemed eager to keep the conversation alive.

The voice turned mellow, as if explaining a sophistication to a child. "Did you not think it convenient that the dinosaurs died out to give mammals a chance at evolving, an action which led directly to humans? Come on, Henry, think about it."

He was no paleontology expert, but Henry knew enough. Dinosaurs thrived for about 135 million years. They were the dominant species on Earth until an asteroid happened.

"You're not saying you were responsible?"

"Not I."

The first reference to the creature's self. *What was he dealing with?* Anth said the Soofysh were some kind of mechanical beings. "That would mean your species have been around since the beginning, but I doubt that any of that is true. Why would you do it? What was in it for you?"

"Yes, yes. Humans always want to know the why of things. Our motivation is simple. We expedite colonization by a more advanced species. In return, we are gifted a modest reward. In the present case, several species have agreed to our terms and will take up residence on this planet."

"What terms? You have an advanced technology. What is so valuable to you?"

"It varies from planet to planet. It might be minerals, certain heavy metals, or even your more than ample water supply. It doesn't matter, does it, Henry?"

"Why don't you show yourself? I'd rather see whom I'm speaking with—or is that too much to ask of my executioner?"

"We have no interest in terminating you, Henry. After all, you represent a successful human brain transplant, or using the terminology you prefer, a stable cyborg."

That bit of news stunned Henry. He thought back to the clinic, the chase at the cabin and afterwards. "What about … Mike and Sandra? I think I saw others."

"All failures. An unexpected incompatibility resulted in unsound personalities. And before you ask, the version of Mike that greeted you—he was upgraded to fully artificial—a flawless construct. How did you find him?"

"I wasn't too impressed. By the way, he's developed quite a flaw. I think you might call him inoperable."

A pause followed, as if the Soofysh was caught unaware.

"What about my wife? What possible use do you have for her … and the others in your collection back in that chamber?"

"We have a continuing interest in human brain function. We expect to keep her and the others in stasis for a while longer."

"Stasis? Looks like you screwed up there."

"A few specimens had internal imperfections such as most biological systems are apt to have."

"I see, so that wasn't your fault." Henry slammed the side of the building. "What do you want from me?"

"A curiosity has come to our attention, Henry. Your wife has been communicating with you during the intervening years since your brain transplant. This observation remains unexplained—thus both you and she are unique to us and worthy of further investigation. It is the reason we supplied you with Seth, your little companion. We wanted to be sure no harm came to you, while we studied the phenomenon. At this point we have concluded that a closer examination is warranted."

"What about that drone of yours—you know, the spider thing that shot out death rays? Was that one of your minions eager for a closer examination?"

"The energy blasts were meant to disable you, nothing more. We have plans for your brain, Henry."

"Treat me like a laboratory curiosity? That's not going to happen." He turned away to see Seth leaning out of the doorway. He needed to digest the news. Although Seth was Soofysh, he was also his best friend.

"Sir, we heard everything you said." A glow appeared in the space between the buildings, casting a bright white sheen on the walls. "It appears the Soofysh may be materializing. What should we do?"

"Everybody, back inside." Henry ran in with the others and heard the sound of sputtering grease on a frying pan. They reassembled in the chamber. Henry opted to leave Liz in her container, hoping that the Soofysh would not harm her. The sizzling outside ceased and an acrid aroma of ozone wafted into the chamber.

"Where's Seth?"

Anth and Genz looked about, but were as much at a loss as Henry. Maybe Seth was done with him—his instructions carried out. The little Soofysh robot probably ran off to rejoin its comrades. "We don't have time to look for him. If you haven't figured it out yet, I was talking with your Soofysh friends."

Anth said, "They are not my friends."

"That thing out there only wants Liz and me, mostly me—for experimentation. If you don't interfere, I think it'll ignore you."

Anth said, "We will not allow it to take you, Henry." Genz nodded, and both reptilians raised their rifles.

"Don't be silly. I'm sure those pea-shooters won't do anything except piss it off."

The chamber's doorway darkened. The apparition standing there appeared as a void—an animated shadow complete with humanoid arms and legs. Its eyeless head reminded Henry of his greatest childhood fear—the boogeyman—stepping out of the closet, graced with an invisible black smile.

It extended an arm. "Come with me." Despite the confines of the chamber, the voice came across as though it was a mystical and distant siren call to a lost soul. Henry's legs stiffened, his will drawn out into the waiting abyss.

He lowered the muzzles of both rifles with his hands. "No need. It's not your fight." He took a step toward the shadow at the door. His resolve to resist weakened with every step. His arms and legs moved as if on their own accord.

"Do not touch my master!" A burnished metal head emerged from between the shadow's legs. A small bronze arm grasped a calf and jerked it backwards.

"How quaint. Your servant robot appears to be defending you, Henry."

Its intonation came across as sarcastic, but Henry had some trouble imagining a heartless Soofysh killing machine having any sense of humor. In the blink of an eye, the shadow picked up the little robot. "Come see what happens to such misbehaving automatons." The robot squirmed in the shadow's arms.

Henry followed it out of the building and used what was left of his mind to scream. "Seth! No, no! He can't hurt you."

The shadow smashed the struggling robot to the ground with such force that it exploded, sending metal limbs, gears and wires flying in every direction. Henry fell to his knees and picked up a twisted piece of metal. "Seth."

Further clanking heralded the entrance of a second Seth, who ran at the shadow and collided with its legs. The Soofysh reached down and grabbed an arm. It swirled the little android once around and launched it into the air, landing it some fifty feet away with a far-away tinny crunch.

When it tried to right itself, it fell to pieces.

Henry's mouth was still agape when another Seth appeared along with another and another. A mob of the little robots streamed into the recess between the buildings. Far behind them, a bat waved in the air.

Henry said, "We need to move fast. Anth, you and Genz carry Liz's container and follow me." They scurried past the thrashing Soofysh shadow, which appeared to be buried under a mob of little mechanical men..

By the time they emerged through the second blast door, Seth had caught up to the group. Henry called out. "Into the rover. I've got an idea."

Genz dived into the driver's seat and they were off.

Anth said, "This is useless. The Soofysh will track us down."

Henry directed Genz onto a side road which led up the opposite side of the Complex. "We're on our way to the last place the Soofysh would look for us."

Chapter 40

It took a few minutes for Genz to reach the Mountain's secondary access point higher up. Henry made sure that Liz was secured at its entry and all their gear was stacked.

Anth asked, "Will we need the rover again?"

Henry said, "I'm not sure. Why?"

"It is a programmable vehicle. We can send it back along the route we took getting here."

Weighing the risk of discovery against the loss of the rover gave Henry pause. The Soofysh might follow the vehicle. "Do it."

With a nod from Anth, Genz ran to the rover.

"Go with him, Anth. Make sure to take it down to the main entrance and set it loose from there. On the way back see if you can cover up the tracks leading up here. Hurry back and don't get caught."

Henry watched the two reptilians descend along the curved road. "What do you think, Seth?"

"Good idea, sir."

"Not that. What do you think about those two?"

"They are in love, sir."

Henry said, "You're doing it again."

Seth laid his bat and backpack down beside Liz's container, opting not to ask what Henry meant.

"Clever move getting those clones of yours to help out."

"They were not clones, sir. They were constructed as I was, but not given any instructions as yet."

"And you told them—?"

"I informed them that you were their master and that their master needed to be rescued from an attacker."

"And they obeyed you without question?"

"I just needed to use my command voice, sir."

"I didn't know you had one, Seth." Henry patted the robot on the back—a habit of his that had no physical effect, but felt good nonetheless. "For a moment there, I thought you—"

"Had gone back to the Soofysh?"

"That, and that the Soofysh had destroyed you."

Seth tilted his head, and pointed his eyeless slit at Henry. "I appreciate your concern, sir. You must have been alarmed."

Genz and Anth returned, gasping, and reported that the rover was on its way.

"That should keep the Soofysh busy for a while. Speaking of the devil, did you see any sign of them, or should I say, it?"

Anth said, "Nothing has stirred."

"I would have thought that the damn shadow thing would be on our necks by now. Let's get Liz inside."

Henry and Seth followed the other two, with Henry casting backward glances every other step. "Seth, the Soofysh hinted that disconnecting Liz would kill her."

"That statement may have been misleading, sir. Other than tubing designed to carry nutrients in and waste out, the rest of the wiring appears harmless, devoted to monitoring her vital signs."

"So, in your opinion, we can get her out of that canister alive?"

"With alien instrumentation, nothing is certain, sir. Two steps will be required—first disconnecting her, and second, waking her. I expect the first to be easy, the second, I would prefer to leave in your hands."

"That's what I was afraid of."

They reached another blast door which was open a crack.

"What is it with all these open doors?" Henry craned his head through the opening. "Damn careless for such a superior species."

Seth said, "Careless—maybe and maybe not, sir."

Anth said, "I am not sure the concept of species applies. I understand that they are not biological."

"Someone had to create them."

Seth said, "A sobering thought, sir."

Anth said, "I agree. All of us had to be created, so why not the Soofysh?"

"That's a curious thing to say, Anth. Do your people believe in a god or gods… an entity that created everything—the whole universe?"

"We are all creatures which evolved on worlds based on survival, mutation, gene flow and migration. Our manner of thinking also evolved and was aimed at survival, not questions of existence. As a result, though we live in a vast universe, we may not have the logic or language needed to consider its nature. In fact, the process of logic itself may not apply to the question or be universally accepted manner of thinking."

"Wow. I didn't expect that—"

"From a reptile?"

"From anyone."

Once again, the cavern lighting was off, and they slowed their pace to allow following Seth's beacon.

Henry said, "I'm afraid I don't know much about this part of the Complex."

Seth said, "Nothing ventured, nothing gained, sir."

"Damn right, Seth."

They plodded along for about an hour when they came up against a second blast door. This one was sealed. Henry sensed they had been moving in a northerly direction, which would put them somewhere above the cavern containing the buildings. He thought about the irony—the all-powerful Soofysh about to be sent on a wild goose chase, while its quarry skulked about in its back yard. At least, that's what he hoped was going to happen.

While Seth probed the blast door controls mounted on the adjacent wall, Henry asked, "Do you think there are others?"

Seth said, "Why, sir?"

"It kept referring to the Soofysh as 'we'."

"That may be a manner of speaking, sir. Like the royal 'we.'"

"There wasn't anything royal about that thing."

Seth said, "Best to assume the worst, sir." The robot tapped a few keys on the control panel. "I detect electrical power behind this board."

"That's a good sign. I think there's a nuclear power source a few hundred feet below us. Only one worry … who the hell has been maintaining it?"

A popping sound came from the door, and a seam between it and the frame appeared.

"Perhaps I found the right combination, sir."

"You're a genius, Seth."

The stale air carried with it a hint of decay.

Henry said, "That stench. This isn't good."

Seth said, "It would appear that this section has been sealed for a long time." A moment later, Seth said, "I found a wall switch," and the lights came on.

The tunnel was half the size of the one below. The walls were rough cut granite, and the layout lacked the elegance of the main body of the Complex. Henry figured they were in a series of access corridors, perhaps with connections to the caverns below.

"The floor, sir."

The hall was filled with bodies—mummified remains of uniformed soldiers. The odor grew stronger as Henry moved deeper into areas which had not seen fresh air in decades. He spoke aloud to no one in particular. "I get the feeling we're the first to come in here since …the genocide. The soldiers we saw outside died of the virus. These guys were running and were dropped in their tracks."

"Sir, there is more."

Henry counted at least ten—each in a position which led to the exit behind them. "It looks as if they were running, trying to get out."

Seth stooped over one of the remains and held a finger out at its moldy uniform. "This is a scorch mark, sir."

"On the back of his shirt."

Seth shuffled from body to body. "They all have similar burn marks. They appear to have been killed while trying to flee."

"Cheery thought."

They passed rooms filled with desks and file cabinets, crates of foodstuffs, many with yellowed and illegible placards. Seth announced their contents. "Rice, corn, honey, salt, pemmican—"

"Wait, that last one. What did you say?"

"Pemmican, sir. It is a type of—"

"Yeah, I know. A dried meat, like jerky, stuffed with animal fat. My father used it on hikes. It has a crappy taste when fresh, but it's great energy food and supposed to last forever. Do you think it's still good?"

Seth lifted up a plastic packet. "Vacuum seal is intact. Looks fine, sir."

"'Fine' is not a word I'd ever associate with it. What about the other stuff?"

"Some of the honey is crystallized, the rice looks good, but the corn is the wrong color."

"We have the makings of dinner."

The undisturbed ashen dust which covered everything, including the bodies, suggested a macabre kind of safe haven to Henry. Not even the Soofysh have ventured up here, at least not since killing the soldiers back in the hallway.

Seth's head leaned out from a doorway ahead of the group. "In here, sir."

It was a kitchen or break room. An empty table with chairs sat at its center. A counter and cabinets were mounted in a corner. A simple wall switch energized one of three fluorescents overhead. Its sputtering added an unnecessary depressing flavor to the already stark surroundings. The doorway leading to the murky hall outside brought up a scene in Henry's mind from an ancient horror movie. "I half expect one of those bodies out there to get up and stagger in here."

Seth said, "Demanding brains, sir?"

The remark raised a dry chuckle from Henry, but judging by the blank stares of the two reptilians, may have lacked universal appeal. In fact, Henry was embarrassed by the thought and even more, saddened by the image. Those were good people.

Anth and Genz came in carrying Liz's container.

"Put her down next to the table." Henry tried the faucet in the sink, which was set into the counter. The deafening groan from its piping, forced him to yank it closed. "That's just what we need."

Seth said, "Not to worry, sir," and pointed out a case of plastic water bottles stacked in the corner. Some had sprung leaks over the years, but most were intact if not a bit discolored. "And we also have this." Seth pointed out several 5-gallon cans labeled 'Potable Water.'

Henry picked up a chair and surveyed the rest of the room.

"Great. We've got a restroom—all the comforts of home." He knelt down alongside Liz's container and lifted its hinged cover. In spite of being impaled with tubes and wires, her face had adopted a surrealistically serene demeanor, as if her mind had drifted off to some far away sanctuary. He remembered that look—back at the cabin, when she sat at the forest's edge. He thought that maybe that's where she might be, waiting for his return.

The longing pulled at his heart. The merciless past worked like that.

"We're going to get you out of there, Liz. Don't you worry."

He was more than worried. He was terrified. The Soofysh skewered you with god-knows what in that box. To those unfeeling bastards she was no more than a brain specimen. Henry put a hand to his head. Whispers echoed in the back of his mind, and rising from those undulating voices, he heard one he recognized. *I am dying.*

"Seth, it's time. Do what you think is best, but we've got to get her out of there right now."

Chapter 41

Seth worked fast—pulling out tubes and wires, discarding them about the floor and over the walls of the container.

Henry said, "She's bleeding." The trickle from Liz's arm gave Henry the impression of a crimson gusher. All the while she remained oblivious, her facial expression unchanged.

"Not to worry, sir. We may have reached the most crucial step." All that was left of the Soofysh harness was a tube which emerged from Liz's mouth and a set of wires attached to her chest. "The tube appears necessary to provide air."

"And the wires?"

Seth touched both and said, "I detect low levels of electricity—in the form of low voltage pulses."

"Could it be a pacemaker?"

"Exactly, sir."

"Deal with the tube first."

Henry leaned in and tugged at the transparent hose and met resistance. "Damn thing is stuck … it's been years. Seth, are you sure this is a breathing tube?"

"I am sure of nothing, sir."

He looked up and scanned the dim room, not knowing what he expected to see, but wishing Liz would show up and tell him what to do.

"Take heart, sir. She trusts you."

"I hope we're not killing her."

"Consider the choices you have, sir."

Henry bore down and continued the pull while applying a slow and steady twist. He fought back visions of ruptured organs and torn flesh. The tube slid out without a snag. He sat back on his heels. "Her breathing. Is she doing that on her own?"

Seth placed a hand on her chest. "Shallow, but regular."

"That'll have to do. The wires are next."

The thin leads led from a panel in a side wall of the container to her chest, right below her ribs. "They are attached to her heart muscle, sir."

"Wait. It might be safer to cut them."

"Good idea, sir. How?"

Henry pulled out an arrow from his quiver. The little robot pinched a loop between two fingers and ran the arrow's blade edge through.

"The wire is strong. This will take a minute."

Liz's chest rose and fell, trembling at times.

"Seth, I think she's having trouble breathing."

"It appears so, sir."

"I have a bad feeling about this."

"I am not without some reservations myself, sir. If I disconnect her, there is a significant risk that her heart may be too weak to contract on its own. Her biological pacemaker may have become dormant over these many years."

Henry held Liz's hand and rubbed her wrist. Her lidded eyes appeared more sunken, her breathing, more labored.

A toaster at the far end of the counter gave Henry an idea. "Anth, you and Genz, rip out the wiring from that toaster. We're going to need two separate strands. Here's another arrow tip to help."

"What do you have in mind, sir?"

Henry lay down along the container. "I will be Liz's backup. You will open my chest with that arrow blade, and access my pacemaker circuitry. I'm sure you can figure out where it is. Check the voltage. We need it high enough to break up any arrhythmia she might incur."

Anth held out two frayed copper wires.

"But sir, I will need to disconnect your pumping system for such a procedure. During that time, your biological brain will be starving for oxygen. You are risking death."

"As I recall, a brain can go on without oxygen for a few minutes before significant damage occurs. Anyway, we'll only need to do this if Liz needs it."

"Sir, I recommend against such action."

"Seth, my good friend, it's not a request."

The robot used the arrow to slice open Henry's chest wall and peel back the artificial skin.

"Jeez, that hurt. What do you see?"

"Metal ribs, similar to human. Below that—your digestive system.

It looks like a garden hose."

"Very funny."

Seth reached under the ribs. "Your artificial heart. A fine design, by the way. And attached to it, I see several wires."

Henry's heart skipped a beat. "Can they be disconnected, and maybe more important, reconnected?"

"It would seem so, sir."

"That's good enough for me. Go for it, Seth."

The robot hunched over Liz's chest, and several beats later held up the ends of two fine silvery wires.

"How is she?"

"So far, she appears—"

Liz's body jerked forward, raising her torso above the lip of the container. Henry swore her eyes blinked open for a moment, and her mouth widened as if pleading. Then she flopped back into her box.

"What happened, Seth?"

"Checking her pulse, sir."

Henry felt the pulsations of his own heart ticking off seconds, desperate seconds.

"We have a problem, sir. She's in ventricular fibrillation. Her heart was not ready for this."

"Do it, Seth. Do it now."

"As you wish, sir. If we don't see each other again—"

"I feel the same about you, Seth. We can talk about it when this is over."

Seth reached under Henry's ribs. He was surprised by the absence of pain. The world dimmed and his thoughts of Liz winked out.

<>

Genz asked, "What's happening?"

Anth watched Seth attach the toaster wires to the Soofysh leads protruding from Liz's chest. The cyborg remained unconscious. Seth placed the ends of the two wires into Henry's torso.

"Seth is attempting to shock the woman's heart into a normal rhythm."

"But without an active circulation, the cyborg will die."

"Maybe. Maybe not." Anth stepped away and pulled Genz closer. "Would you do the same for me?"

Genz shook his head. "There you go again … comparing us to

those two."

"Well?"

"Of course I would."

"I wish I could believe you."

Seth said, "Her heart is not responding."

Two minutes slipped by.

Anth asked, "Do you have enough voltage?"

"Something has gone wrong. I detect no voltage."

Anth reached into Henry's open torso. "I have it. One of the wires came loose." At the same moment, a tic fluttered across Liz's chest.

"That's it. Thank you, Anth."

Seth contacted the leads several times, pausing a few seconds between each shock. Color returned to Liz's ashen face. Seth said, "Pulse appears stabilized, and bit higher than before." He leaned in closer. "Still going."

Anth said, "What about Henry?"

<>

"Are you going to do it or not?"

Seth patted Henry on his shoulder. "All done, sir."

Unconsciousness was a bitch. "Damn, am I just a machine? On and off. Here one moment and—"

"Gone the next, sir. However, in your case, you're back again."

"What about Liz?"

"The good news is that she's taking breaths on her own, and her pulse is slow and steady."

Henry rose to a sitting position and winced. A thin blue line ran down his chest, stained with dark blue splotches. "Looks messy, and did you have to make the cut so big?"

"More room to maneuver inside there. By the way, you can thank Anth for stepping in at the right time. She managed to find a loose wire."

Henry nodded to Anth and turned back to Seth. "And the bad news?"

"She's still unconscious, sir."

"Can we wake her?"

"It's hard to tell if she's sleeping or in a coma. It may be that the Soofysh apparatus supplied her with a chemical agent to keep her this way. It may also be that her body and brain have suffered a shock. She may need time to recover. I recommend we wait and let her decide when to return."

Henry peered over the lip of the container. Separated from the Soofysh tendrils, Liz seemed more at peace. Why wasn't she communicating with him anymore?

"Liz. Can you hear me?"

He studied her face, the tiny wrinkles around her eyes, her mouth. There was no sign that she heard him. Her shallow breathing sounded wondrous.

He grimaced at the pain in his chest. "It hurts to move. I feel I'm going to split open any second."

Seth said, "I used the toaster wires to sew you up. Your lesion will heal given sufficient time, like your ear has. Then we can pull the wires out."

"We may not have 'sufficient time'." Henry lifted himself onto a nearby chair. "It's amazing. She looks the same. Even her hair hasn't grown."

Seth said, "The Soofysh appear to have mastered the science of stasis."

Henry thought back to the bodies in the cube. "Not quite. She was one of the lucky ones. Let's get her out of that box. Anth, pull the other table over here."

They laid out Liz across two tabletops. Henry held one hand and leaned in closer to her ear. "Liz. If you can hear me, give me a sign—"

Seth said, "We need a plan, sir. The Soofysh will return and no doubt trace us here."

Henry kept staring at Liz.

Anth said, "Overcoming the Soofysh may be impossible. They are technologically superior. They are invincible."

Henry broke from his reverie. "Nothing is invincible. Even Superman has his weakness."

Anth said, "Is that someone that can help us?"

"If only." Henry lifted himself off the floor, wobbled a bit, and straightened up.

Seth said, "Careful, sir. A sudden movement could compromise my stitching."

Henry said, "We wouldn't want that, would we? Anth is right. Sooner or later, the Soofysh will find us. And as it is, with me screwed up and Liz hanging on by a thread, we can't run far. The logical alternative is to stay and prepare."

Anth said, "These rifles are not enough. They were not effective on the robot at the entrance. I am certain they are useless against the

Soofysh."

"We need to find something here in this complex to get clever with."

Seth said, "You and I can watch over Liz, while Anth and Genz explore the rest of this level, sir."

"Good idea, Seth, but I'm going along with these two. It may take human eyes to find that Kryptonite."

"Sir, I recommend you stay. That wound needs several days to knit."

"Don't worry, Seth. Anth will carry me."

<>

The traditional solution to solving the maze problem was to follow one wall. They had selected the right side, and had gone through several branching tunnels to find no more than storage rooms containing foodstuffs and water.

Cradled in Anth's arms, Henry said, "This reminds me of when my mother carried me."

Anth said, "We do much the same for our children."

"I'm not too heavy for you, am I, mom?"

Anth's mouth opened and hissed.

"If that's you laughing, remind me not to tell you any more jokes."

Genz muttered something from up ahead.

Anth said, "He's found what appears to be a sealed doorway."

The dim lighting made it difficult to see. Anth stepped up her pace, bouncing Henry as she loped ahead.

Henry said, "Aha, what do you know? It's an elevator."

Genz placed his hands to either side of the vertical seam and tried to pry the doors apart.

"Get me a little closer, Anth." Henry pushed a button to the side of the doorway, and an overhead symbol lit up accompanying by a loud hum. "The damn thing still works. Give it a minute, Genz."

The doors slid apart with a squeal. The panel inside displayed a list of acronyms representing floor levels .

Henry pointed to the lowest button. "That's the one we want."

Anth said, "LL?"

"Lower Level, and I bet that's where the reactor is. At least part of this Complex continues to be powered, and that means that the nuclear core and generators must still be active. It should be in the most protected and remote part of this installation, and that would put it in the basement."

Anth asked, "A nuclear reactor?"

"Is there any other kind? What better place to find a weapon that might work against the Soofysh?"

The descent took a full minute. "They weren't kidding when they labeled it the Lower Level."

When the elevator slowed, Anth hugged a wall to get out of the way while Genz raised his rifle. The doors opened to an unlit, narrow tunnel. At its far end a deep crimson hue added to the morbid ambience.

Henry noted the black and yellow placard bolted over the tunnel's archway. "I was right. That's a warning sign telling us there's radioactive danger ahead."

Anth said, "Is this a good idea?"

"I don't think there's much choice. I'm sure that these things were built with tons of safety precautions."

"Precautions that would last for years?"

"I hope so."

Anth nodded to Genz to proceed.

Henry said, "Don't worry. If there is a leak of some kind, we'll be dead by the time we reach the end of this tunnel."

"That is good to know."

"Your sarcasm is beginning to impress me."

They followed the red glow, which turned out to come from a single bulb illuminating a T-intersection. A sign on the wall displayed a set of arrows.

Henry said, "To the left, we have Reservoirs, and to the right, Reactor."

"Reservoirs?"

"A self-contained supply of water. Some of it must feed into the reactor system … for cooling and to drive the generators."

Once again, Genz led the way. He followed yet another shadowy passage to another red glow. Henry grimaced at the musty bayou odor, and half-expected the two red eyes of a hungry alligator to emerge from the murk.

Anth's voice rose an octave. "Water. There is water on the floor."

Her footfalls turned into sloshing.

Henry said, "That's not good, and the red lights don't make me feel any better. Something's wrong. I think those lights may have been a warning. Who knows what happened to the audible alarms." He wondered if the radioactivity would kill him as it would a normal human. He didn't blame the reptilians for getting anxious.

By the time they caught up with Genz, Anth waded through foot-high water. A rust-streaked door blocked their way. Another warning sign hung over the door along with a message about 'Authorized Personnel.' A metal lever functioned as a doorknob and a steady drip of water oozed out from beneath the lower door seal.

Anth said, "There is still time to return upstairs."

Henry said, "Could be a small leak. If it was critical, the Complex would have melted down by now." At least I think so. "Damn. It does look flooded in there." An image of a ton of water pressing against the other side of the door flashed by. "Genz, give it a try."

Genz handed his rifle to Henry and grasped the lever with both hands. It would not budge. Henry saw a key entry to the door's right. "Hold on, Genz. Let me down, Anth. You wouldn't have a key on you, would you?"

The lack of a reaction set Henry to chuckle. The keyhole gaped up at him. "There's one thing we can try." Henry stepped back and added, "We're going to move back a few paces, maybe more."

Henry aimed Genz's rifle at the side of the key box. "Here goes."

The single shot rang out within the tight confines of the tunnel. Henry felt as if his head exploded. The other two jumped farther back into the passageway. The key hole sported a dent, but otherwise remained intact.

"One more time."

Henry lied. He fired off three more rounds, after which he was certain even his artificial eardrums might have turned into Swiss cheese. When the smoke cleared away, he called out. "Get over here. I need someone with thin fingers."

Anth inserted her spindly digits into the jagged opening. She said, "What am I looking for?"

"I don't know. Maybe a gear or lever—anything that moves."

Anth pushed her hand up through the gap, and a click sounded. Henry motioned for Genz to try the lever again. This time it gave way without effort. A whisper of air swooshed through the door seals, and to Henry's relief, just a trickle of water spilled over the lower frame.

"A small flood."

The three stepped through and into a nightmare. Hot mist cloyed at Henry's face. A pair of yellow emergency beacons winked from the ceiling somewhere, casting a twittering and diffuse sallow glow through the churning steam.

Anth coughed. "We cannot go in there. We cannot breathe such moist hot air."

Unsure of where the reptilian was, Henry yelled out in her direction. "Go back. Go back to the tunnel where it's dry and wait for me."

His hand found a wall. The clammy rough stone contrasted to the heat drifting over his face. The way ahead swirled in and out of view—an effect made more dream-like by the stroboscopic lighting from above. The acrid stench reminded him of Yellowstone and its molten sulfur lakes. He was a bison navigating through a cratered hellhole.

Henry's throat narrowed. Artificial didn't mean impervious, and he wouldn't be of much use as a moldering pile of Soofysh technology. He was about to turn back when a plume of cool air swept across his legs. The sensation lifted his spirits and he waded farther in as the water level rose to his knees.

He leaned down to suck in the cooler air and, for a moment, he was back home, pausing to rest while hiking through the Rockies. The condensation broke up, hugging the ceiling as it spiraled overhead. Other flashing lights, yellow and red emerged from the blur above. His hand rested a moment on a wall-mounted conduit. A vibration ran along its metal skin, and with each step, the sound of grinding grew louder.

The concrete floor rose on a slant, leaving the water behind. Henry emerged from the tunnel onto a raised platform where pipes and ducts led to a set of huge machines inset into an alcove—four metallic behemoths, generators the size of houses. Steam spumed from each, creating small rain clouds that drifted to the ceiling. A closer look revealed three of the generators were dead. The clattering drone of metal on metal came from the fourth. Its gyrating armature, visible through a port, tossed out sparks like a roman candle.

Henry prayed the steam wasn't radioactive. It should have been separate from the reactor, a part of the power-generation system. In any case, he was in for the penny.

The door ahead would tell all. The words REACTOR CORE loomed above its yellow and black warning sign, and it was ajar.

The cold fluorescents emitted a dim light and nerve-wracking hum. A curved handrail led to a pool. The deep blue glow of the water illuminated a half-sunken black monolith—the reactor. The portion above the water displayed a pair of demonic orange-red globes.

Henry resisted the temptation to use the narrow gangway to get closer to the reactor core. Instead, he wandered about the vast expanse, unsure of what he might find. Shelves along the walls offered up hand-held

Geiger counters, bits and pieces of protective clothing, even a Styrofoam cup rimmed with ancient coffee stains—not much in the way of an advanced weapon to use against the Soofysh. The Geiger counters proved to be useless—batteries corroded into a white paste. There were no blasters or ray guns.

Disheartened and weighed down by his yearnings for Liz, he turned back to return, to rejoin the reptilians. On the way, he took hold of a short length of pipe and slapped it against his palm. At least he would have a club to defend himself with. He grinned at the thought—David verses Goliath, maybe he should be searching for a rock and a sling.

When he entered the generator room, his heart sunk. An all-too-familiar dark outline stood in his way.

"Henry, you have proved to be quite an irritation."

Chapter 42

"**I will be more than an irritation** if you don't get out of my way." Surprised at his bravado, Henry stiffened his body and faced the Soofysh square on.

The shadow hesitated before responding as if taken aback. "There is no point to this conversation. We are here to collect what is ours."

"I am Henry Wind In Trees, a member of the free Nation of Lakota Tribes. Thanks to you, I'm one of the last human beings still alive on this planet. And I may be many things to many people, but I am not, or ever will be, your property. I do not belong to anyone."

The Soofysh remained quiet and unmoving.

"You may be technologically superior, but maybe your advanced intellect has lost sight of empathy. Without compassion, you have become an unfeeling machine, or whatever it is you are. It is you who should be the servant—to be owned, and if it was up to me, I'd shut you off and throw you out with the trash. Whoever created you made one damn big mistake."

"Our intellect, as you call it, is a product of evolution over a span of millions of your years. We have ascended to a level your organic brain cannot imagine. Besides, you aren't really human, Henry. We made you. You and your female partner are no more than a curiosity to us—using an analogy you might appreciate—you are specimens under a microscope, butterflies pinned to a wax board, cadavers in medical school—shall I go on?"

"You've been here for quite a while to know about butterflies and medical school."

"Long enough."

"Then you may know something of the natives of this continent. No one has the right to own this land, the Earth. This is as true today as it was during the time of my forefathers. You have no place here."

"We are impressed by your defense of humanity. As a native of this continent, things did not always go too well, did they? Do you remember Big Jack?"

It was a name lost to a past Henry preferred not recalling. "H-how do you know about Big Jack?"

"He was a splendid example of humanity, was he not? Is he the type of person you are struggling to protect, to save?"

"There are always the good and the bad in any population."

"That is not what you thought of Big Jack, is it? You wanted to punish him, maybe even kill him. Is not that true, Henry? The world would have been a better place without his kind. Is that not true, Henry?"

"That has nothing to do with what's happened here, right now."

"Do not deny your feelings, Henry. We are not so different, are we?"

Henry waved his steel pipe in an effort to clear his mind more so than threaten. "This image I'm seeing of you—it's some kind of projection. I bet you're not really here."

"More than a projection, Henry. We understand the nature of matter and have mastered its relationship with pure energy."

"Are you alive?"

"As alive as you."

Keeping the entity talking wasn't a long-term solution to his predicament. That he was shouting and the acrid scent of ozone turned Henry's attention to the remaining and raucous generator. He took a step closer to its open port. "Living things, those that have self-awareness, possess feelings. Without that dimension, you're just a glorified wind-up toy."

"And you, an insect, Henry. You cannot hope to understand us."

"You're not as superior as you claim. Did you enjoy tracking down our rover?"

Another hesitation, then the figure took a step closer. "The time has come."

Henry tightened his grip on the pipe as the air filled with crackling static.. The hair on his scalp prickled and his arms trembled. A thunderstorm approached. The Soofysh was no more than an arm's length away when he tossed the pipe into the generator port. The grinding instantly exploded into an ear-splitting groan. Lightning bolts danced within its housing and arced out, dancing across the ceiling and floor. Then all went black.

<>

Anth said, "Where are you?"

Genz said, "What happened?"

"We lost power. Henry may be in trouble."

"Forget about him, will you? The Soofysh cut the power. We should get out of here."

Anth weighed the alternatives. With the scant lighting gone, following Henry would have been suicidal. They couldn't breathe the air in there. "We need to get back up to Liz and Seth."

"How are we going to do that? No power, no elevator."

"I saw a door on the way here with a picture of stairs. That might be our way out."

"And if it isn't?"

"Do you have any better ideas?"

"Fine, fine, as long as it means we get out of here. The blinking lights are bad enough. I swear the walls are closing in on me."

They held onto each other and felt their way along the corridor. It took several minutes to find the elevator doors.

Anth said, "This must be it. I can feel the pattern on the door's surface." She groped for the floor with her foot and found the stairs. Genz shuffled closer and she said, "Do you recall how much time it took to get down here with the elevator? This is going to take some time so I hope you don't get crazy on me."

A hissy growl acknowledged her warning. They took their time.

Six steps, a turn, six steps, a turn—Anth wondered if she was getting tired from the exertion or the monotonous sequence. They took breaks every hundred steps or so.

Genz gasped. "How much farther do you think?"

"Patience, Genz. I'm sure we'll reach an exit soon. Perhaps on the main level."

"This is killing me."

Anth thought about Henry with a pang of guilt. She should have gone after him and was sure he would have done that for her.

The next flight of stairs ended at a door.

Genz said, "I'm opening it."

Panicked that the Soofysh might be lurking outside, Anth whispered, "Slowly." The thought held her frozen in place.

She ran a finger up the door's edge and swung it open a crack. A draft of cool air caressed her face. She lingered long enough to savor the sweet moment and inhaled. A faint glow from farther within the chamber cast Genz into an opaque silhouette.

"Why don't you answer me?"

The light came from a far corner of an open space. This was not the main level. She tilted her head, and an object came into view that stopped her cold.

Genz said, "It's not one of ours, is it?"

The oddity took shape as her eyes adjusted. It reminded her of the so-called flying saucers humans were apt to witness throughout their history. Unlike the ship she and her people had used to travel to Earth, this one was much smaller—maybe ten paces across—enough for one or two human passengers. *What is it doing here?*

Genz said, "I bet it's a Soofysh craft."

While he continued to gape, Anth moved closer to the ship. Instruments of all kinds encircled the enigma with wires and cables spread out on the floor. "Looks like the humans were studying it." She recognized an electric drill on a table nearby. "And they tried to open it up."

Genz appeared at her side. "No markings. It's definitely not ours. Maybe from another colonization party, you think?"

"I doubt it. What would it be doing inside this complex?" She leaned closer to its hull. "You would think a craft of this kind would have some markings."

They walked to the other side of the saucer.

Genz straightened up. "A door."

"And it's wide open."

Anth pushed ahead of Genz and said, "Move back. Your shadow's in the way." She shifted to the side of the opening and peered inside. "Room for one."

"What else?"

She stepped back. "See for yourself."

Genz shoved Anth aside. "There's nothing else in here. There are no controls, not even a seat."

Anth said, "No markings, no controls, no seat—what does that tell you?"

"I'll tell you what it says to me." Both reptilians jumped at the voice from their rear.

Anth was the first to speak. "Henry. How did you—"

"Get here?

<>

Henry tugged his chest flaps together. "I think Seth's needlework is coming undone." He grinned at his own joke and added, "I'm guessing it's Soofysh. Is anyone in there?"

"Empty." Anth stepped away from the ship and ran her hand over Henry's chest. "You could not have climbed the stairs."

"It turns out that there's a little elevator beyond the reactor core that has but one stop—this level. Maybe it was used for emergencies, That might explain why it has a separate power supply."

"You are fortunate. When the power died, our elevator died with it."

"I'm afraid that was me." The looks of both reptilians begged for an explanation. "I threw a pipe into the one generator that was still working."

Anth asked. "You had a reason to do so?"

"Desperation. The damn Soofysh showed up again and was about to collect me. When I saw sparks shooting from its feet, I figured—"

"You shorted out the generator."

"Many years ago, when I was in college, the campus generator blew up one day. At the time our computer center relied on magnetic storage discs."

"And you lost data."

"You got it. Computers all over the campus were wiped out. I think they called it an electromagnetic pulse."

"How did you know your pipe would do the same?"

"It was either that or throw the pipe at the Soofysh."

Anth said, "So, what happened next?"

"I don't know. Everything went dark. The Soofysh disappeared. At least I didn't bump into it or them. That's when I noticed a bright red light farther along the walkway. I followed it to an elevator, and here I am." Henry walked to the saucer's opening. "All the comforts of home." He gazed at the equipment stacked up around them. "The military must have picked this thing up."

"Maybe it malfunctioned or crashed."

"Maybe, but they brought this thing inside one of our most secure installations." He lifted a dusty set of earphones and threw them aside.

"And no doubt pissed off the occupant."

"That may explain the position of the bodies we found."

"They ran for their lives."

"Do you think your electromagnetic pulse destroyed the Soofysh?"

"No way of telling. If it had anything resembling an electronic brain, it might be scrambled. And then, there's a chance it's just ticked off, maybe skulking around in here right now."

Henry and Anth stood and listened for any unusual noises, while Genz sauntered off.

"Your boyfriend likes to wander."

"He is a free spirit."

"Like you?"

"Not like me."

I see you still have your rifle." Henry pulled out his revolver. "Let's catch up and give him a hand with the search. If it came out of that contraption, then maybe it set up shop on this level."

The single emergency light high up on one corner made it tough to see details, but Henry judged the room to be large enough to be a hangar. The domed ceiling structure stretched across a few acres of concrete flooring. Halfway around the perimeter, Genz grunted and raised his rifle.

Anth and Henry approached on tip-toe.

Henry said, "Another elevator." He depressed a button but heard nothing. "Keep going."

When they passed several military vehicles, including a helicopter, Anth asked, "How did that equipment get in here? I see no doors large enough."

Henry pointed up and said, "The same way the Soofysh saucer did."

The seams of what might be a sealed skylight were visible at the top of the dome.

Once again, Genz raised his weapon, but this time he dropped to all fours. They were in the darkest corner of the hangar, and Genz had spotted something that had him spooked. Henry and Anth moved away from each other in a flanking maneuver.

Henry whispered. "Can you see anything over there, Anth?"

"Yes. Robots, maybe cyborgs, like your Mike back at the entrance."

Henry's abdomen tightened. His hand came up to check that the chest hadn't totally come undone. "How many?"

"I count six."

"Jeez. Any moving?"

"They are all standing still against the wall, as if in a military formation."

Henry rose and headed into the gloom. "Shoot the first thing that moves, but try not to shoot me." The reptilian's hissing laughter did little to quell his dread. Liz needed him, and he'd be damned if he was going allow some ridiculous fear of robots that go bump in the dark stop him.

He passed Genz. The vague forms ahead took shape. Anth was right—six silver sentinels complete with dull green eye sockets, and each was the spitting image of Mike. He drew closer to the nearest one at one end and lifted his revolver to its eye. "Hey, anyone in there?"

Anth said, "They may be dormant."

Henry jumped. She was right next to him. "Sorry."

A flush rose over his face and once again he was impressed by the Soofysh technology. At any rate he was glad that no one else saw it in the dark. "No problem."

At the far end of the lineup, Genz poked one of the robots with his rifle. Nothing.

A glint of reflected light from the workbench caught Henry's eye. "Look at those parts—over there, a half-finished android or robot. And the tools—I don't recognize them, do you?" Henry picked up the item that had glimmered. "Wonder what this does."

Anth shook her head. "I would be careful with it."

Henry turned it over. "It's got a trigger."

"Be even more careful." Suddenly she turned her head and said, "Perhaps we can refer to them in the singular."

"Why would you say that?"

Anth raised her weapon to her shoulder and aimed at the robot next to Genz. A dull glow of green emanated from the its eye sockets. He felt his legs weaken while imagining all the robots coming to life, their emerald eyes twinkling, grotesque smiles widening.

Anth hissed at Genz, who stepped back.

None of the others appeared active as yet. Perhaps they were about to recover from the electromagnetic pulse—one by one. He concentrated on the one with the brightening eyes and cocked his revolver. "So far, only this one. I don't see any movement in the others."

Anth said, "This one is different."

"You're right. The surface is smoother—no seams at the joints. The nose, the mouth—Damn, if it wasn't for the shiny skin, it might even look human."

Its lips parted and a deep, resonant voice echoed throughout the hangar. "I don't know if we should be insulted or flattered." The figure became a shimmering blur and streaked at Genz. In a blink, the reptilian was disarmed and held from behind by a pair of silvery arms.

Anth raised her weapon, but the creature had Genz's rifle jammed up beneath the reptilian's chin. Despite being several feet shorter, the android-like creature held the struggling Genz with no apparent sign of effort.

Henry said, "You're not one of them—one of the robots—are you?"

"How did you like our projection in the reactor room? We must admit that it was clever of you Henry—to generate an electronic pulse. We did not expect such intelligence." The pair edged closer to the tool bench.

"Then you're Soofysh?"

"The one and the many."

"There are others?" He tightened his grip on the revolver, but kept it out of sight to his side. His finger ran over the hammer, ensuring it was cocked.

"Don't you think one of us is enough? Look at your planet." The pair waltzed another half-step toward the bench.

The synthetic muscles in Henry's limbs tensed, begging for release. A number of scenarios ran through his mind, most of which ended with a dead reptilian and worse. They were an arm's length from the workbench. "There is no justification for what you've done. No living species would ever condone genocide regardless of the profit to themselves or to others." Henry hoped he could keep the Soofysh distracted while some brainy plan percolated up through his subconscious.

"Living is one of many states of matter. You are giving it too much importance."

"You might change your opinion if it was I holding a weapon under your chin."

"Not at all. We Soofysh are neither alive nor dead. Your ethical lectures are without interest to us."

"The fact remains—you've killed for profit."

"And profit is what drives all species, Henry. You should know that. What happened to your native brethren right here on this continent? Humans killing humans. You cannot blame the Soofysh on your culture's extermination. I can cite many such genocides."

"That was wrong then. This is wrong now."

The Soofysh flung Genz aside and bounded to the bench. The creature reached out as if expecting to find something and hesitated for a moment, seemingly perplexed.

"Looking for this?" Henry held up a small cylindrical device, while the forefinger of his other hand curled about his revolver's trigger.

"Careful. You are holding a device beyond your understanding."

Anth raised her rifle and trained it on the Soofysh.

"Your weapons will prove of little use. We Soofysh are the most developed, and as you suggested, the most intelligent specie in this galaxy, perhaps the universe. We have existed as such for millions of years, and in that time have evolved beyond what you refer to as biological. Our sole interest is to service lower forms of matter, in particular, animate matter in need."

"What damn need are you servicing right now?"

"We expedite the colonization of habitable worlds."

"Expedite? That's a funny word to use—perhaps sterilization would be more accurate a term."

"As we pointed out, your brain has a simplified concept of the states of matter." The creature moved an inch closer.

"There has to be something in it for you."

"A modest price."

"You're more human than you know. You sound like a damn real estate agent."

The creature hesitated as if pondering the concept, and then moved another inch closer. "A provincial analogy—it is that and more. We are great in number and in resources. We assist evolution. The weak will always fall, seceded by the strong. It is the way of things."

"All very noble, but your actions speak otherwise." Henry raised the device. "That's close enough. You're fast, but I'll wager my finger is faster. I'm not sure how this works."

A white beam of light shot to the floor. There was no sound, no recoil—just an acrid ozone stench reminiscent of concrete walkways before a thunderstorm. Henry's eyes adjusted and a dark circular hole about a foot wide appeared in the cement. "It's a good thing I wasn't pointing this thing at you."

The Soofysh fired Genz's rifle. Anth leaped to the side and Henry rolled to the floor. He was about to fire back, when Genz jumped at the creature. A single, muffled thud sent him to the floor screaming.

Henry was too startled to move.

Anth yelled, "It is running."

The creature was halfway to the saucer when Henry caught sight of it. By the time he reached the spacecraft, it had disappeared. When Anth caught up with him, Henry said, "How is Genz?"

"He will be fine."

"He was brave to do that."

Anth nodded, and Henry was sure she smiled. She said, "Where the hell did it go?"

213

"Anth, such language—I'm afraid I'm a bad influence on you."

Anth chose to ignore the dig. She looked as perplexed as he was, swinging her head left and right. An alarming series of metallic clicks filled the air. Henry peered back to the far wall. The five robotic creatures were gone and the clicking sounds drew nearer. He blinked in disbelief. "Anth, run for the saucer."

Henry aimed the alien weapon back at the workbench, releasing a torrent of blazing energy in a wide arc. Bolts of lightning carved a ragged trail of dark grooves into the concrete and steel bench. A robot appeared, glowed for a moment, and then detonated, knocking Henry to the floor and leaving him partially blinded by the light. A second robot materialized, staggering as if confused. Sparks spewed from its shoulder where an arm should have been. Its body twisted and toppled, spinning on the concrete floor like a Fourth of July pinwheel, sending out streams of smoke in an expanding spiral. The debris cloud outlined yet another automaton.

Henry fired again, and the second explosion's afterimage left the hanger veiled in purple shadows. There were two more and they could be anywhere, including right behind him. Even if they were visible, the rising haze made seeing anything virtually impossible, nor hearing anything through the incessant ringing in his ears.

A tug on his shoulder twisted him around. Anth said, "Come, Henry."

"You don't know how close you came to being vaporized."

"It is something I have become accustomed to." The reptilian led him away from the maelstrom back to the Soofysh craft.

"Can you see any more of those damn golems?"

Anth shook her head while they both picked up the pace. "Golems?"

"Scary men made of mud … not pretty."

"Sarcasm?"

"Way beyond sarcasm, Anth. What about Genz? That scream sounded bad."

"He is a baby."

Henry chuckled. "That baby showed some backbone back there." The Soofysh spaceship loomed large. "Do you hear that?"

"The footfalls?"

"They're being stealthy, trying not to reveal their positions." Henry peered inside the ship. "Nothing. Where the hell did that Soofysh creature go?"

Anth said, "I suggest we—"

Something wrenched Anth away, and in the same moment, she shoved Henry into the ship. His revolver fell from his hand as he tumbled inside. The door slid shut and its walls, ceiling and floor became transparent. Outside, Anth moved her hands over the ship's surface and across the sealed entryway. Two pairs of gleaming green eyes hovered behind her. She called out, but he heard nothing.

"Can you hear me, Anth?"

The reptilian grappled with the phantom on her back, rolling over the surface of the saucer. Henry looked on—powerless and frustrated. The craft had no apparent instrumentation, and if it had, it was probably invisible. He was but a fly caught in a Soofysh web. The thought sickened him. Anth tumbled away into the shadows.

"We are delighted you joined us, Henry."

The voice came from everywhere.

Henry recalled the robot back at the river—the invisible robot. He darted from one side of the craft to the other, feeling about with his hands. "You're not in here, are you?"

"In a manner of speaking, we are and we are not."

"Son-of-a-bitch. Don't tell me you're the ship."

"We are proud of you, Henry—an intelligent, stable cyborg with psychic abilities."

"Isn't pride a human trait? I thought you were above all that emotional crap."

"You should be happy to know you are the only one of all the humans we tested with such an ability"

Henry thought back. "The hospital. You weren't there to save lives."

"In a sense, you might say we were."

"Brains. You were collecting."

"Thousands."

"And the bodies you're keeping downstairs?"

"Potential biological transmitters and receivers—our little experiment. At this point, they are of no further use."

The conversation wasn't going anywhere. Henry searched his rattled mind for something more to say, to ask—anything to stall. "And Liz?"

"Fear not. We will collect her on the way out. The pair of you will expand our knowledge of biologically-based telepathic transmission. Such a rare trait is worthy of our attention."

"The way out—to where?"

Henry felt a subtle vibration beneath his feet. Anth lumbered out of the dark. Her hands slid down along the outer skin of the vessel. The ship rose, and her mouth fell open. She screamed and smashed her arms against the hull. Henry pressed his against the transparent wall, following her outstretched fingers as they slid lower, hoping to somehow reach out, to touch her.

The saucer climbed toward the ceiling of the hangar. Henry fell to his knees. The floor framed what was likely be his last view of Earth which included a distraught alien frantically waving at him, the gloom below swallowing her green outline. A mist appeared below the ship, like the morning fog, rolling in from the Pacific Ocean, blanketing the bay, like his mother covering her babe in a soft, billowy bedspread. Its sweet caress rose and flowed over him. His muscles ached for respite. He sagged to the floor, pulling up the blanket, and closed his eyes.

<>

Warm sunlight danced across Henry's eyelids. The aroma of a wood fire tickled his nostrils. A thin branch swayed outside his window, sporting a jittery set of young green leaves.

He sat up. "Not again." Pivoting off the bed, he staggered to the kitchen door.

"Have a good sleep, Henry?" Liz poured coffee into a mug on the counter and returned the pot to the stovetop beneath which a small fire crackled. His wife looked a bit gaunt but more alive than the emaciated version of Liz back in the Cheyenne Complex. He wondered why the Soofysh had opted to leave his memory intact.

He fought back the urge to embrace her. "You know you're a figment of my imagination, don't you, Liz?"

"Another one of your dreams, honey?"

Good one.

Henry stepped into the kitchen. A waft of cold air slipped in through the curtains at the window. "I have to admit, the Soofysh are good at this."

"Sit down and have some coffee. It's good to see you up. You had a harrowing experience back in that Complex. I'm not surprised you still have nightmares."

Henry ignored the offer and wandered over to the half-open window. The bridge tower pierced the glowering fog. It was just as he remembered it. "Nice day." He took in the invigorating cool air. "You guys tried this once before. What's the deal? Why do this again?"

"You think you're the only one with nightmares? You can't imagine—they stuck wires in me while I was still conscious … and the tubes down my throat. I tried to scream, but—"

"I'm sorry, Liz. I didn't mean—"

"Shut up and have some coffee. And stop thinking for a little while. Do it for me, won't you honey?" She pulled back a sniffle. "I'll put some eggs on."

Henry gazed at her, taking in her lithe figure. She had been everything to him, and still was. *Are you really here?*

"Where's Seth?"

The little robot appeared from behind the counter. "I am here, sir."

No detail left out. "Everything look normal to you, Seth?"

"As normal as the circumstances permit, sir."

That's my Seth.

"I mean … am I hallucinating?"

"If you are, sir, then I am part of that illusion and would say to you that you are not hallucinating. On the other hand, if this is reality, then I would give you the same response."

Liz jerked her arm away as the eggs spattered. "Stop being ridiculous, Henry. Relax. Breakfast will be ready soon."

"Then what happened? I don't remember anything after passing out in the Soofysh craft."

Seth said, "The Soofysh brought both you and Elizabeth here, sir."

"How long ago was that?"

Liz said, "Day before yesterday. The Soofysh claim you banged your head in their saucer thing. This is the first time you've been able to have a decent conversation. Sit down—the eggs are ready."

Henry brought his arms around Liz's back and hugged her. "Damn. I can feel your body. I can smell your scent."

She craned her head and they kissed. "That's enough of that. Even that mechanical body of yours needs nourishment."

Henry slipped into the breakfast nook."But why bring us back here? I thought they were going to study us … to find out how we communicate."

Liz plopped another fried egg onto her plate and sat. "I think they're done here. After dropping us off, they flew off without another word."

The coffee flowed over his tongue, leaving behind a savory bitter taste. "You have to admit, it's hard to believe. Those bastards destroyed our world. We were trying to—hey, what about the reptilians? You know, Anth and Genz."

"I'm not sure. I think they were returned to their colony."

Seth said, "They were happy to go back, sir."

Henry left the table.

"Honey, you haven't touched your eggs."

He sat back down on the bed and slipped a hand beneath his shirt. His fingers ran over the stitched ridges.

Seth appeared at the doorway. "Is everything all right, sir?"

"I wish it was, Seth."

His revolver hung on the wall—longbow and quiver in the corner—all as it should be. "Something's nagging me, and I keep thinking that if I don't do something, the feeling will go away. It'll be too late."

"Perhaps a short nap will clear things up for you, sir."

"Maybe you're right, Seth."

Henry stood up to straighten his bed. "Ouch."

"What is it, sir?"

His foot rolled over the object, but in the shadow, he saw nothing. When he clasped his fingers over it, a silvery cylinder took shape in his hand. "My, my. What have we here?"

Seth said, "Something you brought with you from the Complex, sir?"

Henry raised it to the light. "Yeah, you could say that."

Liz spoke from the doorway. "Henry, put that thing down. It's dangerous."

And how would you know that?

Henry aimed the device at the floor. "A little hole in the floor shouldn't matter."

"No Henry, stop!"

The flash set the floor to shaking. Henry's legs wobbled and he struggled to stay upright. He focused on the hole he created, and saw a dim abyss—the distant concrete flooring of the Cheyenne Complex hanger swirling beneath his feet.

<>

Henry looked up in time to see a massive ceiling support beam filling his field of view. The collision threw him into a wall which flickered—invisible—visible—while the ship spun. The nauseating rhythm persisted as the saucer tilted and adopted a descending arc. Chunks of ceiling concrete struck the craft, sending it tumbling end over end, and Henry with it. Seconds later, the saucer smashed into the hangar's floor.

Henry, sprawled in the dark, was relieved that the spinning stopped and even more relieved that he was alive. After taking stock of his body, insuring it was still intact, he ran his fingers along the walls. A seam or opening might have formed. The muffled sounds of debris striking the exterior added to a mounting fear that the whole complex might soon bury him.

"Henry."

It was Anth.

"I'm okay. See any way to open this tin can?"

No response.

Henry fished about in the dark and found the Soofysh weapon. "Stand back." He aimed away from Anth's voice and fired. A small hole appeared. He yelled though the opening. "Anth, are you out there?"

Hearing nothing and seeing no one, he fired again, and again. The weapon's power seemed to wane with each use. He continued to blast away until the weapon was spent, emitting no more than a faint hum. He had burned a hole large enough to crawl through.

A spindly arm appeared. "Henry!" The reptilian drew him out into a choking plume of concrete dust. "Anth. Anth." He brought his arms about her neck and hugged her.

"What about those robots?"

"I am not sure … when you took off, they let me go."

"They're probably not interested in you."

Skittering debris turned both heads. The Soofysh creature staggered out of the saucer and into a gray haze. "You are correct, Henry. You and your wife are all we want." It pointed back at the ship and said, "You've made quite a mess."

"Me? You're the bastard who made a mess, a very big mess. The time has come for payback." The words felt good, but Henry was painfully aware of his vulnerability and was sure that the Soofysh would see through his bluff. He was an ant talking to a child with a huge foot hovering over it. Who was he to make threats?

"We can repair this ship … repair us."

Two green-eyed automatons materialized alongside the Soofysh. "And what then?"

The creature remained standing as if considering what to say.

Henry said, "I'm putting an end to this … to you. Maybe it's useless, but I can at least try to avenge the billions who died."

"Is violence all you can think about? Henry, rise above your hatred. You are a smart person. Listen to reason. After all, we have a lot to offer—our science, technology—all of it can be yours. We can rebuild this planet together, recreate your home. Think about it, Henry. With such technology you would be a god on this planet."

The Soofysh's voice adopted a mellow, soothing tone. Its words started to sound reasonable, even human-like reasonable. Henry's anger ebbed, his lust for revenge faded, his body weakened. The Soofysh was playing with his mind again and there was nothing he could do about it. He dropped to his knees. A distant part of his being craved to attack the monster, to tear it apart with his hands. A burning desire wasn't enough. Henry reached for the floor with both hands, and as his head sagged, Anth appeared behind the Soofysh.

Henry forced out a whisper even though his animosity for the Soofysh was nearly gone. "Your days are at an end."

The creature emitted a deep-throated witch's laugh. "We shall call you Henry the Last. You do enjoy humor, isn't that true?" The creature turned to the two robots at his side and spoke to them as if they were his aides. "Suitable title, don't you think?"

In one blurred motion Anth's arms wrapped about the Soofysh's head and the two fell to the floor, rolling in the dust. The robots' eyes flashed a bright green as they joined the fray. The fog which had blurred Henry's senses was at once swept away. The melee kicked up a debris cloud. Anth screamed.

Henry forced himself upright and took a step forward as she untangled herself from the Soofysh. Its two robot aides lay on the floor, unmoving. She raised her arm. Two sinuous bundles of wires writhed on their own as they dangled from her hand. Gleaming heads swayed to and fro. "These robots are history." Suddenly, she flew through the air and landed in a heap a few yards away.

A gleaming ghost stepped out of the dust. "You have no idea what you are dealing with."

A crackling sound erupted from the wreck of the saucer. The hole its side rippled for a moment, and then it disappeared, leaving behind a smooth metallic skin.

"Impressed?"

"That must take a lot of power."

"Don't go anywhere, Henry. I'll be back in a moment."

The Soofysh entered the saucer, apparently confident that nothing Henry did would be of any consequence—a sentiment Henry would readily agree with. He sat on the floor and listened to the creaks and cracks coming from the saucer—no doubt more repair work. His head swiveled about almost on its own surveying the hanger. The vague outlines of helicopters, tanks, and armored vehicles loomed into view—all impotent, victims of the passage of time.

Anth joined him on the floor. "What are we to do?"

Genz stepped up behind her, holding his arm.

"I think we're done. I've got nothing. Sometimes you don't win."

Anth shook Henry by the shoulders and her voice raised a notch. What of your wife? Are you so easily disheartened?" She hissed. "I would die before giving up."

Pity was lonely comfort. Anth was right, but what could he do? Henry stared up at her, about to explain that there was no other recourse—that perhaps surrender had the best chance to keep Liz alive. Then something caught his eye.

"That tank."

The three followed Henry's finger.

"It's pointed right at the saucer."

Anth said, "How does that matter? It is a relic, probably unworkable without power and I doubt it has any ammunition."

"Now who's giving up?" Henry ran the fifty feet to the giant war machine with the reptilians at his heels. "I know this beast. An Abrams. Built to last." He took a quick look back. No Soofysh yet.
He leaped up to the barrel, hung off it with one hand and stuck the other in.

Anth said, "What are you doing?"

Henry dropped to the floor. "Damn. It's rusty. We need to clean this barrel."

Anth looked into the barrel's end while Henry popped a tool box on the side of the tank. He rushed back with a wire brush and a bottle.

"I need your help." Henry broke off the mouth of the bottle and poured the contents on the brush. "Shove this thing into the barrel as far as you can and pull it out. Do that a couple of times."

While Anth rammed the brush in, Henry motioned to Genz. The two climbed up the side of the Abrams. Henry was first inside. Genz paused at the hatch opening and said, "Saucer. Make noise."

"Shit." Henry eased himself past the commander's seat into the loader's section. "Sorry about that." The skeletal remains in the seat collapsed beneath him. He fiddled with the loading mechanism and sprung it open. Some oil dripped into his lap. "Genz, tell Anth to move out of the

221

way. Tell her to get behind the tank."

Genz yelled something reptilian. Henry reached behind him. It didn't matter what type of round he chose. At this distance he'd be happy to survive the blast.

The round slipped into the chamber and Henry closed the breech. "Genz, get in here."

Genz appeared in the commander's module and started screaming. "Soofysh come. Soofysh come."

Henry lifted himself up enough to peek out a narrow slit. The Soofysh creature walked toward them. He could swear it had a swagger in its stride. "Damn." He motioned to Genz to slip down to the gunner's module. "Down there. Now!"

Genz's lengthy body scraped by him and dropped into the empty gunner's seat. Henry leaned down and yelled. "The lever. Pull that lever."

Genz contorted his body as he punched at every dial and button within reach.

"The lever! The big thing on your left!"

Henry eased up and looked again. The Soofysh was no more than several paces away-directly in the firing line. Its mouth opened as if to speak.

"Damn it, Genz. Pull the damn lever!"

A bright flash and high-pitched scream filled the air. Henry flew out of his seat and smashed into an overhead support beam as the world turned on its side. Smoke streamed out of the open breech.

"Genz!" Henry hardly heard himself yell over the ringing in his ears. His eyes stung. A blue haze covered his vision. A face appeared through the thick bluish fog that bit at his throat.

"Genz!" Yelling set Henry to coughing. As the smoke thinned and someone dragged him up into the commander's module and then out the hatch. Rolled out onto the hangar floor, he half-expected the Soofysh to be smirking down at him.

"Henry, are you all right?" Anth came into view. It was the loveliest green face he'd ever seen. "You are bleeding."

He brushed a hand over his eyes and his fingers returned coated in a blue stain. "How bad?"

"A small lesion. Nothing to be concerned about."

Henry said, "Maybe from out there. You should see it from in here." His eyes cleared a bit more. "What happened?"

"Genz pulled you out."

He nodded in the reptilian's direction. "But what happened?"

"See for yourself."

Anth helped Henry to his feet. The smoke from the explosion had risen enough to make out the saucer—except it wasn't there. They walked about in a methodical stagger while Henry scanned the hanger—nothing, no saucer, no Soofysh.

"How?"

Henry held himself up at a wall while Anth and Genz jogged around the perimeter of the hangar. When they returned and reported, their findings were stunning. They found no saucer and no Soofysh. All evidence of the two had been erased.

Anth suggested, "Perhaps it was never here."

"That's all I need—another ghost."

Henry couldn't stop looking about, almost certain that the Soofysh would return any second. "Have we really defeated the Soofysh?"

Anth embraced Genz and said, "Only time will tell."

The world had changed. Colonists from other planets were arriving with more in the wings. Whether other Soofysh were positioned elsewhere or more were on their way, were questions for another day. This day was his. This day belonged to the human race, and the new Earthlings—the reptilians.

"We need to get back upstairs. I'm worried about what the electrical pulse might have done to Seth."

Several more lights winked on. "Some kind of backup system is kicking in, maybe from all the explosions and noise. At least we can see where we're going."

Henry heard a chime from across the way. "Is that an elevator?" He retrieved his revolver from near the upended tank. The three hobbled over to the elevator doors.

Anth said, "What if it is another Soofysh?"

"Let's hope not, for its sake."

"Sarcasm?"

The doors parted and Seth ambled out. "Did I miss anything, sir?"

Henry said, "Good to see you're still here, Seth. Where is Liz? Did you leave her alone?"

"Liz is all right, but could be better." It was her voice. She placed an unsteady foot outside the elevator. Draped in a burlap sack, Liz propped herself against the doorframe and gave the two reptilians a stare. "What have you been up to, Henry, and what's with the blue skin?"

Chapter 43

One Month Later

Henry lowered his cup of coffee and watched its condensate swirl across the kitchen window. Seth's reflection bobbed up on the pane—a glossy head leaning in through the door.

"Breakfast is served, sir."

He paused at the window facing the tree line. A figure in a blue dress stood by a headstone and waved at him. Sunlight splashed across her short red hair. Her smile sent a warm glow through Henry's heart and soul. How many years had he stared at her ephemeral apparition? How many nights did he sleep alone, caressing her pillow, dreaming that she lay next to him, waiting for her arm to wrap itself about his shoulders?

He waved back. No longer a dream or a ghost, she was home to stay. He raised the window and said, "Come and get it."

The two sat at a picnic table in the front yard. A late autumn breeze whisked away the few dried leaves on the porch steps and carried them off to join a mounting pile at the foot of the rover parked in the front yard. Henry held Liz's hand and kissed her on the cheek. "How are you this morning?"

"Every day, a little better."

He patted her on her butt. "You're also getting a little fatter."

Liz shot him a lowered brow. "Thanks to your cooking."

Seth scurried around the table with a coffee pot in hand. "I am most pleased that you are happy, ma'am."

"How many times must I remind you, Seth? You can call her Liz."

"I know I can, sir. Will there be anything else?"

"Pancakes, boiled eggs, toast and bacon—Seth, you've outdone yourself."

"Nothing was spared on the occasion of your anniversary, sir."

Henry tried to recall when he and Liz were married. "But—"

Liz said, "Bubble brain. He's talking about our return ... my return. It's been one month since a knight in sparkling blue armor saved me."

One month.

The screen door squealed and three green fingers curled around its edge.

Henry said, "There's room for two more."

Genz slinked out and sat by Henry.

"Where's Anth?"

"She come soon."

Henry suspected Genz's remarkable progress with English was part of an overall effort to impress Anth. The two had grown close, very close.

"And your arm?"

Genz flexed the arm and made the 'okay' sign with two fingers.

Liz hissed out in reptilian. "Please, help yourself, Genz." Just listening to her practice must have rubbed off, though Henry still had trouble with their slithering tongue.

He turned toward the padding of paws on the floorboards. "Someone's caught the aroma of that bacon."

Liz grabbed a strip. "Here, Wolfie. Your favorite." She held it out in her hand and the wolf gently pulled it away. Henry thought back to the grizzly at the cabin a lifetime ago. Wolfie was wild and would always be. The beast had tracked them to the Cheyenne Complex, but it was impossible to convince him to join them in the rover. Whether it was magic or a quirk of nature, Liz managed to beguile Wolfie with a simple gesture—extending her hand, something that Henry was sure would end badly. The four-footed killing machine had opted to sit next to her with his head resting in her lap. Wolfie's visits were his choice and sporadic at best. That he opted not to devour Liz was an ongoing miracle that Henry relegated to his wife's implacable charm.

"I think Wolfie has adopted you, Liz."

"Wolfie is my best friend, aren't you?" Liz used her other hand to run her fingers through his bristly head and behind his ear. Wolfie nudged her to keep up the scratching.

Anth arrived wearing her treasured bear skin and swung a backpack over her shoulder.

"Are you going somewhere?" Henry was careful to keep his voice calm. He had feared that this day would come. The two reptilians had acclimated themselves to a human lifestyle, and cooked food, but it was also clear their hearts belonged elsewhere.

She looked to Genz and asked, "Did you tell them?"

Genz lowered his head.

Liz said, "You're leaving—is that it?"

Wolfie trotted over to Anth and sat down at her feet. She pulled back her bearskin coat and patted her stomach. "I am pregnant."

Henry said, "Now that's something I didn't expect."

Liz embraced Anth. "That's wonderful."

Anth said, "There is more. Genz and I have decided to go our own way … Ahh, my language is failing me."

Henry said, "We understand. You're about to be a family, and you'd prefer to live in your own home. Our way of life is not yours. You would want to keep your customs."

Anth nodded.

Genz said, "And food."

"Oh, yeah—fresh and uncooked."

Liz asked, "Will you go back to South Dakota, to your colony?"

"We do not think that would be a good idea with Fierz in charge. He is not one to forget and forgive." She patted Wolfie on the head. "You two—" She gave Seth a glance. "Excuse me. You three have been kind to us. I have no words to express our gratitude." Anth paused and looked at Genz, who rose and wrapped an arm about her. "We found a cabin a few miles north of here."

Henry laughed out loud, setting Wolfie to howl. "Here we thought you were off to some distant land. Damn, you'd be our neighbors."

"Once we settle down, can we visit you?"

Liz said, "Of course. We insist. Besides, we'll drop in on you too, if that's all right."

Henry added, "We'd like that, besides we need every chance to keep up with your language lessons. Who knows, someday we might bump into one of your cousins. I wouldn't expect them to speak English."

Anth nodded and handed the backpack to Genz. The two reptilians stepped off the porch. After some intense farewell hugs, Liz asked, "Any idea when the baby will arrive?"

Henry held Liz's arm and wondered which it would be—a live birth or an egg—but was too embarrassed to ask.

Anth studied Henry's face, and as if reading his mind, replied, "In about six months. By the way, can we have your permission to name the child either Henry or Liz."

Henry was speechless.

Liz said, "You don't need our consent. We are honored, Anth, and wish you both the best."

The two stepped away and began their hike. Anth glanced at Henry and said, "It is not an egg."

<>

Henry stirred. An afternoon siesta was a habit more than a necessity. Old people needed naps and he was more than old. A sound sleep offered up adventures like no other—jousting with dragons and giant reptilians, dodging glowing spheres, tangling with robots and androids and other distortions that cropped up along the phantasmagorical roadmap of his mind. At times, it was a relief to wake and simply appreciate life. He exhaled and took in the smell of the cabin.

Judging by the darkness outside, he had overstayed his visit to the land of dreams. The cabin was quiet, a feeling he was still getting used to after the reptilians left a week before. He was sure it was the feeling that parents got when their children left, even when in this case it was alien reptilian teenagers making a life for themselves on Earth.

A sweet aroma drifted in through a window, enticing him to get out of bed. His bedroom overlooked the front porch and the yard beyond. The flickering yellow of a campfire drew his gaze to a suspended cauldron. Its sputtering light danced across the surrounding trees—shadows moved among the swaying branches as if sync with the distant thrum of crickets. Liz sat in a rocker next to the black pot, swaying to and fro, hunched over a blanket she'd been knitting for the past week. With Fall fast approaching, she said it was going to be a gift for the reptilians, to help them stave off the coming cold. Wolfie sat next to her, his head nodding, growing heavier as he tried in vain to stay awake. Henry was glad Wolfie had come for a visit, and he was sure Wolfie shared his sentiment. He glanced at the fencing surrounding the chicken coop making sure it was still intact. Wolves were wolves after all.

Liz laid the unfinished blanket on the seat of the rocker and stepped over to the fire to check on her cooking. If Henry had normal skin, it would have erupted into a sea of hackles. The smell. Liz is making red berry soup.

Wolfie snagged her blanket and dragged it off a few feet away, as if the action would fool Liz. He held it down with both paws and gnawed at the knitted end. Liz turned and with arms akimbo said, "Naughty boy,

Wolfie. I'm never going to get that blanket done. I'm forever redoing the stitching you undo."

A chill ran up Henry's titanium spine.

"Sir, I'm glad you are awake. Madam wants you to know the soup is ready."

"Does everything look okay to you, Seth?"

"Of course, sir. Why do you ask?"

"Do you remember my dream about the old woman, her blanket, and her dog?"

"And the red berry soup—the Lakota story of creation. During our adventure—yes, I do."

Henry continued staring out the window.

Seth got on tip-toe to get a better view. "Sir, that dream was a reflection of a myth; this is reality."

"Yeah, reality." Henry put on his moccasins. An image of the last Soofysh-generated wish world floated by. Seth was convincing then too. "Tell her I'll be right out."

A minute later, he had a finger in the berry soup.

"Henry, don't be such a Neanderthal. Be patient. I'll be serving in just a little while." Liz tugged her blanket out of the Wolfie's mouth and sat back down in her rocker. Wolfie ambled over and plopped down next to her. His eyes locked in on her sewing. It was a game—one which involved getting Liz upset. Just a game.

"Fine. Fine. I'm going for a walk."

"Suit yourself. Don't get lost. I'll give you ten minutes."

"Okay, it'll be a short walk."

Henry passed by the rear of the rover and swung around to brush off some leaves caught on its windshield. The last time they used it was a quick trip into the city to raid a grocery store. He looked through the mottled glass, making sure he hadn't forgotten to carry some item into the cabin. A shadow within its dim interior caught his eye. Maybe he did leave something there. He stepped up to the door and as it slid open, he was hit hard in the face. The force of the blow sent him reeling backwards. In an instant, a hand covered his mouth—a scaly hand with three long fingers. He was pinned to the ground, unable to resist or to call out.

"Hello again, cyborg."

Fierz.

The reptilian brought a can up and sprayed its contents into Henry's face. "Fear not, my little prize, this will not kill you."

Fierz pressed a knee into Henry's chest, forcing him to suck in air through his nose. The effect was immediate. His limbs grew heavy and his anxiety subsided. He became distant and detached. Every muscle in his body relaxed. Only his eyes moved, and from his position on the ground, Henry saw the giant reptilian peek over the rover's roof, ensuring that he wasn't detected.

Fierz whispered. "I hope you can understand our tongue, cyborg."

Henry nodded slightly.

"That is good. It will make my work so much more productive when we return to the colony."

Henry struggled to move, but could only wriggle.

"We use the gas to subdue all variety of mammals back at our colony. It works on the mammalian brain and I'm happy to see you're no different." The reptilian chortled, and added, "You do understand what I'm saying, don't you?"

Henry's mouth felt like he had gargled with Novocain. He forced a few words out. "You freak ... frigging ... asshole."

"My, my—and in our language. Very impressive."

Henry croaked out a word. "Why?"

"I have never encountered one such as you. The technology, Soofysh technology, which made you is of immense value to us, to me. I have a laboratory all prepared to take you apart."

Dr. Frankenstein appeared strutting back and forth in his dungeon laboratory surrounded by buzzing electric arcs, big round dials and huge double-throw switches—and Henry was laid out on a gurney next to a bench covered in saws and knives. Igor leaned over him, slavering, while his one good eye wandered to and fro like a Felix-the-Cat clock.

Stop it. His mind was drifting. It was all he could do to remain focused, not on Igor and his ever wandering eye, but on the glaring reptilian hovering over him.

A deep-throated growl interrupted their exchange. Henry forced his head to turn a few inches. Wolfie appeared at the corner of the rover, lips quivering and teeth glistening. The beast took a step forward, keeping his head low and tail tucked.

In an instant, Fierz lunged and seized Wolfie's head with both hands. He lifted the snapping and thrashing animal, and threw it against the side of the rover. The thud could have been a bag of bones slapped up against a tree. Wolfie let out a high-pitched whimper and as he tried to stand, collapsed into a whining ball of fur.

"Henry, what are doing back there?"

Fierz said, "Keep quiet, hero," and snorted. He kicked the wolf, who remained unresponsive. "I won't be needing your wife." Fierz stepped out into the open.

Henry heard Liz speak in the reptilian tongue. "Who are you? Have you come to see Anth and Genz?"

Fierz said, "My, your command of our language is excellent. Why, yes, I was hoping they would be here."

"Are you from their colony?"

"We call it home. I was asked to try and find them, to convince them to return. You see, their family and friends miss them very much."

Henry managed a roll—his head ending up a bit past the nose of the rover. A thatch of leaves blocked his view. He puckered his mouth and blew, but his compromised lungs emitted no more than a puff.

"They moved a few miles north of here. Oh, where are my manners—my name is Elizabeth."

"Pleased to meet you, Elizabeth. You know how it is with teenagers. I'll be sure to pay them a visit."

"Have you met my husband, Henry?"

Her voice faltered. She knew something was wrong.

Henry managed a second roll over. Exhausted, he craned his head high enough to get a clear view of Liz on the porch and the reptilian behemoth with his back to the campfire.

"Oh, I've met him on several occasions. I think it was a month or so ago. How is the old fellow?"

"He's here somewhere. I'll call him for you. Henry! Henry! We have a guest."

She sounded shrill. The panic in her voice was unmistakable. Henry called out, but his hoarse whispers had no chance of being heard.

"Perhaps Henry has mentioned me. My name is Fierz. I am sure he must have mentioned me."

"Fierz, you say? Sorry. I don't recall."

Even a reptilian knew she was lying. Henry rolled once more, giving him an unobstructed view. Liz backed up the porch steps. Fierz kicked away her rocker.

"Run, Liz." The words were mere whispers. Henry strained his arms and legs, his entire body shook. He couldn't lose her again.

Liz backed into the front door as Fierz stepped up to the porch. Henry closed his eyes and buried his head in the grass. He couldn't watch. He couldn't listen.

"Get away from me! We have nothing you want here."

"Oh, that's where you're wrong little human. It will be a shame to waste such a rare find as you, but it would be best for your cyborg husband. We can't have him wishing to return to you."

Henry forced his head up.

"Henry! Henry, where are you!"

Fierz said, "The cyborg is undamaged. I am looking forward to getting that specimen onto my dissecting table. It's a wondrous creation, don't you think?"

The reptilian took a step forward and drew his arms up, unfolding the membranous wings beneath. "Close your eyes. This will be fast."

A shot rang out.

Henry focused in time to see the giant stagger backwards. A second shot jerked his head. His torso arched and his arms curved upward, spreading their wings. No doubt guided by instinct, the reptilian twisted his body round and lurched at the rover. He swung round the wooden post and crashed into Liz's cauldron, toppling its sweet brew into the grass. Fierz's body twitched as it smothered the fire, rolled off, and settled face down in a pool of berry stew.

Liz continued to stare at the reptilian lying at the foot of the porch. Behind her, the screen door swung open. Seth stepped out holding a revolver—Henry's 1873 Colt.

<>

Liz held out a tray of bacon strips. The wolf resembled a mummy with bandages strapped about three legs and his chest. Although prostrate on a rug, the beast managed to open his mouth wide in anticipation.

"Don't get used to this, Wolfie."

Henry and Seth sat on the porch steps watching the show. Henry was convinced that Wolfie was faking. Three weeks had passed. None of the injuries were worse than sprains. Wolfie chewed on a strip and gave Henry a quick glance.

"Did you see that, Seth?"

"Indeed, I did, sir."

"There's more to that animal that meets the eye."

"He likes being here, sir."

"Have I told you yet how much we appreciated what you did?"

"Not today, sir."

"I didn't know you had it in you ... you know, to kill. Isn't there some internal program running around in that incredible brain of yours that prevents you from harming intelligent life?"

"My loyalty is to you and Elizabeth." A pause settled in between the two. Seth added, "You would do the same for me, sir."

"You're damn right, Seth."

"Sir, do you mind if I ask a question?"

"Of course not. Go ahead."

"We are back and Elizabeth is with you—"

"Come on, Seth. I've never known you to be at a loss for words."

"I expected you to be happier, sir."

The statement caught Henry off guard. "I'm okay." The silence that followed begged for more. "I guess you could even say I'm happy."

"There is something troubling you, sir."

"It's none of your business, Seth."

"Sorry, sir. I did not mean to offend."

Henry ran his fingers over the top of Seth's head. "There is something. It's the Soofysh. I can't get them out of my head."

"You are worried they will return?"

"Maybe. But I think it's more—like … all this. Are the Soofysh playing with my mind again? I've been through this crap before. Sometimes I have the feeling that we never got away—that even now I'm laid out on some gurney in an alien lab with wires stuck in my head."

"A perplexing problem, sir. I cannot help you, since your illusion would include me. May I offer a suggestion?"

"Pinch myself and see if it hurts?"

"Nothing so banal, sir. Consider what you said long ago about your hallucination—the image of Elizabeth."

"Yeah, I was either seeing her or I was mental. I think I said it didn't matter."

"Precisely, sir. Why not take each day as it comes? What does it matter if it is all an illusion?"

"That's easier said than done. I keep waiting for something to go wrong, something that pulls me out of this world. The last thing I want to see is that damn Soofysh creature."

"Rest easy, sir. Who knows? All we see and sense may be part of a larger illusion."

Henry smiled and strode over to Liz and her Wolfie. The plate was almost empty. "You know, I think you've spoiled him. I swear he's gained some weight."

"He doesn't mind." Liz edged the plate closer to the wolf and scratched behind his ear. Wolfie yawned and half-closed his eyes, while Liz settled into her rocker. She took up her blanket and started knitting.

Henry hugged her from behind and lowered his head to her ear.

"Can you do me a favor, Liz?"

"Of course, honey. You name it."

"It may sound silly, but please make sure you never finish that blanket."

Chapter 44

23 **Years Later**

"We had a good life, didn't we Liz?"

Henry placed a bouquet of orange poppies at the base of the headstone. A squirrel darted through the pine needles, throwing him a quick glance as it skittered off deeper into the woods. He stared after it and at the empty space that once held Liz's translucent apparition.

"To keep you warm." Henry draped a blanket over the stone. "Didn't I warn you not to finish this thing?" He smirked and wiped a finger across his eye. A weathered white plank with a scrawled set of letters rose out of the ground nearby. "And it's all your fault, Wolfie."

The walk back to the cabin took ages.

Seth greeted him at the porch. "The usual, sir?"

Henry slid into a seat at the breakfast nook and stole a momentary look back at the forest's edge. The squirrel reappeared atop the blanket, jerking its head back and forth. A breeze kicked up, and a school of orange-yellow leaves drifted through the barren branches and settled upon the covered stone.

Henry shuddered at the thought of winter. It was bad enough when Anth and Genz, and their son, little Henry, returned to their colony up in the Dakotas a few years ago. He still had Liz and that's all that mattered. She had never completely recovered from the Soofysh experiment. Even years later, she was always a bit weak, easily catching a cold or flu. She always recovered, until a week ago, when she succumbed. Her will to live was strong to the end, much stronger than he could ever be.

"Henry, you look terrible." Liz laid her head back down and Henry pulled a comforter up to her chest. The woman was incorrigible.

"I'm fine. It's you I'm worried about."

"It's just another episode, Henry."

He was no doctor, but Seth indicated her heart was irregular, making her weak. He called it atrial fibrillation. If the arrhythmia descended to the ventricle, the result would be catastrophic. Seth's technical insight made the look of her rheumy eyes and sunken cheeks even more alarming.

"You need to rest."

She threw him a scowl, followed by a radiant smile. "I love you, Henry. I'll love you forever."

He held her hand and squeezed as she closed her eyes. When he kissed her on the cheek and whispered, "I love you too, Liz," he knew she had left. It was not until the next morning he let go of her hand.

<>

"The usual, Seth."

"He's not here, Henry." Liz's voice made him jump. She was at the range, flipping a pancake. She tilted her head at him, exposing rosy cheeks. She looked alive, very alive—better than she ever did these past two decades. His stomach soured and he turned back to the window at the table. The gravestone was gone.

"No, no. This is not possible. You're, you're …" Henry leaped up and ran out the front door to the forest edge.

Liz called after him. "Your breakfast is getting cold."

A few leaves tumbled over a bed of pine needles where a headstone had been moments before. He blinked his eyes, sure that it would sprout from the ground any moment, that he was suffering some kind of horrible delusion. Then he took notice of Wolfie's marker, rather he noticed its absence. A fit of nausea weakened his legs and he slumped against a tree.

"What do you see, sir?"

"Seth! Weren't you just making breakfast?"

"I may have been, sir."

"What kind of answer is that? Either you were or you weren't."

Seth remained silent, much out of character. Henry noted the smoke wafting up from the cabin's stove pipe. "If you're not cooking, then who's in the kitchen?" He wasn't sure he wanted to hear the reply.

"Perhaps no one, sir."

"Damn it all, Seth. Give me a straight answer."

"I think it would be best if you came with me, sir." Seth turned and marched up a trail headed into the forest. At a loss for words, Henry followed, all the while glancing back at the cabin. He knew the path—one of the many laid out by deer—a narrow trail that ran along the edge of a precipice.

"Talk to me, Seth. What are we doing out here?"

The little robot remained silent as he forged ahead.

"You know this leads to a dead end."

When they reached the end of the path, Seth halted and stared out at a cloudless sky, and beneath it, the deep blue roiling waters of the Pacific.

"Is there something I'm supposed to see out there?"

"Not out there, sir. Down here." Seth pointed to the cove several hundred feet below.

Henry peered over the rim, fighting back nausea. "I don't see anything but rocks."

"Look closer, sir."

He edged closer to the cliff's edge and looked again. The morning sun carved deep shadows among the nest of jagged rocks. They led out in a string from a line of sand and disappeared into the sea. Wave after wave crashed over their toothy black projections, gushing spray and releasing a mist that lingered over the beach. A whispered lament rose up as the sea glided back through the sand and pebbles. Once his eyes adjusted, he did see something odd.

"Damn. It's a body—jammed in a crevice down there."

"Anything else, sir?"

Henry kept staring, willing the haze to lighten. A second shape materialized for a brief moment, long enough to identify a smaller figure glinting in the sunlight. "It's metal … a bronze color. It looks like—" He backed away. "What the hell am I seeing?" Each crash of the waves below sent a piercing chill up his back. The bodies—the bitter cold—none of it made any sense.

"You are resisting your memories, sir."

"Stop with the damn riddles and tell me what's going on."

"It happened after you buried Elizabeth, sir."

Henry placed the shovel up against a tree, and fell to his knees.

"Leave us alone for a moment, will you Seth?"

"I will wait for you in the cabin, sir."

He was drained. Exhausted. Alone.

After covering the headstone with her blanket, he gave Wolfie's marker a nod."I'm done here, Liz. I might last a hundred years more in this Soofysh body, but what's the point? You were everything to me, my reason to live, and without you—" Henry rose and gave the cabin a look. Seth stood on the porch—faithful little servant and a gallant hero.

"I'll miss you, Seth."

He turned away and walked into the forest. Before the cabin was out of sight, he heard the robot's unmistakable footfalls fast approaching.

"Seth, you son-of-a-bitch."

Henry ran. It took only moments to reach the cliff edge. Seth appeared at his side. "Sir, do not do this!"

"Do what? I'm just taking in the view. Go back to the cabin and wait for me there."

"I will not, sir."

"There's nothing here for me. There's nobody left."

"There is me, sir."

"Besides Liz, you're the best thing that ever happened to me." He placed both hands on Seth's shoulders. "I know that somewhere in that electromechanical stew you call your brain, there's an empathy routine. And in that program you will see what I see, maybe even feel what I feel." Seth's eyeless slits remained focused on Henry."What about Anth and Genz? They were your friends. They are your friends."

"Reptilians, colonizing a new world. They've got their own people, their own family to worry about. This world is theirs now. My era is over, a part of a fading history. The Earth is empty of humans, and soon, it'll be empty of me."

<>

"I remember." Henry lowered his head. "And you—"

"I tried to stop you, sir."

"I'm truly sorry about that, Seth."

"With no one left to serve, I would have deactivated, sir."

"There's no need for formality anymore, Seth. And I'm glad you're with me."

"I am also glad, Henry."

Henry shuddered as a cold liquid embrace flowed about his chest. Seth said, "We must hasten."

"I understand, Seth."

When the two arrived at the cabin, Henry felt tired and slow, as if his vitality was being drained. He followed Seth through the door and the two spilled into the kitchen. Liz propped her hands on hips. Wolfie sat at her side, taking up half the kitchen.

Liz said, "About time. And you found Seth. Your pancakes are cold. Do you want me to reheat them?"

Henry lumbered over to the table and slid onto the bench—fingers numb and each breath an effort. "No need. Is the coffee hot?"
With a remarkable knack for anticipation, Liz produced a pot and poured the coffee into the two mugs set on the table. Henry took in its sweet scent while letting the hot liquid trickle down his throat. Liz settled into the seat opposite.

Henry said, "I know what this is."

Liz said, "It won't last much longer, Henry."

He patted Wolfie who nuzzled up next to him and reached over the table, and kissed Liz on the lips. "It doesn't matter, does it, Seth?"

"Not in the least, Henry. Not in the least."

The light in the kitchen dimmed. The sounds of crickets and songbirds waned to a distant, muted harmony, and the wind in the trees joined the gentle chorus of the surrounding forest. The icy Pacific lapped warm against his skin, caressing him with its ageless arms. The last tendrils of sunlight faded into a gray mist. He thought about the lone tower beyond his view, dissolving into rust, waiting to slip into the sea.

ABOUT THE AUTHOR

As a scientist, **Dr. Arthur M. Doweyko** has authored 140+ scientific publications and patents, invented novel 3D drug design software, and shares the 2008 Thomas Alva Edison Patent Award for the discovery of Sprycel, a new anti-cancer drug. He has had a life-long interest in art as well as science, notably writing and painting.

His favorite writing genres are science fiction and fantasy with a particular fascination for Serling's *Twilight Zone* episodes, as reflected in his short stories. He is the author of several award-winning works: Novels *Algorithm* and *As Wings Unfurl* and numerous short stories, many of which appear in his anthologies *My Shorts* and *Captain Arnold*. *Captain Arnold* garnered the 2021 Royal Palm Literary Best Published Book Award (2nd Runner up). Besides fiction, Arthur also writes non-fiction, and his essay, *Five Reasons to Wonder*, took 2nd Place in the 2019 Writers Digest Competition.

Recently, Arthur was honored by winning the 2022 L. Ron Hubbard Illustrators of the Future Contest, a highly competitive international contest culminating in a Hollywood extravaganza attended by some of the best illustrators in the country. His illustrations have graced the covers of more than 20 published books in various genres.

Excerpt from
WIND IN TREES
Upheaval

Henry Wind In Trees, a Lakota Sioux Native American, was born in 2081. Twenty years later the Earth suffered an asteroid strike and an ensuing pandemic that left few humans alive. Henry discovered the apocalypse had been orchestrated by an entity known as the Soofysh in preparation for a subsequent colonization by a reptilian species. The Soofysh had chosen him for an experiment—his brain was transferred to a synthetic body made to look like the original. The Soofysh were intrigued by Henry's ability to communicate with his wife through telepathy. Although he had been told his wife was dead, recurring visions convinced him otherwise. With the help of a domestic robot and a few sympathetic reptilians, he rescued her from the Soofysh and the two lived happily for a number of years. Henry's body could not age, and when she died, he decided to end his lonely existence by leaping from a cliff overlooking the Pacific Ocean. And so it was, until the day he awoke.

Chapter 1

He heard a faint whisper, a familiar voice, followed by three taps of metal on metal. Recollections drifted by. None made any sense. An image of rising waves in a frigid ocean threatened to inundate what little of his mind was left.

He called out to a friend, a close friend. Were his eyes open? The warm embrace of remembrance.

"Try to open your eyes, sir."

Lifting an eyelid, he saw nothing.

"Shh. Someone is coming."

"Wait. Who am I?"

"Why, sir, you're Henry Wind In Trees. I'll be back in a moment."

<>

What an odd name. A faint glow narrowed to a thin horizontal line. His awakening senses shrieked half in terror and half in pain as the line widened and brightened. He slammed his eye shut. The light had burned, but the movement alone told him he had some control.

He was Henry.

Voices came and went. Were they real? A chest muscle twitched. He ran his tongue along the roof of his mouth, savoring its contours, its texture.

He was Henry.

He dared to open his eye again and the strip of light parsed into blurry forms. The shapes merged into a group of figures—familiar reptilian figures. The odd assortment of creatures stood a few feet away, gawking up at him with their wide, sharp-toothed mouths. He knew what they were. A lifetime of memories jostled for recognition as more of his mind awoke. He lowered his eyelid—an instinct for self-preservation, hoping it wasn't noticed. He yearned to ask what happened or how he got to this point, for all he knew, he could be a prisoner or slated for dinner. The invasion had heralded a new age, a reptilian age. He was surprised to find he understood their lispy exchanges. They spoke of history, colonization, and the last humans.

Why couldn't he move?

<>

Tapping—the metallic sound came from below. Henry looked out into the half-light of a broad room. The reptilians were gone. His fingers and arms tingled. His head swiveled down to see a bronze-colored metallic figure standing knee-high at his side.

"Sir, you are awake."

"Seth. It's you. How?"

"All in due time, sir."

"What happened? Where are we?"

He lifted his head. A pair of humanoid figures came into focus from some twenty feet away. A man and woman stood in front of a cave and appeared to stare back at him. Both were covered in hair, wearing little clothing, and motionless, much like himself.

"Seth, where the hell are we?"

"I'm glad you're regaining your voice, sir."

"Seth?"

"We are in the Museum of Natural History in Atlanta, sir."

Henry fought back the urge to ask a million questions, and instead whispered. "And what's wrong with me? Why can't I move?"

"I'm afraid you are one of the exhibits, sir—quite a popular one I might add."

"Are you kidding?"

"I suggest keeping your voice down, sir. A night guard comes by once in a while."

Henry paused, his mind enthralled by a small parade of events marching past—the search for his wife, Liz, and years later, her death—the view of the ocean from a cliff. The realization that he was still alive angered him. He should be dead. Liz had passed away yesterday and he was alone—the last human in a world populated by reptiles. And now he was a museum exhibit. Things had not improved.

His blue-skinned hand protruded from the sleeve of a stiff deerskin shirt. "I think I can move my fingers. Where did you come from?"

"Like you, I have been on exhibit. A week ago I was revived, and have been working on you, sir."

"We should both be dead."

"We were retrieved, sir."

An image of a swell of water emerged, followed by the crash of a wave against rocks—large boulders at the base of an ocean bluff. He struggled to move, to breathe.

"We were brought here and put on display."

"I remember the water. You were there, too. The cliff—"

"We fell, sir. Do you remember your cabin back on the Marin peninsula?"

"We didn't fall, Seth. You tried to stop me from jumping."

"Perhaps so, sir."

"Damn it all, Seth. You know what happened."

The lights came on. A tall, gangly, green creature wandered in. It paused at each display, bobbing its scaly head up and sideways, reading the placards. After a minute, it left and the room became dark once again.

"Seth, are you still here?"

The small robot stood in front of Henry outlined by indirect floor lighting. "I am glad to see you are returning to the living, sir."

"I'm afraid I don't share your enthusiasm."

Seth paused as if mulling over what to say next.

"It's not your fault, Seth. Last I recall, we were both drowning, isn't that right?"

"That is correct, sir."

"Maybe this is a dream ... you know, last thoughts and all that. Maybe we're still under water."

"This is no dream, sir."

Henry ran a hand over his leggings. "I can move my hands and my arms." He gave a tug at his ponytail.

"We were saved by a group of reptilians. By the way, they call themselves Batrans. I believe that may be derived from the name of their planet, Batra."

"I don't care." An image of Anth and Genz flashed by—two reptilians who helped him rescue his wife, Liz. "Are the Soofysh still here?" Henry recalled the strange creature, more mechanical than biological, referring to itself in the plural. Even the reptilians feared it. The Soofysh were responsible for killing off humans to make way for the reptilian colonization, and they were adept at playing with one's perception.

"It does not appear that they are. However, it would also appear that many Batrans have arrived in the years since."

"Wonderful."

"Can you move anything else besides your hands and arms, sir?"

Henry wiggled a foot. "As a robot, I can understand how you survived, Seth. But me ... I have a human brain in this titanium pot. It needs oxygen. How the hell did I survive?"

"I've repaired most of the damage to your legs, sir. Apparently, the Soofysh technology that went into your construction was more robust than we thought. I must surmise that the Soofysh built in some safeguards. Your brain may have entered a kind of stasis, probably triggered when the rest of your body discovered the end was near."

"Damn convenient. So, how long have we been here?"

"You and I were placed in this museum … part of a tribute to the technology of the human civilization that once existed here on Earth."

Henry shook his head. Although he and Seth were the products of Soofysh technology, the choice of becoming a cyborg was not his own.

Seth said, "According to my internal clock, we've been here for about one hundred years."

Henry swore his legs buckled, but he remained the steadfast statue he had been for a century.

"Are you sure?"

The surrounding shadowy recesses in the hall took on a ghostly veneer—the impression of a mausoleum—Henry's final resting place—a perpetual testament to a morbid choice made several lifetimes ago.

"Quite sure. But do not despair, sir."

"Why the hell not? I'm supposed to be dead. I don't like being here, and I don't want to be here."

"Perhaps you will reconsider, sir."

"Not likely."

"Things have changed considerably since you—"

"Since I committed suicide?"

"Tried to, sir. Although you were a bit damaged from the fall, I'll have you fully operational in a few minutes."

"And that's supposed to make me feel better?"

"I was not able to help you until I was powered up myself."

"Powered up?"

"In a moment, sir."

"Why am I propped up here anyway?"

"The placard announces you as a human-like robot probably because of your blue skin tone. Apparently the Batrans mistook you for an automaton, much like myself."

"Nice." Henry swung his head around. He was surrounded by a variety of mechanical wonders, including several small robots that looked a lot like Seth.

"Anybody in here?" The guard stepped into the hall once again.

Thanks to Liz and her tutoring, Henry understood the hissing tongue. With so many years gone by, her memory lifted his heart. He missed her smile and unflinching optimism. When she died, he had spiraled downward. There wasn't anything left for him.

"What do you mean 'things have changed'?"

The guard came nearer. "Who's there?"

Henry narrowed his eyes and felt Seth snuggle up behind his legs.

The Batran stopped across the way and cast a beam of light over Henry's display. After a few moments it shuffled away, all the while muttering what sounded like incantations to ward off museum spirits.

"He is gone for the moment, sir."

"I can feel my legs, Seth."

"Excellent, sir. Let me close you up, and then we can be on our way."

Henry wiggled a toe for confirmation. "On our way to where?"

"How do you feel, sir?"

"After a hundred years propped up like a manikin, I'm not sure I can walk. And I'm hungry. And thirsty."

"I'll be back shortly, sir." The little robot leaped out of the display and disappeared into the surrounding gloom.

Henry tried to follow, but found himself stuck in place. A tall figure cane into view. "You remember me, Henry?"

He recognized the raspy mechanical voice. A green pinpoint appeared where there should have been an eye. A silver sheen flashed across its human-like form and its bright ceramic teeth.

"You're Mike, aren't you?" A chill ran through Henry's titanium body. He studied the creature—not exactly a cyborg—this one had its human brain replaced with an artificial one. He recalled their last encounter. Mike should be missing most of his brains.

"The one and the same. You don't look happy to see me, Henry."

"It must be resurrection day at the museum. The last time we met you tried to kill me."

Mike pointed to his missing eye. "You tried to do the same to me."

"Yeah. I shot you in that eye. Your brains flew out the back of your head like silver confetti."

"Shooting me in the eye was a stroke of genius. I ended up with some brain damage thanks to you. Now, don't get me wrong, I'm not upset. I'd have done the same if I were in your shoes."

"I don't get it."

"Lucky for me, your shot only took out half my brain. It took a while for the Soofysh technology to knit and repair what was left."

"Damn amazing. You know you should be blind."

"How so?"

"The optic nerves in human brains cross over. Each eye uses the opposite side of the brain."

"Ah … so my left eye gets shot out along with the left side of my brain, leaving a right eye that shouldn't work."

Henry craned his head for a better look. "Got to hand it to those Soofysh."

Mike said, "They knew what they were doing."

Henry looked out beyond Mike's gleaming hulk, anxious for Seth to emerge from the shadows. "They were experimenting, leaving behind lots of dead human beings."

"Look at you, Henry. You're back. You owe your life to the Soofysh."

"You call this a life?"

Mike extended a hand and patted Henry on his shoulder. "We're both here for a reason."

"So, what now? We shake hands and forget about the past?"

"The Soofysh are gone, Henry. I take orders from no one. You might say I'm my own man."

Mike was no more a man than a wind-up doll, despite what the Soofysh promised. An artificial brain would never be human and could never be trusted, except in the case of one small but loyal robot.

Seth peered out from behind Mike and held up a bag. "Unfortunately, the vending machines only carry uncooked meat."

"Did you know about Mike, Seth?"

"He was the one who brought me back, sir."

"I know someone's in here." The silhouette of the guard framed the entrance to the hall.

When the guard approached again, Mike slipped into the shadows of an adjacent display. Henry wondered if he should shout out a warning, but only looked on while the Batran collapsed to the floor.

Mike shoved the body to the side and said, "He's not dead, if that's what you're worried about."

"It's not so much the guard. It's the display you came out of."

"What about it? Some dinos in a kitchen. They kinda look happy."

A family of Batran reptilians sat at a kitchen counter ready to have dinner, while mama filleted a chunk of fresh red meat. A window at the rear of the diorama displayed a pastoral scene of rolling fields of green and a traditional red barn.

"Look at what's in the corral next to the barn."

Mike moved closer. "Those are people … humans. Maybe they came for dinner?"

Henry said, "Yeah. Maybe. Considering this is a museum, that scene is probably old, I wonder if they were the dinner. Seth, you said you were activated by Mike a week ago?"

"True, sir."

"Did you have a chance to look at the other exhibits here? Maybe they tell a story we should know."

"As I mentioned earlier, sir, things have changed. I cannot be sure, but—"

A high-pitched intermittent wailing filled the hall.

Henry lurched away from the troubling display and stumbled. Mike moved in a blur and caught him. "Gotcha, Henry."

Being held up by the very creature he had tried to kill gave Henry the willies.

Mike said, "You're in good hands, Henry."

Seth offered up the bag and said, "Eat up, sir. You'll need your strength."

They entered a hallway which led out of the display area. Henry squirmed out of Mike's embrace, snapped up the bag and staggered ahead.

"Sir, where are we going?"

"I don't know about you two, but I'm going to finish what I started."

<=>

Printed in Great Britain
by Amazon